Barbed Wire Fence

Barbed Wire Fence

Stories of Displacement from the Barak Valley of Assam

Edited by

Nirmal Kanti Bhattacharjee

Dipendu Das

NIYOGI BOOKS

Published by
NIYOGI BOOKS
D-78, Okhla Industrial Area, Phase-I
New Delhi-110 020, INDIA
Tel: 91-11-26816301, 49327000
Fax: 91-11-26810483, 26813830
email: niyogibooks@gmail.com
website: www.niyogibooksindia.com

Editor: Mohua Mitra/Niyogi Books
Design: Nabanita Das/Niyogi Books

ISBN: 978-93-81523-29-2
Publication: 2015

This is a work of fiction. The names, characters and incidents portrayed in it are the work of the author's imagination. Any resemblance to actual persons, living or dead, events or localities, is entirely coincidental.

Printed at: Niyogi Offset Pvt. Ltd., New Delhi, India.

Content

Introduction

Robert Frost

> ***"Something there is that does not love a wall ..."***

The history of human civilisation has time and again witnessed collective migrations driven by political upheavals, dictatorial coercions, home wars, economic depressions or natural calamities like epidemics, floods or earthquakes. The oldest such example in history is perhaps the exodus of the Jews led by Moses, 'And Moses said, we will go with our young and with our old, with our sons and with our daughters, with our flocks and with our herds, will we go....'. This arduous journey happened by defeating the pursuing horsemen of the Pharaoh of Egypt, and by crossing the bifurcated Red Sea. It is signified in human history as the journey of liberation.

Another devastating migration took place in Ireland in the nineteenth century not because of political suppression but due to the damage of harvest by natural calamity. Between 1845 and 1851, ten lakh people died in Ireland because of the potato epidemic. As a result, millions of people abandoned their home and hearth. While the population in 1851 was around 80–85 lakhs, in a decade it came down to sixty-five lakhs. Loss of harvest, famine and epidemic forced regular migration so much that by 1921 the population of the country had been reduced to only forty-three lakhs.

But these are only two examples, one from ancient Biblical mythology and the other from recent history. In between such upheavals there are many other occasions of historic and pre-historic migrations, and as far as our age is concerned, it is already being called the 'Age of Migration and Exile'. Edward Said has called the present age 'the age of the refugee, the displaced person, mass immigration'. From countries like India, Bangladesh, Thailand, Indonesia, people are moving on in search of livelihood to Taiwan, the gulf countries, Saudi Arabia, UK and the USA. But when people migrate en masse, they do so because of political turmoil and suppression or economic disaster, ethnic clash or natural calamity or a sustained epidemic. Such a huge en masse cross-border migration took place from the then East Bengal to West Bengal and the Barak Valley of Assam in the wake of India's Partition (1946–47). Never before or since, in human history, has there been such a mass exodus of people.

This great current of humanity crossing from East Bengal to West Bengal and to the Barak Valley of Assam—some on foot, others by train, steamer, boat; some with few belongings, others penniless; some accompanied by near and dear ones, others losing all their relatives—never found due creative expression in Bengali literature. Sankha Ghosh in his poem, 'Rehabilitation' (*Punarbasan*) writes:

Whatever was around me
devasted,
arrows and javelin
home and hearth—
All tremble together towards the west
Memory is as if a long queue of distant travellers.
Broken boxes lie abandoned under the mango tree.
One step, two steps and suddenly all are homeless.

It is Adorno who uttered that famous sentence: 'Writing poetry is barbaric after Auschwitz.' The devastating experience of the bombing of Hiroshima and Nagasaki or that of the holocaust at Auschwitz benumbs the imagination of man, and hence it becomes impossible to create art out of such experiences. They demand silence. In the language of George Steiner, 'The world of Auschwitz lies outside speech as it lies outside reason.' Rudolf Borchardt in his book, *In May, In May Cried the Cuckoo,* advised the poets to go to a forest, catch fish, cut wood, 'and do your most heroic deed: Be silent.' And yet poets and authors like Anthony Hecht, Primo Levi, Paul Celan and others attempted to discover a language for this atrocity. Based on the terrible experience of spending days in the nightmare of reality, they tried to construct a new 'art of atrocity'. Like the poet Hans Magnus Enzensberger they also realised that giving in to the urge for silence will mean 'surrendering to cynicism'. Unfortunately, Bengali writers chose to surrender to silence, if not to cynicism.

George Lukacs' *Theory of the Novel* has shown that the epic is written in 'settled culture' where identity is stable, life unchangeable; but the novel is the imaginative picture of 'transcendental homelessness'. If this is true, the days of homelessness during Bengal's Partition and the huge migration of people contained all the ingredients for great novels. But those novels remained unwritten. This makes Hasan Azizul Haque lament in his book *Kathasahityer Kathakata,* 'When lakhs of people in whose wildest imagination the question of leaving the motherland never occurred had to flee their country, uprooted, homeless and reduced to refugees, no one wrote about this most dreadful story of terrible pain and suffering in our recent history. It never seriously featured in Bengali fiction.'

Let us now turn our attention to the particular situation in the Barak Valley of Assam. The barbed wire fence on the porous Indo-Bangladesh border, apart from demarcating the boundary of the two nations created out of undivided India in the wake of independence, stands as a wall between the peoples sharing a common culture, tradition and language. Naturally the fact of border-crossing, migration and displacement has become one of the most important issues in the post-independence period in the eastern part of India, particularly Assam, the state that shares its border with Bangladesh at several points.

The nature and the consequences of the social phenomenon, such as migration and displacement that remain central to the post-colonial and globalised world experience, acquire further dimensions as one seeks to delve deeper into the issues concerning displacement in Assam. Naturally not merely the mirroring of the context or the representation of the issues involving dislocations and relocations inform the expressive traditions of the diverse cultures of the state; rather they, emerge out of such a context. One of the important components of the expressive traditions, the literature (both oral and written) of the different languages in Assam is no exception to that.

Owing to the many reorientations of the boundary of Assam and the migration to the state in the colonial and post-colonial periods, Bengali today is one of the largest linguistic groups in Assam. The Bengalis are concentrated more densely in the Barak Valley of Assam comprising three districts, Cachar, Karimganj and Hailakandi. It needs to be mentioned that dislocation and displacement, often voluntary and mostly under duress, and the resulting human crisis are inseparable parts of the history of the Bengali community. One of the largest displacements took place after the referendum in Sylhet district on 6 and 7 July 1947. The probity of the manner in which the referendum was conducted was questioned and the scar remained alive in the heart of the displaced. The referendum and the partition on the basis of religion created a sense of betrayal among the religious minority in East Pakistan, and a sense of insecurity crept in. This was intensified by organised threat, physical violence and reports of violation of women.

All these prompted a large section of the religious minority of East Pakistan to migrate from their homeland to the other side of the border. Thus in the wake of independence, a large number of citizens of undivided India became homeless, uprooted refugees in independent India. A portion of them sought shelter in various parts of Assam. The exodus into Assam was repeated twice in 1965 (during Ayub Khan's regime in Pakistan) and in 1971 (during the Bangladesh Liberation War).

The state of Assam already had a significant number of Bengali speakers (both Hindus and Muslims) in the pre-independence period. A section of Bengali-Muslims was in fact persuaded before independence by the state government to migrate from East Bengal and settle in the large tracts of unused arable lands of the Brahmaputra Valley. The state newspapers often reported incursions of immigrants through the porous border.

It must be mentioned that Bengali-Hindu immigrants (different classes, educated and uneducated) to Assam were mainly refugees, who had to leave their homeland under duress. The displaced

Bengali-Muslims were mainly uneducated poor people who crossed the border and settled in Assam in the quest of better economic possibilities. They were mainly concerned with more immediate problems of securing economic stability and displayed little interest in establishing their distinctive linguistic identity through the pursuance of literary activities in Bengali. The dispossessed Bengali-Hindus from East Pakistan had inherited a rich cultural and literary tradition and were keen to nurture and protect that distinctive cultural and literary identity.

However, displacement, the pang of being uprooted and the crisis of identity rarely became thematic concerns in the Bengali literature of Assam for the first two decades following partition. The landless and uprooted destitute people were so engaged in earning their livelihood, and so recent and close was the experience of being uprooted that they failed to distance themselves from their immediate context and explore the themes in literary productions.

The inclusion of a large number of Bengali speakers (both Hindus and Muslims) created resentment and apprehension among a section of Assamese intelligentsia and political leaders. The enemy was identified in the 'other'—the immigrant, and this tension found expression in several agitations (often violent) in Assam. Once uprooted, the apprehension of getting displaced once again created a crisis of identity not only amongst the immigrants, but the entire Bengali community in Assam. This fear of dispossession destabilises any evolving sense of belonging, and as a result, a search for a socio-cultural centre ensues. Bengali literature of Assam till the 1970s reveals a distinctive attempt to shape itself in the mould of a Kolkata-centric, seemingly mainstream Bengali literature.

Significant changes can be perceived in the Bengali literature of Assam during the 1980s. The tension resulting from migration and displacement, and several agitations in Assam accompanied by violence created a sense of despair among the displaced. Gradually, more and more Assamese as well as the displaced began to express their voice against the senseless violence. There was now a renewed hope, a feeling of solidarity and a sense of emergent belonging. Instead of turning their back to the problems being negotiated, Bengali writers of Assam began to address the issues pertinent to their marginal existence, their disturbed sense of belonging and their peculiar crises, and thus succeeded in evolving a distinctive identity.

The establishment of the tea industry in Assam in the colonial period entailed immigration of a large number of lower caste poor people to the state from places such as present day Jharkhand, Chhattisgarh, Bihar, Andhra Pradesh, Odisha, Uttar Pradesh and West Bengal. They were recruited by the British tea planters from between the mid-nineteenth century and the early decades of the twentieth century to work as indentured labourers in the tea plantations. Often the attempts of labourers to escape inhuman torture, hardships and adverse physical conditions prevailing in the tea gardens would prove futile, as any such attempt was met with severe torture inflicted by the tea planters and the colonial masters. To return to their homes was no longer an alternative as the lands left behind were occupied by the villagers back home. No marked difference could be perceived in the plight of the tea garden labour community even after independence.

The issues concerning displacement in the context of the tea industry finds representation in the Bengali literature of Assam. It must be noted that the tea garden labour community of Barak Valley of Assam uses a dialect that reflects the influence of Bengali and Hindi dialects. The literature they produce is mainly written in Bengali and also in Hindi. It must be mentioned that the early evidence of literature written in Bengali by the tea tribes reveals some hesitation in the use of the tea garden dialect in the literary compositions and in the dialogues. However, the more recent compositions reveal that the writers have begun to be unapologetic about their use of the dialect not only in the dialogues but also in the narration.

The selection of short stories for the present anthology has been made on the basis of the context given above and the negotiation of the issues of displacement and marginalisation ingrained in the texts.

Nirmal Kanti Bhattacharjee

Dipendu Das

Of Human Bonding

Shyamalendu Chakraborty

Luit, which is also known as Lohit, was deeply engaged in its own sport with mighty whirling currents. They were on this side of the sloping bank sitting under the shade of a tree. At a distance, in the greenery of hillock, plants and herbs with the temple of Umananda Bhairab, the island floated on the river like the back of a tortoise. And on both sides ran the Luit or Brahmaputra, creating strong currents that eddied around.

Rupali had been looking in that direction for quite some time with Hiren nibbling at a blade of grass. At times he cast a glance at Rupali. The peacock-coloured sari matched her fair complexion and radiated an excellent splendour. Hiren was in no mood to utter anything at that moment. He was deeply engrossed in a feeling of fondness at the depths of his consciousness.

The wall by the roadside concealed them completely. Such moments of tranquility at noon were not their first. Hiren sometimes came out of his office during the day. Rupali might have just started her work then. On such occasions Rupali chided him—

'Why don't you first ask me over the phone?'

Hiren would sometimes pretend not to hear her. At other times, he would tell her colleague, 'Kindly look after things on her behalf for a while. I'm taking her out for tea.'

Rupali had to willynilly come out with indignation writ large on her face. Sometimes the teasing remarks of her colleague would make her blush furiously.

Of course today neither of them had office engagements. The two came out for the sole purpose of meeting each other. Consequently they met on the road.

Keeping the Judges' Field by the side the two walked along the road darkened by the shadows of big *sal* trees. After advancing a little, they reached the riverbank by an entrance through the wall.

They had been sitting in silence for a long time. On spotting a seller of tender coconuts, Hiren gestured towards him. The man came up to them, chopped off the top of the two coconuts with the chopper in his hand and offered them the cool refreshments along with two plastic straws.

'How much?'

'Just a-rupee-and-a-half,' the man replied with a smile.

As the man departed, Rupali exclaimed, 'Can you read my mind? Just what I desired—'

When they were alone together, Rupali spoke in Bengali. She was yet to fully master the pronunciation of the letter 's', otherwise she spoke, in Hiren's words, 'flawless Bengali'.

Quickly pouncing upon Rupali's compliment, Hiren replied, 'Then give me a toffee in return.'

'Hey, bad boy—if you have toffee, you'll probably end up with terrible toothache.'

'Why didn't you tell me in advance that you have got pyorrhoea?'

Rupali flushed in anger, 'Don't you dare, I say.'

'I beg your pardon—see I'm twisting my ears. I quite forgot your love for those milky white teeth of yours. All right, now I shall forget about that toffee.'

Rupali smiled at Hiren's funny gesture; throwing up dimples in her cheeks.

'If you smile such dimpled smiles, I'll be unable to control myself from snatching a toffee.'

Rupali hastily turned her face away. They whiled away the entire afternoon in such childish bickerings.

The declining sun's reflection on the waters of the Luit, lent it a red hue.

Hiren urged, 'Get up, let's go to an evening show.'

Rupali did not warm up to the proposal. At Hiren's insistence, she said 'Won't *deuta*[i] be waiting for me?'

'Why didn't you tell your father that you're going out in order to seek me?'

'Ha! What a *mahapurush* (great man) you are that you should be sought!'

'May not be a great man but certainly your *purush* (man) and would-be *giriek* (husband, but also literally a mountain), you understand? I'm your one and only mountain.'

'I understand mountain-king, now let's go.'

'Why, let's sit here for just a little longer. Watch how the soft darkness approaches.'

'Why, do you wish to be a glow-worm in the darkness?'

'The name of my glow-worm amidst the darkness is Rupali.'

'Khagen Mahanta also said something similar.'

'Ah, why speak of that *khoga* (bird) on this nice evening, dear? He left long ago.'

'True, he has left us but it seems he is coming back in a bigger way.'

'What's the matter, tell me?'

'Why, didn't you hear the clamour "*Jai Ai Asom*" (Victory to Mother Assam)?'

'Why shouldn't I? Mother Assam is mine too.'

'No, Hiren Ghosh, Mother Assam belongs to Rupali Bora, Khagen Mahanta—not to Hiren Ghosh and Dipen Bose.'

'Oh, do they say so? Let them say. What does it matter?'

'No Hiren, this time it won't stop so easily. They are setting up organisations in schools, colleges and offices.'

'Let them do so. Come on, let's make a move. Otherwise your *deuta* will be really angry.'

After escorting Rupali home, Hiren hired a cycle-rickshaw.

For some days now, he had been noticing that people in general appeared to be more serious than usual. The newspapers too have been singing a similar tune. It was time for the Brahmaputra to overflow. His mind was filled with sadness.

Next morning he woke up to find posters written in red ink pasted on all the walls. The same slogan—"Drive Outsiders away."

He came out on the road with the toothbrush in his mouth. When did they write these posters? "Outsiders leave Assam"; "We want Independent Assam"; "Sever Assam from India," etc., etc.

Like a hounded man Hiren came back. Had so many people gone mad at the same time? What did independent Assam mean anyway? Was Assam dependent?

He was about to leave for office after his morning meal when the sweet little son of Naren Saikia from the adjacent house emerged. Hiren had great affection for him. The boy was in class three at a convent school.

'Uncle, aren't you a Bengali?' Hiren was taken aback by this strange query.

'Oh my dear! Why do you ask this?'

From his explanation Hiren gathered that the previous day a few people had come to his school. They had asked the students to boycott their school from today. The students were told that Bengalis were at the root of Assam's misery and so on and so forth.

'They would drive Bengalis out of Assam, they said.'

'My darling, you needn't think about these things. Carry on with your studies like a good boy.'

After locking his house he hired a rickshaw. He found boys and girls of different ages in a procession on the road. Their destination was the Judges' Field. How could everything change overnight? Hiren could hardly grasp the situation. Rupali called him over the phone at three o'clock.

'Do be careful. You have a habit of moving about without prior notice.'

'Don't worry. I'm coming over to see you in the afternoon.'

'What's the need? It would be difficult for you to return at night.'

'But I have not met you for so many days.'

'Hey! With whom had you been last afternoon?'

'That was with Rupali Bora. Today I wish to spend time with Rupu—*Jai Ai Asom*!'

It wouldn't be possible to prevent this crazy fellow. Rupali put down the receiver. She decided, she wouldn't allow him to return home tonight.

When he reached Rupali's home in the afternoon, Hiren almost found himself in a cauldron of hot oil. Khagen Mahanta and some others were engrossed in a heated discussion about something.

At Hiren's entry everyone fell silent. Their facial expressions suggested that they were not willing to make Hiren privy to that discussion.

'What's the matter, Mahanta? Why have you stopped the discussion? Does my presence disturb you in any way?'

Rupali herself caught the end of the thread—'I cannot agree with your opinion, Mahanta. Your objective may be good, but you cannot keep a whole lot of people under control for too long. The people who are shouting for independent Assam today may not listen to you tomorrow.'

'May I ask a question, Mahanta?' Hiren joined the conversation.

'Sure.'

'Do you consider the non-Assamese people who are residing permanently in Assam to be outsiders?'

'No, we did not say so. The people who came after 1951 should be branded outsiders.'

'And what is the reasoning behind this? What wrong have the post-1951 settlers done?'

'It's not a question of wrong-doing. The problems of Assam multiplied due to the arrival of these people. It has become difficult for us to get jobs.'

Rupali abruptly said, 'That's it, we cannot cope up with the competition—we should admit this. All the anger is due to this.'

Hiren counters, 'No Rupali, I wouldn't say that too. With the rise in population the unemployment problem has increased. But this is not a problem faced by the Assamese people alone. Also, besides the oil refinery there is no other industrial development in Assam. Isn't the entire matter a problem of Assam as a whole?'

'That's exactly the point,' said Khagen Mahanta, suddenly finding direction.

'But you are not saying this. You are trying to make the problem of Assam into a problem of the Assamese people only.'

'Isn't it one and the same?' Mahanta laughed triumphantly.

'Not the same, Mahanta, not one and the same. If it is treated as the problem of Assam then you would not keep the large number of Bengalis living in Assam out of it and treat them as enemies. Remember they are equally involved in every moment of Assam's prosperity as well as trials and tribulations.'

'In our movement we invited all the people of Assam,' Khagen Mahanta responded in a feeble voice.

'No, that is your deliberate error. You are exploiting a cheap sentiment to push a real problem into the dark.'

'You did not get the point, Mr Ghosh. Assamese language and culture today are in deep crisis; they are approaching annihilation. And for this the Bengalis are to be blamed.'

Hiren burst into laughter, 'Mahanta, for a culture and language which are not dynamic, death is inevitable. Your perception about Assamese language and culture cannot be supported. A dynamic race has a dynamic language and a culture that would be refined through evolution.

If you analyse Assamese language and culture deeply, you will realise that they are not stagnant like inanimate objects. Its dynamism can never be eclipsed by any culture of the world, not to speak of Bengali culture alone. If only some people like you did not keep it in narrow confinement.'

Rupali observed Hiren in amazement. He appeared to be a different Hiren altogether. She was as if, meeting this new Hiren for the first time. Her mind was filled with a loving sense of pride for him.

Khagen Mahanta kept silent for some time. Then he said, 'I don't have the kind of faith that you possess. The programme which has been charted out cannot be abandoned now. We shall have to advance with that.'

'It will not be an advancement, Mahanta. You are driving back Assam's development by at least fifty years. I am aggrieved at that.'

Rupali rose, 'Please sit a little longer. I'm bringing tea.'

The tea session finished in silence. They left. Hiren remained lost within himself for some time longer. Sitting beside him, Rupali continued to gaze at his face.

'No Rupa, the result of these blockades will be disastrous. The trade and commerce in Assam will be severely disrupted. In this turbulent situation some profiteers will take undue advantage of the situation.'

'Nothing can be done, Hiren. They won't listen to you and me. A tense situation prevails throughout Assam. At any moment a conflagration may start and some innocent people may lose their lives and properties.'

Three months elapsed. The movement was now at its peak.

Rupali's attention made Hiren almost a captive at home. School-college-office—everything got disrupted. They declared it to be their last struggle and vowed to fight till the end.

The over-enthusiasts even considered it to be the second battle of Saraighat, the first of which took place when the independence of Assam was threatened by the Mughals. But did the struggle now hold any merit after years of independence? Hiren's troubled mind raised rhetorical questions. The horse of the legendary *Ashvamedha yajna*[ii] galloped ahead. The *ghee*[iii] for the sacrifice came via an invisible, secret path.

Everyday there were disturbing occurrences—both big and small incidents. A panic-stricken situation was being meticulously orchestrated. Law and order was ten fathoms under the Brahmaputra. The waves of malice filtered into Meghalaya and Manipur like floodwater.

'Rupa, in which country do we live?'

Rupali felt his agony.

'You shouldn't worry yourself about this anymore. Let things unfold the way they are meant to and take their own course.'

'I should allow whatever is happening to continue? What rubbish! Are we going back to the sixth century? Is this justified? Someone is attempting suicide. Shall we allow it in spite of knowing about it?'

'How can you tackle it alone? Moreover, even if you say this, who would listen to the enemy? Don't you see how all the leaders have shut their mouth out of fear? No one dares to play with fire while sitting on gunpowder.'

'None has the daring? Not a single one among one crore Assamese people? Are we to believe that? No Rupa, it can't be. It can't be true that everyone's thought process has become turbid. In fact, it is a question of who is to bell the cat. The hesitation lies there. Someone must speak out first.'

It did not take much time for the fire to flare up. The over-zealous had their way. The people who came from across the border for the safety of their lives, leaving their motherland behind, now met their end at the hands of their own people. Jesus was crucified for the second time.

Hiren became extremely restless, 'Rupa, stop them!' he exclaimed. They will extinguish all rays of hope. They are disgracing themselves.'

Rupali was alarmed. She didn't know what to do. She continued to turn over the pages of newspapers and magazines. Suddenly she exclaimed excitedly, 'Hiren, just see, there are people--people who dare to say—see what's written in *Kalakhar*.'

Hiren went through the magazine thoroughly. His eyes welled up with tears as he read it.

'No Rupa, it is a sin to lose faith in men.'

Rupali felt reassured at his exuberance. The bird of hope soared, spreading its wings for some days.

But truth is often unpalatable. The editor of *Kalakhar*, Hiren Gohain was assaulted for speaking the truth. Nirupama Borgohain was shown the door for committing the crime of impartial reporting. Dr Anjan Chakraborty paid with his life for not giving false statements.

Hiren was dumb-founded. Was this what they called a movement? Would these humiliations and deaths solve their problems?

Around this time, Udayan arrived from Shillong. Hiren, as if, got his life back. For Hiren, it was like a shot in the arm.

'Well professor, off from college suddenly?'

'Don't speak of college, my friend. I received seven days' ultimatum. On the sixth day I was reminded that it was the last day of my tenure there.'

'And you ran for your life!'

'What could I do—it is foolhardy to embrace death senselessly.'

'Udayan, is this region within India?'

'I don't think so. From what is happening throughout the region, it seems there is no constitution or law here. Let it go to rack and ruin.'

'Who'll go to rack and ruin?'

'We are the scapegoats of Independence! It is our destiny to scurry along the whole length and breadth of India like a football being kicked around.'

'All right, but for how long? Should it continue even after thirty-three years of Independence?'

Udayan kept quiet. Hiren rose and went to the kitchen to cook rice on the stove.

Rupali arrived just then.

'Hey, Udayan babu! What's the news?'

'The usual news.'

'Where's your friend?'

'Possibly busy cooking something for me.'

'Then let me go and help him.'

'Ah, the meal will be enjoyable today.'

'Why hanker after food? We are feeding you Bengalis so much, yet your belly wants more! You're all gluttons. Would you like some tea?'

'Is it a question that needs to be asked?'

Rupali entered the kitchen. 'Go, chat with your friend, I'm making tea.'

'What a relief!'

After an initial hesitation, Rupali asked 'Did you go through today's newspapers?'

'No, I've given up reading them altogether. Why, is there anything special there?'

Rupali did not answer immediately and tinkered with this and that. Later she managed to spell out in a trembling voice, 'We are not even worthy of being called human beings. I just cannot think of it—the way they stoned a living man to death!' There was a lump in Rupali's throat.

Hiren stared at her in silence. Hearing no sound from the kitchen for a while, Udayan came in to check. He was surprised at finding the two standing with an awkward silence between them.

'What's the matter? Is it a lovers' squabble?'

'Udayan, have you read today's newspaper?'

'Are you referring to the news about Rabi Moitra?'

'Rabi Moitra?'

'Yes, the oil refinery expert. He was hired to help find petroleum deposits in this region. Yesterday he was—'

At this moment someone called from outside. Hiren opened the door. Two or three young men entered. Hiren asked them to sit down.

'Hiren babu, we must do something.'

'What do you want to do?'

'In the name of agitation, organised eviction of the Bengalis is going on. The police is either with them or remaining a mere silent spectator.'

'What can a few of us do together? They've almost built up a parallel government all over Assam. Haven't you heard them shouting "Kerosene Government"? We are under the rule of this Kerosene Government.'

'We know. Let the Kerosene Government run. We have toured through the entire Nowgong and Goalpara belts. Everywhere there is the same wave of rising protest. It is not right to put up with this quietly.'

'I understand. But can you build up resistance? Protests must be launched everywhere simultaneously and large-scale riots breaking out as a consequence is not an impossibility. We must act only after taking every aspect into consideration.'

'After conducting the tour, we realised that people are ready to come out on the streets to protest against this massacre; they are ready to take every risk. It is better to react than spend day after day in severe tension. Their main argument is: this is their state too and it's time the Assamese people are made to realise that.'

Udayan listened in silence all this while. Now he joined in. 'You shouldn't think of the Bengalis alone. You must approach the enlightened Assamese people also and make them your partner. You will always have such people who do not support racial sentiments. Along with this, you should raise a demand for the annulment of the bill that led to the formation of states on the basis of language.'

'It is not possible to communicate with everybody within this short span of time. We have already talked to many people belonging to the Assamese intelligentsia. Everyone realises that closing down schools, colleges, cancelling examinations, creating chaotic situations all over the state is tantamount to inviting total destruction unto themselves. Even they are apprehensive of greater dangers in the way the students are spending their days. But no one is willing to face the gun. We shall bring out a protest march this coming Wednesday. Hiren babu, please join us with as many people as you can on that day.'

'All right. But take care, it should not be a poor turnout.'

They left. Rupali had been listening all this while, standing at the door. Now she came in with tea.

'I'll be going with you on Wednesday.'

Hiren protested, 'You don't have to. If anything happens, you will be in trouble.'

'I don't think there will be any trouble. Besides you, many people will be attending the procession. I know.'

'How do you know?'

'Khagen Mahanta and his group have come to learn about the procession. They are going door to door, warning people that participants in the procession will be socially censured.'

The procession could not be stopped with the threat of fine and censure. The protest rally spontaneously turned into a tidal wave of protestors. The breaches which created the wave were felt at Nowgong and Goalpara. This was perhaps beyond one's imagination. Khagen Mahanta and the party became scurrilous in their protests. But it could not be said with certainty that their voices missed the tremor of fear.

That was the topic of discussion in Hiren's office. The agitators had cleverly invited this inevitable reaction. The offices remained open for a few days every month to disburse the salaries. During those days, conversation flowed among the colleagues in hushed voices.

A few applauded Hiren for the speech he delivered on the day of the protest. At this moment Rupali called him on the phone, 'Return early from office in the afternoon.'

'Why, will you come?'

'Yes.'

'Then let me leave right now.'

'Don't make fun of me.'

'Is there any room left for fun after all those serious events?'

'Forget this topic. I'm coming home.'

'Then should I order sweets?'

'Look here, I'm getting angry now.'

'For God's sake, show your anger in front of me. It's worth seeing your face when it becomes scarlet—like a Kashmiri apple!'

'I'm coming within an hour'—Rupali put the receiver back on the cradle.

Udayan had gone to Maligaon to meet a friend. The two sat facing each other accompanied by cups of tea. Rupali appeared to be grave today. Hiren occasionally glanced at her out of the corner of his eyes. He wanted to tell her something. Right at this moment the uproar reached their ears, 'Bring the Bongal out!'

Stones rained down on the door with those words.

Rupali stood erect. Anxiety was writ large on her face. Hiren was astounded at first. The sound of shouting increased manifold. Hiren's face became tense. He stood up and approached the door, but Rupali pulled him back. Both stood for a while looking at each other. Rupali suddenly opened the door. Before Hiren could make any move, he heard her cry out in pain—'Oh!'

Rupali pressed her forehead with one hand. Like *krishnachura*[iv] flowers, blood flowed like a stream through her *champa*-[v]yellow fingers. Grasping her with one hand Hiren came out of the door. He found a group of young people standing defiantly. His cold, firm voice broke the stillness, 'Who's looking for me?'

There was no response from the crowd. He challenged them again, 'You are looking for the Bongal, aren't you? You want to drive him out of Assam? Keep in mind, I too belong to Assam. If anyone dares to, come and drive me out.' His voice reverberated in the air and floated above the gathering.

Translated by Ashok Kumar Nandy

(Endnotes)

i Father.

ii Ritual horse sacrifice.

iii Clarified butter.

iv A red flower belonging to the Magnolia family.

v Golden flower.

Food Giver

Badarujjaman Choudhury

On my way back home from school, while I am cleaning my feet and dust-stained flip-flops on the steps leading to the pond outside our house, a few yards from our co-shared Panjegana mosque, I hear my Borochacha's[i] voice blaring from the neighbouring house, 'Keep aside your religious strictures and tall talks! How much have you seen, little suckling! You are still a green horn smelling of mother's milk.'

It has been excessively hot for some days. The scorching sun is burning the earth. Borochacha's temper is in tune with the sultry weather. His peevish, waspish temper makes him infamous among relatives and neighbours. There is a long stretch of verandah alongside the eastern room of the mosque. A small parlour has been improvised there by a separation made of bamboo fencing. The Mullah resides there with his belongings: cot, chair-table, etcetera. The son of one of our relatives, he is a young chap of seventeen or eighteen. He studies in a Kowmi Madrasa (Islamic school) in a rustic town, a few kilometres from here. In fact, I am a little concerned about the different classes of madrasa. However, upon enquiry, I have come to know that he still has around eight months of pupilage there.

Ours is a small hamlet. Here Mullah is generally addressed as 'Mullah beta' (a male son) instead of only 'Mullah'. The ladies confined in the inner chambers never really regard him as their own son though they tag the word 'beta' with Mullah. My third son is of the same age as Mullah and is a good friend of his. But my wife still maintains *purdah* before him when he comes into the inner-house to have lunch or tea. It is considered a vice for the *bepurdah* (without *purdah*) ladies to show any tinge of voluptuous joviality before an unknown male visitor. But my wife appears freely before our daily workers, hawkers, fishmongers, pals of my daughters and sons. At the hour of need, she even cordially welcomes them with tea and *paan*.[ii] One day, I lightly put a question to her, 'Why do you maintain *purdah* only before *mullah-maulavi-talebads*? Are they the only worthy males in your eyes?'

I have heard that this year the Mullah will sit for the high-school-leaving examination. He prepares lessons and attends classes in the madrasa along with namaaz (religious prayer of Muslims) in Panjegana, tutoring kids in the verandah of the mosque up to eight or nine in the morning after the completion of morning prayers. It is difficult for him to find time for his own studies. However, somehow he finds the time. I have heard that he has general proficiency in all he studies. Perhaps, returning from the madrasa now, he has just settled down to read, amidst which Borochacha decides to yell at him.

Once home, I request my wife to give me a cup of tea. I take off my clothes–damp with sweat–and drape only a *lungi* around my waist. I try to switch on the fan but there is no electricity. My sapient Borochacha, the oldest living member of our family, ignites my irritation with his loquacious prattle directed at an examination candidate. In addition, the roasting, wicked heat instigates me to utter a piece of expletive just as my wife takes the lid off a *handi*,[iii] brimming over with frothy gruel.

Taking a palm-fan I straddle on a chair. Staring disdainfully at my wife I ask, 'What are you staring at? Is my charm bursting forth today?'

She twists her lips slightly in an exotic charming gesture, 'Oh! My Prince Charming!'

I say, 'In the past devoted wives would fan their dear husbands for hours when they returned home in the boiling heat. Alas, those days are gone. Why was I not born in those days! Nowadays Shah

Banu and Taslima have brainwashed you. Bring the tea with some lemon or tamarind squash and biscuits.'

Firoza does not deign to reply, only stares queerly. As she moves, I repeat, 'Three cups of tea; one for that Mullah beta, another for Borochacha.'

'Who is this Borochacha?'

'Why? Borochacha of that house—chief of our family. He has nothing to do. And that poor chap—his exam is knocking at the door. But Borochacha's relentless wrangling will never end.'

I don't have the habit of fanning myself. My Chachi[iv] would do that. The day her son departed from this world was the day of my arrival in the same. On my third day, I was told, when my mother was in deep slumber and I was whining and restlessly flailing my legs and arms, she came in quietly and lifted me from the bed. I did not have much need to feed on my mother's milk and soon that chance was also lost forever.

My mother lived with my father somewhere else. Father sent her home before my birth. Forty days after her death, Chachi celebrated *sirni*.[v] Many people were fed. *Maulavi-maulanas* came, read from the scriptures and blessed us. They ate *korma-pulao*[vi] and were also offered valedictory tribute. My father also participated with his new bride. Chacha[vii] told him, 'You have remarried. Allah will give you more children. Please, give me this ill-fated child, a mother-devourer at birth.'

My father had no objections.

One day, I was trying to sneak my way into her room, trying to steal my Chachi's *aam satwa*[viii] jar when she was taking her siesta. Surprisingly her palm-fan was gently moving in an alternating rhythm of slow and swift with occasional pauses. Sometimes, it sloped down onto her chest. Concluding that she was gradually slipping into deeper slumber, I unbolted the almirah-door but it banged in an odd manner. I looked up and saw that her fan was not on her chest but had started swaying once again.

When I think of those days when I was breast-fed by my Chachi, I am often reminded of the popular Bengali proverb about milk coming out from a squeezed-nose. Was it possible? It is generally said that after the burial, when the people who gathered for the event, retreat some forty odd steps away from the buried body, the soil smothers the corpse and squeezes out all the milk that the deceased consumed since birth from its mouth and nose. I switch the fan from my right hand to the left and squeeze my own nose with my right hand. Some dusty-sticky snot comes out. Pondering over this, I wonder how a large amount of dust is inhaled everyday into our body through our nose.

Recently a benumbing thought of death has started paralysing my senses. Last night I saw myself dead in a nightmare where Chachi asked me, 'When did you come? It is like returning to your own abode or some relative's house.'

I woke up sweating. By my side, Firoza was in deep slumber snoring loudly as usual.

Firoza brings a tray with tea, squash, biscuits and some peeled pears. Looking at me she shouts in disgust, 'What are you doing? Go to the bathroom and wash your hands and face with soap. Don't touch my glasses and cups with your filthy hands!'

After washing up, I first drink squash and then eat the pieces of pear. Taking a sip of tea, I tell Firoza, 'Last night, I saw Chachi in my dream.'

Chachi did not have any more children. After Chacha's death, her daughters took their mother with them and sold the property. I requested her to live with me. But she didn't. Moreover, my relationship with her daughters had soured in connection with the buying–selling–splitting of movable and immovable property. So I never went to visit my Chachi after that. But I heard that she often asked about our well-being.

Firoza's hands are preoccupied with knitting needles. I am not sure whether she has been paying any heed to my words or not. I know that she often goes to visit Chachi without informing me. I pretend as if I know nothing. Some days ago, she sent *sadh*[ix] to our daughter's house. Now she is busy knitting a pullover for the expected child. In the meantime, electricity returns.

I request her, 'Switch on the fan.' At first she pretends not to have heard me. When I again ask her, she replies 'Can't you see I'm busy with my work?'

'Your work will not be hampered if you do this trifle of a task.' She does not move, but says, 'You can easily do this, why are you asking somebody else?'

'Is it the same to ask you and to ask somebody else?'

'Yes.'

I switch on the fan myself. After that I go to the verandah and stand beside the banister. It becomes difficult to look at the sky. I ask without looking at her, 'Well, do you believe in *Quayamat*?'[x]

'Yes, being a Muslim, I do. But why are you suddenly asking such a question?'

'On the day of *Quayamat, Hashar*[xi] or last judgement, everybody is supposed to assemble in the same field. Is it so?'

'Yes. Why?'

An unknown bird is chirping somewhere in the distance. All thoughts associated with Chachi are trickling down the lanes of my memory. Her query in my dream, 'When did you come?' is incessantly drumming my ears. I am trying to remember her profile–features, voice. Oh! My dearest. Alas! It has been a long time since I met her. Her heart-rending voice, coupled with a sense of guilt, starts pricking my conscience. I am trying to drift off into other thoughts. I say, 'You know about my Chhotomama,[xii] though you have not met him, only heard about him from me. When he gave *talaaq* to Chhotomami,[xiii] his son Ahmed was a boy of hardly five or six years. Then, ladies like you, who have no work of consequence, unnecessarily used to ask that little kid, "Well Ahmed, do you remember your mother? Don't you miss her?" Do you know what his answer used to be?'

I presume Firoza will ask about Ahmed's reply but she remains silent. She is standing behind me. I turn back and see her eyes are focused on her knitting needles; her fingers are moving very fast. I say again, 'He is now head of the department of English in Victoria College in Kumilla. After Partition, when my other maternal uncles fled to East Pakistan, now Bangladesh, this boy said, "But father does not allow me to go." However, he hoped to meet his mother in the field of *Quayamat* where his father would not be able to slap him.'

Firoza stops knitting and says, 'But upon growing up this same stripling will beat his wife and give her *talaaq*.'

'There is nothing left for him to grow up further. Didn't I tell you that he is now head of the English department in his college? I have heard that he has already given *talaaq* to his first wife and become engaged to one of his students from his private tuition.'

'I've already said so.'

Her nonchalant shrill-sharp, piercing tone has a glistening steely modulation.

I ignore that and ask, 'Do you know the reality?'

'What?'

'When men burn their wives, the mothers-in-law and sisters-in-law of those ill-fated wives, celebrate the occasion.'

'I know that you will say so.'

I have finished the cigarette. I sit down.

'Chachi is not at home now, I suppose?'

'Who?'

'Borochacha's wife of the northern house.'

'She's gone to her sister's granddaughter's house.'

'How many days does she stay at home?' I become contemptuous.

'What will a young lady like her do with such an old man? Will she pluck out his silvery hair?' Firoza says with burning gusto and rancour.

Hanif Mian, my Borochacha says that he is ninety-eight years old. But, we assume that his age is a few years above eighty-five or eighty-six. I light up another cigarette.

My Borochacha's first wife was Firoza's Fupu (aunt). She is dead. When she was alive sometimes Firoza came to stay with her. I saw Firoza then, for the first time. Adolescent, youthful Firoza sometimes came with her Fupu to visit our house. I was in college then. However, there was no opportunity of knowing her better. Many years after the death of her Fupu, we had an arranged marriage.

It's been a good while since the bird has stopped chirping. Perhaps it has left the place or has become tired of straining its voice. My teacher had once presented me with his own pen because

I had captured the essence of the poem 'To the Cuckoo' in my own language. But my youngest brother misplaced it. I feel sad when I wonder why people also lose their happiness in the same manner, somehow, somewhere.

I notice silvery shades among the locks on Firoza's forehead. Her scalp is visible through her receding hairline. But once she had dense hair. After our marriage Chachi frequently engaged one or two maids for oiling, combing and braiding her hair into a bun or plaits. I called her Chachi, but Firoza addressed her as mother.

I remember those days. Firoza always says I have two mothers—one gave birth to me and the other nurtured me. Both are mothers.

Sometimes I have some peculiar wishes and thoughts. One day somebody told me 'You are an ageing man now. Don't bother yourself about everything. Don't try to mingle your past with the present. You cannot enjoy it and subsequently cannot derive happiness from it.' It is true. I feel extremely depressed when somebody calls me an 'old man'. But in reality, that I have indeed become an 'old man' can be deduced by looking at Firoza.

In our village there is a poor land-labourer named Mutlib Sheikh. He dotes on his wife and does whatever she says. Everyone teases her and calls her 'the mirror of Mutlib'. The poor woman always retorts furiously, though. I have been taken aback after looking at my own reflection in the mirror. '*Hori din to gelo* ...' ("Lord, my days have come to an end...")

Suddenly I ask Firoza, 'How are your days passing?'

'What?' she is startled. I realise that she had been completely engrossed in some deep thought, taking her mind away detached from her immediate surroundings. That is why she is startled by my voice. It shows that my presence in her mind's world is insignificant.

She asks, 'What do you mean?'

Actually, she does not know that my question is based on my recollection of the song, '*Hori din to gelo*...' I ask, 'What is your age now?'

'Oh!' she becomes irritated, her knitting needles become active again. 'Why do you ask such peculiar questions? I do not like it.'

'Do you remember Fupu? What a gracious lady she was.'

'Quite often I used to see Chacha, after completion of his Zohur namaaz, sitting down to a meal of hot rice and curry. After serving rice, Chachi offered him some large pieces of fish, "Please, eat these also; you like to eat *hilsa*."[xiv]

What a pleasing sight: picture of a perfectly happy family.' I pinch Firoza. 'However, you never like these things.'

She responds laconically, 'You can see! People see what they want to ...'

'What do you mean?'

'I mean it was not something meant to be observed by you. Do you know that when Chachi used to slice fish, your Chacha would come and simply order her to give him a *paan*? Chachi would say that such errands would further delay her cooking . He had a habit of blowing the entire situation out of all proportion if he did not get his lunch immediately after *Fazir-e-namaaz*.[xv] *Paan-chun-*[xvi]*supari*[xvii] used to remain properly arranged on the dish. He only had to make his own *khili*[xviii] ...'

I flip through the daily newspaper.

Firoza says, 'You men! You regard your wives as mere maid-servants! Fupu would be slicing fish. After that she would wash her hands. Then she would arrange *paan-chun-supari* as an offering before 'God' who did not have hands or legs. He could not make his own *khili*. But when the time came to beat his wife his hands and legs became active all of a sudden. At first, he kicked and punched her and ultimately he hurled the *paan*-container aiming at his wife's forehead. I was there, even when she was given her last bath after her demise. The deep scar and the wound on her forehead was still visible even after it had dried up long back.' Fixing her eyes on mine she asks sarcastically, 'A happy ideal family? Is it not?' This said, she resumes her knitting.

There are some postal cards and envelopes on the table. I have already read them. Again and again I arrange, rearrange, and read them. An editor has requested me to send a mini-story. I wish to ask him, 'What is the matter, sir? Will you request me after some days to send a micro-story?'

Some blank sheafs of paper and a pen lie on the table. I pick up a sheet and scribble 'Dear sir' and two more lines but my writing does not proceed beyond that. I tear the paper to pieces.

Firoza stops knitting and observes my actions. I expect her to say something since the torn shreds of paper are now strewn all over the floor. But to my surprise, she asks in a bitter, caustic voice, 'Will you please tell me what the differences are between a man and a woman? These breasts, these …' She utters some obscene words in an offensive manner. I can understand her anguish, but her impudence embarrasses me. She finishes her sudden outburst by concluding, 'Yes, there are some physical differences. But what does it really matter? Why do you behave in such a brutish, disgraceful way with us?'

I cannot sit there anymore. Gathering my *gamochha*,[xix] *lungi* and soap, I go to the pond to take my bath. Firoza is in the kitchen now. Today a hen has been slaughtered. The hen was ready to hatch eggs. All the eggs got broken in the process. Its inactivity and reluctance to eat compelled us to butcher it. Firoza is scolding and blaming the cock for the whole situation. I expect to have a large meal today. I have asked Firoza to prepare *pulao* as well.

The *Zohur-namaaz*[xx] is recited by the Mullah. The remaining portion is recited by me. After completing his recital he walks up to me. I realise that he wants to say something. I ask, 'Do you have something to tell me?'

He almost shrivels up in shame, 'Today I am supposed to dine at your Borochacha's house.'

'So what?'

'Actually the grandmother at Hanif grandfather's house is not at home.'

'I know.'

'In the morning he ate chilled stale rice from last night as he hadn't cooked in the preceding afternoon. In the morning I went to the madrasa without having my breakfast.'

I observe that Borochacha is engaged in *Kabar Jiyarat*[xxi] after completing his namaaz. The graveyard is just in front of the mosque. Noticing that he has finished his reading of *dowa-darud*,[xxii] I address him, 'Chacha?'

'Who? Oh, Rahmat, what's the matter?'

His tone is very much acrid. It is said that when mango ripens, it becomes sweeter but when man ripens he becomes bitter. Unless there is an emergency I generally avoid talking to him.

I answer, 'Nothing serious. I have come to invite you to join us for lunch at my home.'

'Why, all of a sudden?'

I blurt out, 'As you know today is the *okat*-day[xxiii] of Firoza's dead Fupu.' He looks strangely at me without uttering a word. He contemplates for some time. Then he accepts the invitation and says, 'Well, I will come. Let me visit home once before that.'

We send Mullah beta's lunch to the mosque. After that, I sit down to eat lunch with my three sons and Chacha. Firoza's face turns dark and glum. She serves the food. I tell Borochacha, 'I remember how carefully and tenderly my late Chachi used to fan you and how dotingly, she placed all the large pieces of fish on your plate without leaving anything for herself!' He had once thick-set eyebrows. The weight of age has pushed his eyeballs inside the sockets and his lax skin makes them invisible from others' sights. Lifting his eyes he first stares at me and then at Firoza. My sons are nudging, pinching each other and sniggering among themselves. I warn them with a glare. He notices them, too. Then he looks at his plate and says, 'All days don't pass by in the same way.'

He heaves a deep sigh.

I move on to a different matter, 'Chachi is seldom at home. You can cook well even at this age whereas I am not even used to preparing a cup of tea.' I try to smile.

He remains silent. Nowadays Firoza does not address Borochacha as 'Fupa'. She relates herself to him in accordance to my relationship with him. Suddenly she asks, 'Do you have *paan-supari* even now, Borochacha? Do you make the *khili* yourself or is it prepared by our present Chachi?'

He can understand the jibe implied in the question. He is mixing the rice with curry. His fingers start quivering. His voice is choking with helplessness, 'I remained hungry this morning. I had some left-over food from yesterday. I did not cook out of sluggishness. While eating, I noticed some ants in the rice; I washed it, but there still remained some. I do not even see well anymore.'

I look at Firoza. For the first time in my life I feel like beating her up. She is grinning. She comes near me and asks, 'Do you want some more *pulao*? After all we are having *pulao* at home today after many days. You love it, that's why ...'

Translated by Susmita Chakraborty

(Endnotes)

i Uncle; father's elder brother.
ii Betel leaf.
iii A utensil like a saucepan.
iv Aunt.
v Ceremony after the death of a person.
vi Delicious food items.
vii Uncle.
viii A thin cake made of dried juice of ripe and sweet mangoes.
ix Ceremonial offering of food to a woman expecting a child.
x The day of judgement.
xi The day of judgement.
xii Uncle; mother's younger brother.
xiii Aunt; mother's younger brother's wife.
xiv Fish available in eastern India and Bangladesh.
xv First prayer in the morning before sunrise.
xvi Slaked lime.
xvii Betel nut.
xviii *Paan, chun, supari*, etc., packed and wrapped together in a triangle.
xix Thin towel.
xxi First prayer in the morning before sunrise.
xxi Visit to the graveyard.
xxii Prayer to Allah for his blessings and the praise of Prophet Mohammed.
xxiii Ceremonial observance in the memory of the departed.

The First Order

Mithilesh Bhattacharjee

On a certain winter afternoon, when the sunshine takes the colour of a ripe banana, when an unpolluted breeze gently blows through the suburb, when fearless sparrows and blackbirds nibble at grains from the field or on the dusty road, when a dove sends out plaintive caws from a denuded tree, when the bodies shrunk with cold are back to life after a sunbath at the courtyards and terraces of scattered houses—on such a lazy timeless afternoon Haranath Das, the fishmonger, got down from the bus and set foot on the suburban neighbourhood. His short, dark frame moved in rhythmic steps with the burden of the fish basket on his shoulders, his veins showing the creased skin of his hands. He wore a half-sleeve, tattered, blue shirt, a pair of khaki pants and a pair of *hawai chappals.*[i] A basil-bead garland adorned his neck.

Although it was rather late for vending fish, Haranath was totally relaxed. Not a trace of anxiety was seen on his face. He was confident that his fish would sell in any case. Fresh, large, silver-coloured *sarputis*.[ii] Caught this morning with cast net from the private fishery of Basudeb Das. Usually, Basudeb did not catch fish from this fishery for selling outside. It was for domestic consumption. But if there was an emergency requirement for hard cash, only then did he touch this fishery. The plump and tasty fish of this fishery were carefully preserved through the year for feasting the dignitaries. Basudeb was the *panchayat*[iii] chief of the Baluchari Camp. Highly placed people regularly visited his office. People like the loan officer of the bank, bureaucrats and sundry government officers, MLAs and their cronies and so on.

Haranath had carefully picked and chosen his fish one by one today. Of course, he had to pay more than the others. But he was sure about one thing: he would not have to dole out a free polythene bag to the customer with this lot of fish. There was such a craze about free gifts these days. Even the ramshackle shops of their slum were not immune to this craze. A balloon came free with a one-rupee lozenge wrapped in shiny colourful paper; a comb with a bottle of perfumed oil, a ribbon with a band of hair clip. And many more offers such as these. This had become a pain in Haranath's neck. The demands of his wife and children haved increased manifold. On the other hand, he could hardly make both ends meet by whatever he earned at the end of the day by selling fish.

In the ether waves of the quiet lane, meandering into the distance like a narrow stream, Haranath's full-throated voice reverberates, 'F … i … s … h, who wants f … i … s … h!'

Binod has been expectantly waiting to hear this call right since morning. He was actually a little surprised that no fishmonger had entered their lane since morning. He was at a loss to guess the reason behind this exceptional situation, especially when fishmongers thronged their lane by turns everyday from early morning. They did not come from afar. They collected fish from the fen, marsh lands, lakes, canals and fisheries falling within ten to twelve kilometres of this suburban settlement. Then they rushed towards the town in buses or in trucks ferrying sand. Those who could start early sometimes even covered the distance on foot. The rhythm of their fast pace while balancing the fish baskets on the shoulders was worth a watch. Their whole bodies swayed to the rhythm as they moved. Binod has watched their steady gait with bemused eyes on many occasions. At times, mishaps also happened on the uneven road full of ditches and pits. Maybe something similar had happened today as well. Maybe the wheel of a vehicle had got jammed in the pitfall of a tottering wooden bridge.

Be that as it may, Binod now called out loudly to the fishmonger and asked him in. His typical Bengali heart leaped up when he observed the fish piled high and laid out in the wicker-basket. The silver-coloured phosphorus-rich *sarputi* fish should have become delicious this winter after having acquired fat during the month of *Agrahayan.*[iv] A full-grown *sarputi* fry, steaming hot rice, bright green fresh chillis of Halflong—what more could a connoisseur of food ask for!

Sitting on his haunches before the wicker-basket, Binod eagerly asked, 'What's the rate today?'

'A hundred rupees per kg, babu.'

'Hundred!' Binod raised his eyebrows in feigned surprise.

'I'm offering a reduced rate, babu. I would have sold it at hundred and twenty if I could come earlier.'

'Why couldn't you come in the morning? Was there any problem on the way?'

'Twenty-four hour *kirtan*[v] is going on in my locality, everyone is damn busy. Haven't you got the programme details?'

'Tell me, what's the name of your place?'

'Why, Baluchari Camp, babu.'

'Oh, I see. I went there last evening and had *prasad*[vi] from the *kirtan*.'

'Have you really?'

'Yes, piping hot *khichdi*,[vii] curry and chutney.'

Hearing these words, Haranath instantly became happy and contented and his eyes turned misty in a strange rapture. He folded his palms and touched his forehead, glancing at the sky with half-closed eyes, falling into a kind of momentary trance.

Hearing the news of twenty-four hours *kirtan* taking place in Baluchari Camp, his God-fearing colleague Sandip was eager to pay a visit. He invited Binod very sincerely, 'Come, lets go there and listen to the *kirtan* for a while.' Binod was happy to learn that on the occasion of the *kirtan*, a fair was also being held. He was always drawn towards the romance of a fair. He enjoyed wandering about aimlessly and anonymously in the crowd of humanity.

Along with Sandip, Rajesh and Nibaran, Binod worked in the rural branch of a bank a little distance away from the Baluchari Camp. The area was off the gravelled road. As such a sleepy, colourless and glamourless place inhabited by low-caste people, it had come alive by the excitement of the twenty-four hours *kirtan* and the hullabaloo of the fair. People of all descriptions—young and old, men and women, boys and girls, the housewives, the children—from the surrounding villages had flocked there to lap up the rare pleasure provided by the *kirtan* and the fair.

A huge *pandal*[viii] of bamboo poles and corrugated tin sheets was set up in the open space before the permanent pavilion near the main road. This is the space where every evening a makeshift bazaar took shape with the villagers selling fruits and vegetables grown in their own backyards and fishermen selling tiny fish caught from ditches and canals with their scoop nets. When Binod and his friends visited the place the previous evening, buying and selling was on in full swing at the rows of shops in the fair. A large crowd had also gathered at the space for the *kirtan*. Even in the midst of this sea of humanity, a young *kirtaniya,*[ix] clad in *dhoti* and *fatua*[x] stood on the dais raised in the middle of the pavilion and played a lively tune, his nimble fingers deftly moving on the reeds of a harmonium tied around his neck with a piece of yellow cloth. While doing so he said in a voice charged with emotion, 'The song I am going to sing now speaks of the mind and the body, of desire and passion and above all of the love of Radha and Krishna …'

Sandip was particularly happy seeing the overflowing crowd of men and women in the assemblage of the *kirtan*. Walking slowly towards that direction he muttered to himself, 'Wonderful! These people have devotion to God and religion. Good … very good.'

Rajesh and Nibaran followed him.

As Binod slowly moved towards the fair, he noticed the small hutments made of bamboo, straw, twigs and occasionally tin and lime-washed mud. He noticed the rough and rugged terrain bereft of trees and plants, the muddy ponds, the barren land covered with dry saffron sand. He could imagine the relentless struggle for survival that these people were engaged in.

With a variety of goods for sale the fair attracted a large number of enthusiastic crowds. There were cheap eateries, shops selling cigarette-*bidi*-[xi]*paan*, shops of clothes and shoes, of toys and cosmetics and what not. In the midst of all these wares, suddenly Binod's eyes were drawn to a young woman placing a tea-kettle on the bluish flame of a Janata brand stove. Her well-endowed body, her wheatish complexion, and perhaps her striking posture of a slight stoop towards the stove, immediately engaged his attention. She was wearing an unclean yellow sari, and a blouse without any bra inside, thus accentuating the charming swell and curves of her breasts. Binod noticed all this in one sweeping glance. The fall of dusk was imminent at that time. Like a man in a trance Binod found himself stepping into the mystery world of light-and-shade inside that makeshift teashop.

Exactly at that moment the deep voice of the announcer on the microphone resounded above the din of the fair: 'The devotees present in the assemblage of the *kirtan* and the fair, please listen. We are extremely happy to announce that our Chief Guest and patron of this Annual Festival, Honourable Shri Rajat Shubhra Das, former minister and present MLA, has kindly agreed to give a brief discourse on religion for our benefit. We request you to kindly maintain silence for a while and listen to his words.'

A few moments after the announcement, the voice of the former minister and present MLA was heard over the microphone: 'Friends, I will not deprive you of the pleasure of the *kirtan* and the fair by giving a long talk. I want to share only a few words with you about religion and the practice of it. I believe that following the path of religion is the best way to safeguard man's moral character in this age of restlessness. Only religion can unite and strengthen humanity. Friends, it is only through the right practice of religion that the salvation of your souls can be possible. So I would strongly recommend that you devote yourself to the practice of religion as far as possible through *kirtan*, worship and holy rituals ...'

The four of them found themselves in a spot while returning from the Baluchari Camp. Movement in villages and semi-urban areas at night can be fraught with hassles if you don't have a vehicle at your disposal. Standing by the side of the gravelled road, they were anxiously looking around in the hope of finding a conveyance. The sonorous sound of the *kirtan*-songs, the din and bustle of the fair and the dazzling light—all were far behind them. Here as far as one could see there were only clusters of darkness with occasional relief provided by a few fireflies. Suddenly a man appeared as if piercing through that darkness fraught with fireflies. It was so sudden that they were a bit frightened to begin with. A lean and thin man of nondescript appearance, with a cloth band tied around his forehead. Had a mischievous petty thief of this rural area followed them? But waving aside all their apprehensions, the man indulged in a formal salute towards them and said in a light vein, 'If there is no vehicle, why don't you take an auto?'

'Will an auto be available?' all four asked eagerly.

'Of course, it will be available. Wait, let me call one.'

Having said so, the man vanished in the darkness. Naturally, they did not attach much importance to his words. They thought the fellow must be a nut. But a little later an auto materialised before them to their utter amazement. None of them could gauge whether the fellow was a madcap or a good samaritan.

The local auto driver satisfied their curiosity about the man. Once upon a time he owned a sizeable amount of land and property in the Baluchari Camp. He was intelligent and reasonably educated too. But there was one fatal flaw—he was headstrong, obstinate and rash. That ultimately spelt his doom. A few years back at the time of the harvest, an errant bull damaged much of his paddy field. The enraged man tied up the bull in a confined space for three days. The bull suffered a lot and finally died of starvation and thirst. This disturbed the equilibrium of his mind and within a few days he turned cranky. People of this region believe that the man lost his head because of the curse of Lord Shiva whose carrier is the bull.

'Babu, how much fish shall I give you?'

Binod's spell snapped and he replied in a normal voice.

'Maybe half-a-kilo. But you are charging me way too much.'

'No babu. Okay, I'll give further discount specially for you.'

'How much, tell me?'

'Ninety rupees per kilo. As a result, my profit will be minimal. But after all you have visited our *kirtan*. I am a member of the committee. How can I charge you more?' Haranath smiled broadly.

'How long have you been in that Camp?' Binod changed the topic.

'Many years, babu. The country was partitioned. We were also relocated from one land to another.'

'You people originally belonged to the vast region of marsh. You've got similar surroundings here too, right?' 'Yes, and that's why we are struggling to survive.'

'Why somehow? The government has taken up many projects for your upliftment and is pumping in a lot of money too. Are you aware of all this?'

'One does hear such things from time to time, babu. But one does not see any result anywhere. Anyway, we don't hanker after much. By the grace of Lord Govinda, our days pass by reasonably well.' Having uttered the last words with deep conviction, Haranath closed his eyes and with folded palms paid obeisance to the unseen God.

Binod wondered if Haranath knew the young woman he met at the fair. While talking to Haranath, he was repeatedly reminded of her. The woman took good care of Binod. Such a personal touch in serving tea and her frank easy demeanour while engaging in a conversation with Binod, surprised him a little. After all, he was a stranger. Of course, it could be explained away as a part of business conduct. The young woman had adopted the style quite well. But Binod was surprised for a different reason. The place was a grossly backward village. If it were a suburb or semi-urban place, the woman's frank behaviour would have been inconspicuous. Maybe she instinctively realised that Binod entered the shop fascinated by the intoxicating attraction of her buxom physique. That is why she had been so expansive: 'Come, come, please take a seat. Tell me what you would prefer to eat. Have you come to listen to the *kirtan*? Well, in that case you are our guest now. You must stay till *prasad* is distributed. Have you received initiation?' The woman chattered without break. All the while Binod's wayward eyes had been grazing on the different parts of her desirable body like a pair of persistent flies.

The moment Binod broached the topic of the young woman, Haranath started off in a torrential speed, 'You are speaking of

Sabita, right? Wife of Girin. Now they are separated. The man is an alcoholic, keeps boozing day and night. Whatever the girl does for the sake of survival, selling tea or selling her body—she is very pious by nature—a real devotee. That is the most important thing; what do you say , babu?' Haranath called upon Binod's judgement.

An astonished Binod realised that everything pertaining to mankind–body and soul, wealth and poverty, sin and repentance–everything was harmonised and reconciled at that single point—*dharma*. What he witnessed with great surprise at the Baluchari Camp yesterday now turned into an unfathomable mystery at Haranath's words.

Translated by Nirmal Kanti Bhattacharjee

(Endnotes)

i Slippers.

ii *Puti* is a kind of fish small in size; *sarputi* is *puti* bigger in size.

iii Local self-government at the village level.

iv Ninth month of the Hindu calendar: 22nd November to 21st December.

v Singing of devotional hymns in praise of deities accompanied by traditional instruments.

vi Food offered to a deity.

vii A dish prepared with rice and lentils.

viii A temporary structure made of a variety of materials, usually related to a religious ceremony.

ix One who sings *kirtans*.

x Indigenous informal male upper garment.

xi A kind of cheap indigenous cigarette made with unprocessed tobacco wrapped in leaves.

The Tale of Dunduburi

Ranabir Purkayastha

The slim fingers of Champa – resembling flower buds themselves – danced in circles like a peacock. The little fingers – gathered together to shape a peacock's head – had formed a beak too. The peacock's beak pecked at the earth, digging up dust. Light streamed in from the space between two houses on the south and reflected on Champa's beautiful dark face. She shook her greasy face to drive the flies away. The knots at the end of her braids played silently on her back, cutely jumping up like ping pong balls on a table. The six-year old's voice chanted a quaint folk rhyme – '*Dunduburi dances; Salutes the sahib and prances*'. With the bizarre words of her rhyme, Champa, the little daughter of Amalkanti lent a new air to the mundane urban morning.

Suddenly Amalkanti's toothbrush slipped out of his hand and fell to the floor. While stooping to pick it up he exchanged glances with Chandra. Chandrabali Dutta – this pretty young girl crossed eighteen around four years ago. She attended classes of Sankha Ghosh at the university. Chandra watched Champa at play. The precocious little child neatly arranged the strange words of the folk rhyme to a rhythm and set it to melody. Amalkanti had taken his daughter to Karnamadhu village, where he had spent his childhood. He had pointed to an anthill and told her that chanting those verses in tune while moving one's fingers lightly around that hill would induce a nice, slim and young ant to come out and do a little dance with its hands over its head. His daughter had asked in amazement, "Really? Is that true?"

"Certainly," Amalkanti had replied. We made them come out so often."

He withheld the truth of his childhood from his daughter. He had taken his wife and daughter to Karnamadhu at the onset of winter to refresh the memory of his lost and forgotten rustic roots. Champa derived immense pleasure in getting her father's childhood tales verified with the old stories of 'amma-dadu'. In the process of assimilating the truth of her father's tales into her own childhood, she had started the game early this morning.

In his haste Amal again dropped his brush. This time Parna emerged from the kitchen, picked up the brush and applied some toothpaste on it. Bowing down, she noticed her daughter. The face of her neighbour's fashionable daughter also drifted into her view in the process. Glancing furtively at Amalkanti from behind her glasses of minus seven, she uttered an 'Oh' with an indulgent smile on her lips. Drawing the window curtain she said, 'Now brush fast and return a little early today. I am going to Hatibagan with Ramola boudi from "Shukhneer"; leave some money for me."

The words sprang out at Amalkanti like four bullets from an AK-47 rifle, establishing her authority; merely informing him of her perfect plans for the day and setting the stage for a *jizya*[i].

Parna knew that it was difficult to contain Amalkanti by mere sweet words. So she had planned a 'direct action' since morning. Instigate, irritate, … and you were safe. You would achieve everything you needed to. This was an excellent composition and the right dose. Amalkanti also knew about this virtue or vice – call what you may – of his personality. But where does one get the money at the end of the month? Six more days to go. And after six days it was Champa's sixth birthday on the sixth of February. Parna was to go and buy a dress for Champa with Ramola boudi who was supposed to have good taste in clothes. She was familiar with the shops as well. Rather than her being known as Subhas da's wife, Subhas Chaudhury enjoyed the status he had due to her. As of now, he was a public leader. There were hidden ambitions. Amalkanti knew, shopping was not the real purpose of the trip. This was the opportunity to roam about, free of cost. Maybe they would watch a movie starring Victor Banerjee at Radha theatre. But Ramola boudi had no appetite for Bengali movies; buying a seven-rupee ticket for fifteen , they would probably watch *Khuda Gawah* – a Hindi blockbuster. They would also eat out at Golghar: a spicy meal of parathas and keema curry. They would have fun at the cost of his love for his daughter.

Amalkanti was at the moment thinking of his wife in terms of money-making schemes. He would inform Mamaji of his requirements over the phone before going to office. A timely S.O.S., which would ensure a free hand over a choice of good food and new clothes. He would ensure that Mamaji Electronics got the dealership. They would perhaps be able to go to Diamond Harbour on their daughter's birthday. They would have got the dealership anyway. Mamaji would readily earn a little more profit to ensure the happiness of Amalkanti's wife. Everyone took commissions; it was his due too. And genuine enough. Anyway, a supplier of the cash had been found. But he could not bear to surrender to Parna so easily. A slight resistence was imperative.

As a prologue to displaying his anger, he drank a glass of water after brushing his teeth and, avoiding the regular morning cup of tea, went downstairs. Champa was playing Dunduburi in the sun. He wrapped a new handkerchief on his fingerless left hand. Amalkanti did not foret to brush his hair, by running his left hand though his hair before going down.

Champa had ended her game by then. 'Won't Dunduburi dance again? See there! Chandra di is also dancing!' Amalkanti pointed his finger above at Chandra's window. Caught in the cross fire between his wife, the neighbour's daughter and his own daughter, Amalkanti in his confusion, mentioned 'dancing' and not 'watching'. Champa did not protest but said, 'She herself is Dunduburi'. Amalkanti did not want to know the cause of her sudden anger and led his daughter upstairs. He had to telephone Mamaji before going to office.

Parna knew it was useless hurrying Amal for anything. She had asked Amal to come back early, merely as a way of extending their conversation. He returned at three, at his usual leisurely pace. To offset the ugliness of one useless limb, he tried to keep the rest of his body fit and active, and his mind unstressed. The absence of fingers in one hand did not disturb him any longer. Keeping all worries contained within his mind, he kept his body agile, quick and free of undue burden. The day one-year old Champa fell from the bed, he had criticised Parna's shrieks and running helter skelter. He had been successful in making Parna realise that hysteria was not the perfect solution to the accident. Now they usually avoided unnecessary hurry and rush, even when attending to phone calls and doorbells.

Amalkanti's entire weakness centred round his hand. He kept it covered in a white handkerchief at all times. Some suspected it to be eczema or some other contagious skin disease, others considered carrying the hand inside the pocket to be a style statement of sorts. There were always a thousand questions about his left hand. Few knew the answer. He avoided the curious eyes and questioning looks, confronting them with a strict visage. Gravity had become his second nature. It earned him the negative epithet of being 'vain' but also the attribute 'smart'.

He did not misuse his mask of gravity to cheat or confuse people. It was simply a strategy on his part to hide his own weakness. There was only one such instance when he joined his job. The interviewer couldn't detect his handicap and Amalkanti consciously kept the secret under wraps as getting the job was important. The company had also not lost in the bargain. Amalkanti had proved to be quite a successful sales manager. He did not select Mamaji for their dealership merely for the commission. The company has been convinced that the Mamajis mean hard core business.

Amalkanti's family did not cheat Parna too. As per the protocol of an arranged marriage, his father had informed them of everything and it was a gentleman's agreement. Parna of course, did not quite believe in such protocols. Arranged marriages always involved facts that were to be brushed under the carpet and concealed from public view. After the first meeting, to bridge the gap of three meonths, Amalkanti had written a letter from Calcutta to Parna Chaudhury of Silchar. 'I'm a one-handed, crippled man. I don't know how and why you chose me,' Amal wrote romantically.

Was that honesty in his writing or illusion? Betrothal and wedding were supposed to take place in November. Feigning many excuses, Parna's family had postponed the wedding for three months. Parna also wrote back. Amal was mesmerised by the style and impeccable Bengali of that letter. 'I too am a flat-nosed girl, without much of a nose, teeth or hair.' But he had seen Parna with his own eyes and she was beautiful and still is, with fabulous teeth, hair and nails. Who could solve this puzzle? He couldn't possibly complain to Parna's family or anybody else for that matter, that his wife's front teeth were false! In their later life, this little falsehood on Parna's part often led to much discord.

Amalkanti ignored the first ring of the doorbell. It was near about five o' clock. Should be Sita, the maid. He asked Champa to open the door. But Champa, the unmindful, adamant child, refused to open the door. Like her father, she could do only one thing at a time. Now she was busy listening to fairy tales. When requested for the second time, engrossed in the story of Tepai, she unwillingly touched the latch lock and turned around to ask her father, 'What did the parrot say, papa?' From the bedroom Amalkanti called out, 'Open the door as I tell you.' He continued in the same breath, 'Then the parrot said "Get up Tepai. Serve rice, the seven brothers have come."' Both of them knew the story of Tepai by heart. Champa did not like stories without birds playing major and funny roles. So Amalkanti kept on repeating the tale of Tepai.

Champa was very fond of birds. Apart from the birds surrounding her, like crows, sparrows and magpies, the birds in the zoo and the ones found in books were her friends. Her father could spend only a little bit of time for her. Her mother was busy throughout the day. Uncle Shyamalkanti had given her a Barbie doll which she kept in the showcase. Her uncle had promised to take her to the bird house. He knew stories about many beautiful birds and knew quite a range of Bengal's own variety of birds. *Holde gal, kalokopal, photikjol, nilkatkatia, lalgal, moutushi, munia, tuntuni, chandana, benebou* – these had enchanting names which she loved; while the birds from the fairy tales were fancied for their achievements – the *shuk-shari* and *bangoma-bangomi* could accomplish fantastic things. The fabled *pakshiraj* flew like a bird in spite of being a horse. *Lakka, fakka, loton* and other tricksters performed games and delivered letters. You could send a letter with a swan too. Her uncle said even the clouds could carry news like the flying birds.

Like the birds, the tiny ants were also Champa's playmates. Amalkanti enjoyed his daughter's pranks in the closed-door bedroom, watching the blue horizon take on magical sunset hues. His eyes and ears were focused on his daughter's prolonged attempts at making friends with a sad, love-lorn mynah perching on the terrace of Chandra's house. His little girl created the spell of the Bhimpalashri – an evening raga – in her conversation with the bird, 'Oh mynah dear, are you the queen of the sky?'

As the doorbell rang again, Champa threw a glance at the irritated face of her father and asked, 'Do you know what Tepai said after that?' She mumbled as she opened the door, 'O wretched parrot, why do you keep calling? Oh God, it's you!' Chamapa ran away keeping the door open. She whispered in Amalkanti's ears, 'Dunduburi'. He guessed from the girl's discomfort that it was not the maid. Coming to the door with his hand in his pocket, he too was taken aback, taking a little time to gather himself and say, 'Strange! Is it you!'

She was dressed like a film star – wearing a loose skirt and a colourful blouse with pink petals printed on white – snugly fitting to her frame. With the lipstick on her full lips and dangling ear rings, the morning's Dunduburi had returned at dusk like a fever for him. He was taken over by fear – an exciting and beseeching one. Undecided whether to call her in or let her be where she was, he started talking to the door itself, 'Parna is not at home. They have gone shopping to Dakshinapan. There is a dance performance there where one of her friends is taking part. I am baby-sitting Champa.' He muttered these lies with relative ease, still standing at the door.

Chandra pinched Champa's soft cheeks. She was a chit of a girl but she disliked people pinching her cheeks. 'Hello,' said Chandra. 'Is your Dunduburi finally out?' Champa pointed a finger at her angrily, 'You are Dunduburi'. Amalkanti was embarrassed and quickly asked, 'Do you have anything to say to Parna?'

'No, it's okay. I'll come again...'

Champa slammed the door shut even before Chandra could finish. Amal opened the door once again, scolding her. Chandra stood there. Amal apologised on Champa's behalf, 'For some unknown reason she is upset with you,' he tried explaining. 'Please don't mind.' He still couldn't muster the courage to ask her in. Chandra left, smiling. Did she leave unwillingly, in a huff? He could have called her in, no harm there. He had wanted to, in fact. Fearing a misunderstanding with Parna he had to let go of such a golden opportunity. The way Parna had dramatically uttered 'Oh' in the morning, spotting Chandra through the window, she was surely going to whip up a storm if she heard Chandra had actually dropped in and had also been asked in. Chandra, the university girl, was indeed different from all other girls who came to Parna. She came just as a neighbour and did not form a part of Parna's circle of friends. She was not particularly different or special, but there certainly existed a grace in her gait and talk. She was bright and exuded a comely beauty; she would be able to stand comparison with Parna who was generally considered a beauty. The company of such a woman, even for a conversation, was highly desirable to Amalkanti.

In Parna's club, there were quite a few slim and trendy young girls but they were far from being bright and intelligent. Amalkanti had not been successful with any of them. So Parna actually had nothing to worry about. And Ramola boudi, president of the women's club where Parna was the joint secretary, was quite an aged and plain woman. Amalkanti was often forced to ask her in and entertain her when Parna was not around. To be with the lady who was the local gossip queen and the wife of politician Subhash Chaudhury, was to belong to the zed category of security. Parna realised that full well. It was only Chandra that Parna was excessively touchy and wary about. The mention of Chandra's name annoyed her.

'I understood the real meaning of the proverb "Better late than never" from your book-gifting ceremony today.'

'What is the matter? You are becoming rather touchy and emotional these days. You were never so formal. And why do you call it a ceremony either?'

'Why not? One book is launched at a book fair and the preparation for the following year is over. The third volume of the poet is also probably waiting to be published.'

'No. To the utter disappointment of my detractors, only the two old books will be available at the magazine stalls this time.'

'That's quite reassuring then; there is someone after all, willing to serve old wine in a new bottle and read out old poetry in new jackets. Will you actually recite poetry or whine about your new soul-mate not keeping her promises?'

'What a suspicious non-believer you are! I'm carrying the book with your name written on it!'

'I bought this bottle about a couple of months ago for a lively *adda*[ii] and poetry session with you. I was waiting for winter to set in.

'Do I display greed and lust?'

'That is exactly the report from every quarter.'

'Oh I see. And what about you my dear? You don't soil your hands, do you? Sink deep without touching the surface of the water. There is a gift in the box. That is mine.'

'That is already in Subhashda's pocket. There is a pen with an electronic watch. Your dear friend has gifted that to Ramola boudi.'

'Great! The charming glance of a well-endowed woman past her prime will perhaps inspire a good poem.' If she comes, she will drink, throw a drunken fit and relate my name to your wife's, will spread rumours and pollute the morning's enviromment. Pass it to me…'

'You needn't worry about the affected environment. She will not come. It being Saturday today, she has rushed for the *puja*'.

This conversation was taking place between Amalkanti and Paramesh, at nine o' clock at night. Amalkanti had drunk one-and-a-half pegs. Parna too had been following her husband's example. Champa's Photik kaku, the poet Paramesh Majumdar, was still sober. Champa had gone to sleep. Though looking sober, he had finished the first peg like a factory labourer. He called it 'a quick single' a street slang. As a result, he reached a 'high' very quickly.

'Why do you play so defensively, Amalda? You are a complete flop. You should consider scandals to be a credit to your name; they should be a part of your prized collection. What's the harm if a man is known to be a drunkard, a flirt and a debauch? It is the night that counts. "*Atandrila, when moonlight suddenly descends on my white bed, I find you missing*." Isn't that by Amiya Chakrabarty?'

'You are right, buddy. Just a while back, a portion of a hit movie was filmed in the life of this flop star. The girl next door – by the way, why does Parna call you my friend? Friends are supposed to be contemporaries, childhood buddies. Are you old? An old, lecherous man of forty-six? You know – a girl – oh... '

He deliberately behaved like a drunkard, looking at Parna and pleading, 'Please don't misunderstand dear. I'm not talking about myself. I'm dedicating that fetching girl to Param. What a stunner she is! Like a petite sonnet bursting forth from a poet's pen. My, my, don't I empathise your misery?'

The bottle of soda toppled and fell on the carpet from one corner of the table, pushed deliberately by Parna. It was not easy for Amalkanti to be high and happy, in spite of drinking. Just a glance from Parna could turn him sober. He took the cue of the toppling soda bottle; he was forbidden to talk anymore; simply had to continue drinking quietly. While he just wanted to inform Parna that Chandra had dropped in, he enjoyed himself at the same time and didn't want to spoil the good mood.

Paramesh had come after a long interval and Parna knew very well how happy that had made him. In spite of all his inconsistencies, Paramesh was a favourite with all three – Amalkanti, Parna and Champa. They could not come to terms with the fact that Paramesh was now a divorcee. It was difficult for them to think of Paramesh and Seema as not husband and wife. Even now their deserted home invoked the dream of a happy family. It was difficult to gather how in the desert town of Jamnagar, the happy family of Paramesh and Seema got destroyed by a sudden storm. Now both of them lived in this city, but separately. Amalkanti has often thought of dropping in at Seema's office – the red brick building in Dalhousie Square – but Paramesh has made it very clear that he shouldn't be doing that as Seema was not a part of his life any more. Amalkanti wished to see Paramesh happy. He now lived a carefree, reckless life and had dedicated his latest volume of poems to his new girlfriend, Diya.

On the pretext of picking up the soda bottle from the carpet, Amalkanti glanced at Parna and mentioned in an almost dreary, apologetic voice, 'Chandra came in the evening, looking for you. Your daughter angrily called her "Dunduburi"'.

'Amalda, if I write more poetry, I would dedicate the next collection to your daughter. I can't carry on like this for long, boudi. I can't write poems without women and nature in mind. What kind of a poet am I? Women are fast disappearing and along with childhood memories, nature has also been fading away. I often thought of bringing you people into my poems but I couldn't. It's also true that I understand you two very well. You're a happily-married couple.

His last words were swallowed with half a peg of alcohol.

'Happy couple! Yes, that's what we are, even without your Bagpiper label. What do you say to that?'

Parna's face was expressionless; only her glass hung limply from her hand. Amal's drunken speech continued. 'Let me tell you a Chinese proverb,' he told Paramesh. Parna banged the glass down on the table with a harsh, grating noise. Amalkanti looked deep into Parna's eyes and shook his head. 'No I'm sorry, I can't', he said. 'I had better relate it to the hollow of a tree. A drunken poet should not be regaled with old proverbs.'

Chandra came on Sunday as well, dressed beautifully, much to Amalkanti's wonder. She wore a handloom silk sari with an orange-and-green border. Her face was devoid of all makeup. Amal tried his best to keep her away from Paramesh. It was always Champa who took the caged bird near the free birds in the sky. Paramesh had been trying to leave before it was dark but Champa had stopped him ffrom doing so, requesting him to sing or recite one song or poem after another. Chandra's entrance caused a moment's break.

'Photik kaku, please sing that song, "The forest bird lived in the forest..."'

Finding herself at a loss as Paramesh didn't quite oblige, she struck at the core and Paramesh was more than willing to tow her line now. Finally approaching Chandra, Champa pleaded, 'Chandra didi, Photik kaku is not singing. Please ask him to sing.' Uneasy with a complete stranger, Chandra looked at Paramesh and then moved her eyes to Parna and Amalkanti. She looked around quite helplessly, almost like the uncertain eleventh batsman down the batting order coming in to bat before the fall of the last wicket. Realising that she would have to play along, she pulled Champa close to herself and said, 'Yes, if Champa wants, you must sing Photik babu.'

Except Champa, everyone burst into laughter.

'Are you sure his name is Photik?' asked Amalkanti, the game's umpire.

'That's what Champa told me.'

'Sorry, we haven't introduced him to you. He is Paramesh. Paramesh Majumdar, the writer Samaresh Majumdar's brother. Champa calls him Photik kaku, after the little yellow bird 'Photikjol.''

'*Photik* means clear, transparent. Boudi believes that I have qualities akin to the name. So I became Photik kaku. Just as you are Dunduburi. *Namaskar*.' Paramesh's words raised another round of laughter.

'Though he's not as great a writer as his brother is, he has a pretty decent reputation as a poet. He is an amateur actor and practises Leninism but wears gems on his fingers. He has also been part of a television serial produced by his brother's friend.'

Even a smart young man like Paramesh was surprised by Amalkanti's quick wit. He didn't even get the chance to protest. Watching him sitting, quite taken aback, Amalkanti started all over again. 'Are you joking, man? Didn't you know she had a proper name? Their surname is Dutta. Champa calls her didi and Parna is Chandra's boudi. Parna knows the rest, over to Parna...'

Parna decided to play along. Like a seasoned TV anchor, she carried on, 'Thank you Amalkanti. Chandrabali Dutta is the only daughter of the famous theatre actor Bhairab Dutta. She's a post-graduate in Bengali.' Chandra's half-uttered 'boudi' restrained Parna for a while but she carried on.

'She is actually due to appear for her finals after a few months. And though she is keen on theatre, she never watches *jatra*[iii] shows. Learns driving at Khanna Motor Training School and the photographer Sunil Das has visited her home a couple of times and taken her photographs. They are sold at a charge of three hundred rupees per photo. A few of them have already been sent to the world of showbiz.'

'Wow!' exclaimed Paramesh. 'This is almost like a crime thriller where the private detective is on the trail of a murder mystery even at the most innocuous, sleepy suburb town. I am a broker by profession, kindly remember that.'

Amalkanti intervened with a timely explanation. 'Paramesh works at the Royal Jordanian Airlines. You only have to wish to go somewhere and you'll be there in a moment!'

'Since everything has fallen into place, why should Champa's request remain unfulfilled?'

Paramesh was full of unrestrained energy after this and sang on till dusk set in. And Chandra signed off with a soulful old Bengali number. Champa didn't call her Dunduburi any longer.

On Mondays and Wednesdays, Amalkanti went out intending to return late. But he forgot his intention during the course of the day and on both days, returned earlier than usual. On Wednesdays, Champa went to a dance school in Lake Town on the city's northern fringes and on Wednesdays she went for English coaching from five to seven in the evening. Parna decided to open a children's coaching centre at home with a simple plan of a three-month contract at one thousand rupees per head. She would take in about ten children per session and convert the big drawing-dining space into a temporary coaching class. Amalkanti had suggested the name 'Shishusamity'[iv] for it. Parna was not discouraged by this jibe at her women's club. But now her project was on the back burner. Champa had to be admitted to a good school and after a great deal of effort Parna had been able to procure a birth certificate for the child showing her to be a couple of years younger than she actually was.

A set of duplicate keys lay in Ramola boudi's house. Amal collected the keys and entered the house. He was very hungry. There was no food anywhere except in the fridge. Why did she keep the fridge running even on such cold days, he wondered. One of his bad molar teeth suddenly throbbed and ached. Had he asked the driver to stay back, he could have asked him to get a cup of tea from outside. He opened the south-facing window after walking about aimlessly. It was a cold winter evening and everything was shut tight. He couldn't decide whether he was happy or unhappy at that, putting N. Rajam's cassette back on the shelf without playing it.

Parna returned with the much-awaited food, smelling delicious. Brushing past her husband, she entered her bedroom, settled her daughter down with a picture book and flopped down on the sofa after changing into a house coat and a cotton shawl. Eventually she served the parathas cut into squares with a sprinkling of tomato sauce. She didn't give her daughter any of that food as it was not home made.

Amalkanti used his right hand to eat. 'Why did you box your daughter's ears?' he asked.

'Because she wanted to come to this room and listen to our conversation.'

'Please don't spoil my mood today. I'm in a transcendental state, neither happy nor unhappy. I can almost feel my heart beat!'

'Is that your heart beating or is it the beat of your Dunduburi's dance? She would easily be your daughter's age, had you not married late.'

'Please Parna. Why don't you take a joke in the right spirit? You have so many women in your club. Have I ever shown any undue interest in them?'

'Of course you have. Nobody but me can detect your lechery…'

'Oh God!'

'But how can possibly flirt with a young girl for hours?'

'For hours? How do you…oh…this is the information supplied by your spies I guess? Making mountains out of a molehill! She came looking for you but I sent her back because I feared you'd be upset. You can ask Champa.'

'Don't involve Champa in this. You should be happy to realise that the fish has actually jumped to your lap even before you had spread your net. What compliments you get! "Dada has such an imposing personality; he walks so smartly with his hand fashionably in his pocket..." I did not disclose your little secret. They have just arrived, they'll get to know the truth soon enough!'

'Please, please Parna.'

'You want me to stop? Did you stop last Saturday, when you mentioned the story of that old proverb to Paramesh? About the grand betrothal of the snub-nosed bride holding a bunch of flowers before her nose?'

'I was drunk then...'

'That's a lie. You are never drunk. You only pretend. You think I don't follow your sarcasm about snub noses and false teeth. You knew everything when you married me but it was only after the wedding that you confided to your bosom friend your secret, unfulfilled desire of a proper kiss! What filthy language! I know what I am and what I lack and I never pretend to be something I'm not!'

'No more, please.'

'Why should I stop? You are not the only one who is frustrated! Does the woman not need a man's touch...his hand...during love making? One needs to be a complete man to have a fulfilling conjugal relationship. Are you a man?'

Amalkanti left the drawing room. He didn't know how to battle his depression. No matter what he did, he would have to spend the rest of his life within the four walls of this house. Was it really a life worth living? His little girl read aloud, 'I have ten fingers on my hand.' Amalkanti minutely observed her ten little fingers which resembled the buds of the champak flower. So perfect, so beautiful...he was filled with a sudden surge of love for his daughter.

Embracing his daughter, Amalkanti took time to think over. How could Parna talk like that? Jumping at the gentle touch on his back he looked up to find his lovely wife caressing him. Trembling, he tried to put the recent past behind him. And Parna too, surrendered herself completely.

'Why do you allow me to say the things I do?'

'What do you mean?'

This was no doubt an oft-repeated set of questions.

Amalkanti felt equally guilty; he had also hurt Parna on several occasions. At least, that had been balanced out. Women were a capable lot and Parna was well aware that she ruled over family and home. After a bout of crying, she returned to her normal self and ran to switch on the TV, calling her daughter on her way. Laying out the food – which had gone cold – on the table, she beckoned Amalkanti to join them at the meal. 'Ma, Dundu…ma Chandra didi,' cried Champa, on spotting a particular face on the television. Chandra appeared on the TV screen. Of the two songs she sang, one had been sung last Saturday in this house- *Mono pothey elo bonohorini* ("A wild fawn ran into my mind's eye"). The earlier rendition of the same song had been much better; her throat was now parched in front of the television camera. The second song went much better – "*I shall not hold your hand my lord, you hold mine.*" Amalkanti found her unattractive. Should she have applied the cakes of makeup just to be facing the TV camera? And the green sari…ugh!

'Don't know why she chose that particular colour!' muttered Parna. 'She proudly believes all colours suit her complexion! This was her first television programme and the tension was writ large on her face. You're extremely rude; you should have asked her to come in; she had run to us to give us the happy news! She would naturally not have told you but informed me about the programme. She had rushed to our house to tell me. Actually that old hag put me off by saying that the two of you had great fun and stood frolicking at the door. And you too, have no regard for morals, right and wrong! '

'I do care. This is nothing but a little fun.' Amalkanti gave Parna a chance to laugh it off after having shed copious tears a while ago.

'How can you call it a little fun? You dragged it far beyond that. I had been to Hatibagan while you told her I'd gone to Dakshinapan; there was no dance programme at Kala Mandir. You lied to her. And Paramesh is no better, exactly like you. You said he was writer Samaresh Majumdar's brother and he accepted it! What were these and so many other lies for?'

'It's okay dear. It's perhaps wise to spend this short span of life in fun and laughter. You can then see what is not there. Why do you hate swimming with the tide so much?'

'Well, I don't hate swimming. You can swim as much as you like but be careful that you don't drown me in the process, with all my belongings.

'But I haven't drowned yet.'

'Leave your jokes aside, will you? You people are great… intellectuals, supposedly the friends of a great writer's brother. You're capable of doing many things. Can't you take Miss Chandrabali Dutta to a good play…one of those group theatre plays? Go and get two tickets.'

'Only two? For whom? You and Chandra? What about me?'

'You can go in that case. I shall have to stay with Champa; she won't be allowed to enter the theatre.'

'Oh why not? She'll be allowed entry alright. We won't go to theatres which say "Children below eight years are not allowed." Some of these plays also write "Bring your children with you."'

Paramesh's phone call had induced Amalkanti to inform Parna of the evening plans. Paramesh's proposal had been a simple one. Amal da, boudi and Champa were very dear to him and they would all go to a good hotel for a chat, drinks and later, dinner. And since he had met Chandra during the weekend, he was keen that she joined them too. But Parna turned the offer down as she didn't wish to drink in the presence of her daughter and she rejected the last proposal straightaway. Amalkanti got the permission to go.

Amal had been looking for an occasion to drink. At six in the evening the two friends sat in Amber restaurant, facing each other. Amalkanti was quite prepared to deal with Paramesh's possible queries but he read a new calamity in the latter's eyes that evening. He was quite sure that the queries would be one dimensional. Was Chandrabali Dutta really Bhairab Dutta's daughter? But the gentleman had married twice. So why didn't the daughter stay with her father? Did they own a huge property? His cautious replies to these pointed questions wouldn't satisfy Paramesh, he was quite sure. For Amalkanti, he simply wanted to keep talking to his heart's content to Chandra every time he set his eyes on her. That was the only relation between them. He went on to relate to Paramesh all the trivia he had heard about Chandra, courtesy his wife. Chandra didn't belong to Parna's club. Chandra and Champa often sang and danced together. A prospective suitor was on his way from Germany or Japan. Did Paramesh want to join the long line of suitors too? Compete with them? His beautiful boudi would surely help him out. Thanks to his boudi, Amalkanti was also quite a popular man. People found him smart and 'manly' with his hand in his pocket.

American chopsuey was his favourite dish at the Amber. He hoped the noodles would be piping hot, as he continued to drink to his heart's fill. On previous occasions, he would mainly chat with Paramesh about Seema, reviving memories of their past life in their house in the desert country. He would bring out the romantic side in Paramesh. But it was different today. He drank to apply balm to his hurt emotions and felt an irresistible urge to pronounce himself as 'manly', looking at the empty glass held in his right hand. He slapped the table with his left hand wrapped securely in the handkerchief, rambling on almost incoherently about a hundred odd things. How he could ill afford a car but still maintained one – which was of course not possible by fair means – because he hated public transport; the seats of trams and buses repulsed him. Chandra was a simple girl, without airs and very honest; very different from Parna.

Finally he came up with the offer of the play by Bibhas Chakrabarty—he had a spare ticket for the Friday 6.30 pm show at the Academy. He would give Paramesh his ticket. Why did he want to bring Chandra and Paramesh closer to each other in spite of himself? Certainly not because he adored Paramesh! Was it because he was too angry and upset with both Parna and Chandra? Why did the anger take root in the first place? Why couldn't a man appreciate a woman for being a woman? It was true he was married but it was also true that he had desired many other women. There was certainly no age bar as far as appreciating women went. Parna thought he was too old but people sometimes married women who were their daughters' age. Granted that he himself could not explain the strange fascination he had with this girl next door, he wasn't even allowed to speak a few words with her! However, he didn't quite wish to get entangled in something which would yield no positive result. Complex relationships meant no escape. In college, he would often sit and chat with his female classmates over a cup of coffee or sometimes pay their bills but this couldn't be repeated with Chandra. He inwardly felt old himself and knew that Paramesh was young enough to enjoy himself.

After a few drinks, Amalkanti was ready to retrace a few steps backwards and consider his own failings. Perhaps Parna was right. What love or pleasure could a disabled person give to a young woman's body? So he induced courage, desire and the illusion of beauty to egg him on. Finally he refused to part with the theatre tickets that he had promised Paramesh and reached the theatre by five-thirty. This was the time of the day when the Academy complex bustled with activity and groups of art students left on buses with their cloth bags and long rolls of art paper slung on their backs. This was followed by the entry of men and women dressed in nice jeans, jackets, coats and cardigans. Amalkanti detected a solitary figure moving amidst the crowd, through the movie camera of his eyes. Salt-and-pepper beard, *khaddar kurta*[v] paired with jeans, Jawahar coat[vi], bag hanging from his shoulder along his side, the gentleman scanned the display board and ran his eyes down the names of the plays, one after another. Moving his glasses and placing them firmly on the bridge of his nose, the man approached the ticket counter and asked for two five-rupee tickets in the last row. There was another man getting off the bus and joining his waiting wife, trying to catch his breath while exchanging niceties with her and ordering two cups of tea with nankhatai biscuits. The cup of tea brushed across Amal's arms as the man tried to move closer to his wife. Amal didn't quite mind as the tea didn't spill over finally. He was amused instead. While sipping his tea he noticed Chandra getting off a minibus; a youth waved back at her from the window of the bus. Amal quickly moved to the back of tree; he needed some privacy to deal with the sudden blow to his happiness.

He hadn't ever considered the possibility of Chandra having someone else already marked out for her. Chandra found him after a while, sitting by the side of the lotus tank. Amalkanti made room for her to sit but he hardly had anything to talk about. He pointed out the small fishes to Chandra under the lily leaves in the tank.

'Have you seen? So many fish in so little water?'

'Haven't you seen the tank behind Nandan? The children from the slums catch fish there with threaded hooks.'

'But the fish are no fools. They must be given food'.

'That's right!' Chandra's eyes twinkled and her entire body language was one of amusement. Amalkanti wondered why Chandra went to that part of Nandan? Who took her? Maybe it was that boy in the minibus who taught her how to catch a fish without a bait. Today Amalkanti did not glance at Chandra's body; he only watched her face covered with soft and silky black hair. He did not look at her directly but stole glances. Modern girls probably did not use kohl anymore, but Chandra's eyes were outlined by dark kohl. Her red lips wearing a hidden, detached smile could be quite destructive. The corner of Chandra's lips moved, 'Lets go, we will walk to that side. There is enough time still. When boudi and Champa come, they will be surprised upon not finding us.' Amalkanti was puzzled. Where did she want to take him? There was truce between them now. Did Chandra want to wilfully lead him down the path of destruction? Chandra looked into his eyes directly, taking him by surprise. A young girl of twenty-two mesmerised and paralysed a middle-aged man. They walked together. She did not hold his hand, yet they walked hand in hand; their bodies didn't touch each other, yet Amalkanti was elevated to another world by the smell and touch of her body.

'Do you know why I did not come with boudi?' Chandra pressed him without actually touching him, in a happy gesture of dependence.

'How would I know that?'

'Who else would know?' Amalkanti forgot that he might have to pay a heavy price for any act of reckless bravery. It was his day today.

'Why did you send me away from the door? Not due to lack of courtesy? You must have been afraid. Of whom? Me, boudi or Ramola boudi's spies?

'Everyone. But since I like you, it was only for your good...'

'That's a lie. As soon as I got off the bus, I realised that you feared Chandra the most. I have come to watch the play today only to find out the reason behind your snub. Why did you hide yourself once you saw me get off the bus?'

'You are so confident, and your analysis is spot on. Who has taught you to tackle the complexities of life at such an early age? Naughty girl—if you could feel the love of an elderly man for you, why didn't you hide it?'

'I also want to talk to you. Your eyes keep on talking to me, but you behave like a stranger when I come near you. Why dada, am I not a nice girl?'

'Not at all; in fact, you are very naughty.'

'Oh, that is indeed a compliment.'

'Compliments are the real achievements of this age. The word 'sweet' with 'naughty' is another compliment. Had you not been sweet, other evil thoughts would have come to my mind. Now lets put an end to this episode of observing fish without bait. Let's go back.' Amalkanti returned from Nandan with Chandra.

Exactly at six, Parna and Champa arrived. Champa had an amusing accusation up her sleeve. Pointing her finger at Amalkanti, she said, 'Baba, you are a big cheat. Dunduburi never comes out or dances.' Amal put up one last resistance, 'Is that so? Who told you?'

'Ma, oh no, Chandra didi.' 'Oh your Chandra didi is also a cheat. She is the Dunduburi, she dances to your song.'

Both Parna and Chandra enjoyed the exchanges between father and daughter.

Saturday came. Amalkanti returned home at three o' clock. A suitor had come down to see Chandra from Germany or Japan and Parna had been given the responsibility of dressing the prospective bride. Amalkanti narrated to Champa the story of Dharmamati shuka bird and Kajalrekha. 'Kajalrekha removes all the needles from her dead husband's body. Asking the maid to grind juice from the tree leaves, she goes for a bath … '. The doorbell rang. Champa ran to open the door. Parna was back with Chandra, who was dressed in an ironed yellow handloom silk sari, and a shawl. Her face appeared as though it had been cleansed free of makeup. Looking at Chandra, Amalkanti asked Parna.

'What happened? The interview is already over!'

'Yes, it's over. Everything went smoothly. Her father has left the decision to her. She is now playing games with everyone. I brought her over because you might be able to gauge her mind.'

'How can I succeed where you have failed?'

'Because you can. That is why I brought her along. The boy seems to be good. Very good, in fact. So please counsel her. Not like that day—when you went for the play.'

'What did I do?'

'I heard you hassled her by talking about fishing. She, told you whatever she learnt from friends, without thinking.' Parna sounded relaxed and easy in her mind.

'I will be back in a minute. Ramola boudi is supposed to get me Champa's birth certificate.' Parna left two bottles of Pepsi for them and went out chanting '*agnaye swaha*' (oblation to fire). Amalkanti was quite surprised by Parna's behaviour.

Did he really go crazy when he looked at Chandra? He always scanned his appearance in the mirror before going out. This time he didn't, but he should have checked whether he looked smart and manly. He moved his hand in the pocket to its proper position.

'Well, how was the play? Did you know that Bibhas Chakrabarty is from our place? A Sylheti.'

'Couldn't follow most of the dialogues. Was that in Sylheti too? I heard it was taken from *Maimansingha Gitika*.'[vii]

'How did you like my friend? He is a fine guy. He was interested in you. We sat together till very late on Saturday night. So he stayed back on Sunday. Do you know that we often have a drink together?' Amalkanti did not quite know how to start off the conversation. Parna had entrusted him with the task of counselling Chandra about marriage.

'I heard about it the other day', Chandra replied. 'I am the daughter of a theatre director. Nobody holds me in high esteem. My father married twice. My mother is a village girl. He lives with his other wife—the actress. Since I like you, love to talk to you, I often stay here till ten at night. I feel greedy when I see you.'

'What have I done to make you feel greedy, my dear? Rather, you are the one who has been pulling me towards you like a hooked fish.'

'No, no, I didn't mean that. I was referring to your happy married life. I too want to get married. The boy is slightly short, not tall like you.'

'Go ahead, get married. It doesn't matter if he is short; good things in life should not be delayed. You will be happy if you want to be. Dear girl, this happiness of ours is the result of much pain and suffering.'

He had been playing quite well till now, like a good bowler in a game of cricket. But a good bowler was often a poor batsman. At the reference to 'happiness', he got drunk without having consumed a drop of alcohol. 'My dear girl', he said. 'Let me tell you the story of a Chinese proverb—please listen.'

Champa had been silent for a long time. When Amalkanti mentioned the word 'story', she returned to the story of Kajalrekha.

'What did the Dharmamati Shuka bird say, Baba? Kanchanmala's story is different; she stays beyond seven seas and thirteen rivers, in the golden country.'

'Oh yes, I didn't finish the story of Kajalrekha.'

'Dada, the story of the proverb?'

Amalkanti looked up: this was a perfect cricket field—his daughter's young face at long on; Chandrabali's face full of complexities at fine leg; and Parna's stable home and hearth at silly point. The half-empty bottle of Pepsi lay on the carpet. The bottle did not break, but a little Pepsi spilled out. His right hand reached the centre table just in time. In the light of the new faith acquired, Amalkanti admitted to Chandra, 'My tale is over.'

Translated by Jaydeep Chakrabarty

(Endnotes)

i A special tax imposed by Aurangzeb during Mughal times.

ii Informal chatting session.

iii Bengali folk theatre.

iv Children's association.

v Loose upper-garment made of handloom cotton fabric.

vi A kind of vest popularised by Jawaharlal Nehru and hence named after him.

vii A folk musical play from Mymensingh district in Bangladesh.

Fire

Arijit Choudhury

As soon as Atul sees Mahendra, he becomes grave. Mahendra asks him, 'Where are you going?' Atul moves on without answering him.

Surprising how this movement to oust foreigners has lent bitterness even to a generous and kind-hearted man like Atul. Not only did Atul and Mahendra sit for their Matriculation examination together, there was great intimacy between the two as well. Both are farmers; both of them have set up their own shops. They sit in their shops when they are free from their agricultural occupations. None is well off; somehow they manage to provide for their subsistence. In order to buy things both of them go to Nalbari either by riding bicycles or in a bus; once they even went to Gauhati together. They have other similarities too—they are-both dusky men, their surnames are 'Das' and they have large families including parents, brothers and sisters, wives and children. There is only one point of dissimilarity between the two and this has been breeding only in the last few months. Mahendra is a worker of the Farmers' Association and Atul is not connected with any organisation, but then like other villagers, he is a great supporter of the movement to oust foreigners. But Mahendra is against this movement; as a consequence of which, everybody calls him a Communist, though he is not affiliated to any Communist party. Actually, he works for the Farmers' Association, and in this connection, he is acquainted with some of the Assamese–Bengali politicians of the party. He does not understand all their ideologies, but

Mahendra has realised that spotting a Bengali-Hindu or a Muslim or a Nepali, immediately branding him 'foreigner' and inflicting torture on him is inhuman and unjust. Even if one is a foreigner that does not mean that he should be driven away or his house and belongings should be burnt down—Mahendra would never support this.

Mahendra has earned the ire of most of the villagers because he has been publicity vocal about his views of late. Even Atul has stopped talking to him; the well-known faces of the village, always mild mannered and innocent, have turned factious. The sons of rich and influential personages visit the villages occasionally and make the chiefs of the villages the profitable elements of this movement. They realise that about fifty to sixty lakh 'foreigners' reside in Assam and if the migrants leave, their land and property would rightfully belong to the local Assamese residents. The village chiefs are incited by this theory and they form the local committee of the *Ganasangram Parishad* (Popular Struggle Association) and also form the Students' Committee with the help of the prompt and clever local youths. Even the number of members for various activities in Mahendra's Farmers' Association is on the decline. Terrible summons such as, 'Come, come! Come out! Chase out! Chase the Foreigners!' are very frequently heard in chorus. In the midst of this atmosphere of dissent, a few reasonable argumentative voices like those of Mahendra also rise to the surface. Many people come forward and quite plainly accuse them of wanting to remain as an agent of the Bengalis! They allege that the Communist party is merely a mouthpiece for the Bengalis. This party has already captured West Bengal and Tripura and now if it captures Assam, its dream of forming a larger Bengal will come true to a great extent.

In one gathering, Mahendra had remarked that if this was the case then why was this Communist party known as the party of the tribes in Tripura? In the midst of such a discussion Khagen Barman raised his voice and said, 'I am a simple villager and I can never understand where, when, and for what political gains a party manipulates power.' He added 'I only understand that the Bengalis have devoured Assam. What do you have to say to that?'

Everyone present at the gathering nodded their heads in Khagen's favour. Khagen took out from his black bag an Assamese newspaper published from Gauhati, which he had brought from Nalbari that very day. Uunfolding the newspaper he asked Mahendra to read what was written there.

Mahendra could guess what was written there even without reading it. The headlines in most of the Brahmaputra Valley newspapers were: 'Frantic activities of the foreigners in Assam'; 'Rule of the Bangladeshis over the local people'; 'Permeation/Migration of the Bangladeshis: Apprehension—Assamese to be turned into Minorities.'

These stories and articles published in the newspapers were all falsehoods or half-truths. Sometimes incidents taking place in the nearby villages were also reported. These reports in the newspapers surprise Mahendra. He failed to understand why these newspapers tried to create animosity between people, making men animals by exaggerating the issues. And Mahendra would never have realised this, had the incidents not taken place in his own neighbourhood.

In Mahendra's house also, division had set in. His brothers wanted him to dissociate himself from the Farmers' Association as well as the CPM party and declared that openly in 'Namghar' by organising a meeting. They have otherwise threatened to ostracise him. But Mahendra's wife, Arati was against these hostile surroundings and she was determined to support her husband although she was expecting their second child. Mahendra spent his nights outdoors these days; sometimes strangers came and asked for Mahendra but Arati remained unperturbed. Arati's father, Anandamohan was a primary school teacher and, during the 1942 freedom movement, he even went to jail. He now spent his retired life in a village near Barpeta engaged in vegetable and fish farming; he was no longer interested in politics. But he had his own opinion regarding this Movement. He once told Arati that killing people could be someone's policy, but it was not a good policy. 'The Congress is bad, Communists are bad, all the all-India parties are bad—what kind of language is this? These hypocritical words cannot be sustained very long. Let Mahendra work according to his own conscience.' Arati told her father, 'I am very scared.' Her father had replied, 'Don't be afraid, they have not seen Mahatma Gandhi; I have seen him—he only had one stick in his hand but he did not fear the mighty British.'

One day Mahendra, finding his father-in-law alone, said that he should not continue to publicly voice his opinion everywhere because the times were bad. Not paying heed to Mahendra's advice, his father-in-law instead told him that he was too old to be afraid of death.

Mahendra decided it was better that the elderly did not keep track of all the information—his father-in-law did not know that even the old and respected people had to undergo physical torture and atrocities if they even slightly criticised the AASU (All Assam Students Union) Movement. Mahendra told his father-in-law about a lecturer of Gauhati University, who had Leftist affiliations, and had to bear the physical assaults of the AASU agitators for just running a small newspaper, which revealed the tortures inflicted on the people by the agitators and the ill effects of such a Movement. These small criticisms against the Movement were insignificant compared to those who were in favour of it, but the agitators refused to be reasonable. The professor lived in the Gauhati University campus, but his paternal home was in Chandmari (Gauhati) where he was attacked by the ruffians.

During the day, Mahendra moved very cautiously, but even then very often he was subject to the reproaches of the agitators; and during the night, he did not stay in his house and village most of the time. It so happened that the supporters of the Movement hunted out their victims; if not found at home, the victim's house was set ablaze. But Mahendra did not want his paternal house to turn into ashes and rubble.

Ministerial rule had collapsed in Assam. There was President's rule in its place. After the 1978 Elections, there were two ministries. One was of Janata Dal and the other one was of Assam Janata Dal. Within two years both the ministries collapsed. A few days ago a very tough officer, H.C. Sarin joined as Chief Advisor to the Governor, but the situation had not improved. It seemed as if the Government was being swayed by AASU and *Ganasangram Parishad*. In a remote village, one of Mahendra's co-workers was physically assaulted, but he did not have the guts to go to the police station because the policemen were present at the spot when the incident took place.

And he was also threatened by them that all his teeth would be smashed if he went to the police station to file a case.

That day there was no working schedule for the Movement; even then with Atul's initiative a meeting was organised including some village chiefs and youths. The news was that the Communist Mahendra had not been in the village for a long time and that he had been seen returning home today by Atul. Old Mahajan Debeshar Das had said that they should also adopt the policies being put in practice elsewhere. The enemies of the country who were against the Movement, that had emerged in order to retain the origin of the Assamese race, should be wiped out. And moreover, Mahendra was very clever; today he had returned, the next day at the crack of dawn he might run away. Therefore whatever was to be done should be done without further delay.

Mahendra had come with medicines for his pregnant wife. He had no plans of staying the night but suddenly his four-year-old daughter was down with fever. They always stocked medicines at home; nowadays they kept a larger stock because of the *bandh*s (strikes) and road blockades. But tonight there had been no medicines for fever because Mahendra's nephew suffered from fever a few days ago and all the medicines were exhausted then. Mahendra decided to go to old Biren Ayurved's house to get some medicines. The shadows lengthened and night fell; it grew extremely dark. His younger brother offered to go instead. But even before he could step out of the house, a terrible hullabaloo reached their ears: 'Traitor Mahendra, come out!' '*Jai Ai Asom* (Victory to Mother Assam)!' 'Foreigners' agent, Mahendra, come out, come out!'

They were about fifty in number; most of them in an inebriated state. Something occurred to Mahendra and instead of trying to escape he stood up to confront them and asked them what they wanted. They replied, 'We want your life.' Only after a while did they draw blood—they struck Mahendra on the head with an iron rod, they also tried to plunge a dagger in his stomach but they did not not succeed. There was no dearth of men in Mahendra's house—and they came out with sticks in their hands, but it was impossible to fight with so many people. Mahendra realised that if he stayed on, his family would be under constant attacks. The mob had come with the express intention of murdering him. They were repeatedly vowing that they would finish the Communist enemy of the state and only then would they leave.

Suddenly Arati caught hold of Mahendra's hands and pulled him into the house. She opened the back door of the house, took Mahendra to the side of the pond and told him, 'Go, run away, otherwise they will kill you!'

Mahendra ran through the plantation garden, crossed the canal, swam across a swamp; then while running through the furrows of a bog stumbled on innumerable occasions. He did not stop though the pain in his head resulting from the injury increased. If he could manage to reach the big road and successfully cross the jungle on the right side of the road, then at a little distance, there was a Muslim village—Mahendra wanted to reach this village. The road was almost deserted with one person turning and looking back again and again in the dark; some people began to walk fast out of fear of this curious figure.

Before fainting and rolling down, Mahendra managed to bang only once on the door of Samsul's hut. It was through the Farmers' Association that Samsul and Mahendra were friends. Samsul was also a worker of the Farmers' Association. Long ago Samsul's forefathers used to live on one of the banks of the Brahmaputra river; when the Samsuls were young, they came to the Nalbari area. In the eyes of the agitators, their village belonged to the foreigners. Twice they tried to burn down houses in that village, but they were not successful. The Samsuls kept watch in rotation. Earlier, this whole area was a jungle; Samsul's forefathers had cleared the jungle and made it fit for cultivation. But nobody cared for such facts anymore. Now, the Samsuls were called Bangladeshis, though they had never been to Bangladesh. The Samsuls spoke in Bengali at home, but three or four Assamese words inevitably croped up in any sentence spoken. Moreover their children received education in the Assamese medium schools.

When Mahendra regained his consciousness, he found himself lying on Samsul's bed. His head was swollen up like a drum, but the bleeding had stopped. Mahendra heard from Samsul that two-three days ago, the supporters of the agitation stripped naked some of the Communist farmers and students and after beating them brutally took them to the office of the Students' Association. Two Communists—Madhab Deka and Madan Barman hid themselves and later cycled to the Mukalmoa Police Station to inform them about the atrocities taking place. But within a short while they were found by the agitators because the chain of one of their bicycles slipped up. Then began the most inhuman torture on Madan and Madhab. They soon fainted. Thinking Madan and Madhab to be dead, the assaulters left them, though they were not actually dead. When they regained their consciousness they took shelter in the nearby *Bodo*[i] home. Getting this information the rowdy agitators attacked the *Bodo* house. Then a rope was tied around Madan and Madhab's necks, their hands and legs were tied up and then they were dragged along the uneven roads for about one-and-a-half kilometres and brought to the office of the Sangram Parishad. While being dragged along, the fingers of their hands and legs got shredded into pieces and, later in the office, salt was sprinkled on their bruised skin and their eyes were clawed out. They died slowly, all the while shouting in unbearable agony. Then both the bodies were placed inside sacks, tied up and then thrown away in a far-off paddy field.

Samsul said, 'You are lucky to have escaped. Even if you were killed nothing could have been done for you.' Samsul also told him that Madan and Madhab's news had not yet been published in any of the newspapers.

Samsul's economic condition was very fragile compared to Mahendra's, but even then Samsul spent a lot of money for Mahendra's treatment, comfort and pleasure. Mahendra stayed there for three days and three nights; he got some news of his home as well. That evening even after he had escaped, the agitators were there in his house for a long time. They insulted his family members. They even tried to insult the womenfolk, but since Arati and the other women took up scythes in their hands, it did not go beyond that. Before leaving, the agitators' final warning was that Mahendra should not be seen in the village again.

One night Mahendra went to Gauhati along with a policeman, who was known to Samsul. In Dispur, Mahendra had to take shelter in the house of one of the leaders of the Workers' Union of the CPM. But here also, there was a great problem—the person himself was a prime target of the agitators. In order to chase away the foreigners, strikers were picketing in front of government offices. Some boys regularly came and threatened the leader, so that he did not report at office again. Looking at Mahendra's unshaven, haggard countenance, they were curious about his identity.

Mahendra went out to see the picketing. He noted that the police and CRPF *jawans* were chewing tobacco right in front of the offices while the office staff stood there with smiles on their lips. But some boys and girls roamed on the streets. People asked each other, 'Where are you going? Don't enter the office.'

Nobody obstructed anyone. If the police wanted, they could compel everybody to go inside the office and work, but they were not doing so. The atmosphere was one of a holiday. Suddenly Mahendra stopped. In front of him was Nripesh from his village, a worker of the Ganasangram Parishad. He stared fixedly at Mahendra and said, 'You here?—Wait.'

That day itself Mahendra was sent to Silchar along with a young Communist Bengali boy by the leader in whose house he had taken shelter.

Mahendra made himself comfortable within a few minutes after he boarded the train and fell asleep. This train was bound for Cachar where most of the people were Bengalis and most of the passengers on the train were also Bengalis. The passengers were mostly all 'Sylhetis', originally from Bangladesh. Mahendra could neither speak pure Bengali nor the Sylheti dialect perfectly. But in this train he felt secure. To begin with, no one looked at him with hatred and suspicion; nobody reproached him. Instead, noting Mahendra's bewildered face, one person gave him his own place to lie down. The compartment was reserved; after passing a few stations, Mahendra's companion managed a couple of berths in the reserved compartment.

Mahendra woke up from deep sleep when his companion called out to him. He sat up but suddenly felt a stab of sadness. Where was he going? Cachar? He had never been there before. Leaving behind his house, wife, children, parents, brother, sister—in short everything, he was running away and escaping like a common thief to an unknown place. What was his fault? He was a worker of the Farmers' Association, he could not tolerate injustice and cruelty meted out to innocent people, be it murder or arson. It was because of this attitude of his that he had to leave his house. He remembered Arati and realised that in her poor physical condition, this great anxiety would slowly consume her. Mahendra was responsible for Arati's poor state. If he had been a supporter of the AASU Agitation Movement, then he would not have had to leave his home and family behind. But it was not possible for Mahendra to work with people who didn't believe in any expediency, who believed in hostility and hatred, and who were easily incited by popular events to wreak ruin and destruction. If his family, his house went, then let it go.

The train was late because it moved with difficulty since the railroads to Cachar were very old. Many tunnels had to be crossed in between Lumding and the Borail range of hills—it took almost twenty hours to reach Silchar. His companion took him towards the villages on the outskirts of Silchar and left him at the house of one of the old workers of the Farmers' Association. His companion's house was further away from there.

Mahendra didn't know the full name of the old worker; everyone called him Bhuluda. Mahendra also called him by this name. The house was an ancestral *pucca* house, but was in a dilapidated condition due to long drawn neglect and lack of maintenance. Bhulubabu's wife was also a worker of the Party. Once upon a time, she was a gutsy and courageous woman and had even gone to jail on a number of occasions. Now old age and a number of ailments have confined her to her kitchen.

Bhuluda was childless, but someone or the other from the Association, always stayed in his house; meetings also took place there at times. Bhuluda was more or less conversant in Assamese but he was taciturn by nature; his wife was agarrulous woman who always spoke Sylheti. Mahendra did not face much of a problem because of this. Rather he seized the opportunity of mastering many Bengali words and phrases during his stay there.

Within a few days, Mahendra grew familiar with the people of the village. Towards the beginning, most of the villagers suspected him to be a member of the AASU or Ganasangram Parishad, but when they came to know that he was staying in Bhuluda's house, their suspicion vanished. In the Barak Valley, Mahendra noticed something—the Movement to oust foreigners did not have much impact upon the people, especially in the villages, whereas, in the Brahmaputra Valley, all classes of people were being tortured; they belonged to all religious groups and minorities. In the Barak Valley, hardly anybody knew about the movement properly. Examinations were not being held in schools and colleges, students lost out on one whole year—because of these factors. In Cachar, there was a demand for a separate university, but this uproar was not very strong.

What was gathering strength was the ethnic violence between the Hindus and Muslims. The Lok Sabha elections had taken place a few months ago. As a result of the obstructions created by AASU, it was not held in the Brahmaputra Valley, but polls were held for a couple of seats in Cachar. In Silchar, this election took the shape of ethnic violence and riots. Though the riots stopped, the resentment continued to accumulate in the minds of the people. Bhuluda and his comrades were deeply concerned about this and were trying to organise meetings in their area to discuss this. But just like the anti-agitators, in the Brahmaputra Valley, who were against the Movement, and didn't have sufficient power and support, in the Barak Valley, Bhuluda and his companions were an ostracised few. The violent Hindus considered them to be the agents of the rioting Muslims and the violent Muslims did not like their peaceful ways.

A fortnight passed in Bhuluda's house; the food served to Mahendra was plain and simple. But even then he started feeling uneasy. How long could he stay like this taking advantage of Bhuluda's hospitality? But for Bhuluda and his wife it was nothing unusual because they were used to the fact that outsiders often came and stayed in their house. Whenever Mahendra spoke of leaving, Bhuluda smiled and replied in the Sylheti dialect, 'Where will you go? AASU has made you an agent of the foreigners, your *boudi* (Bhuluda's wife) was also displeased with your plans of leaving us.

Stay for some more days, let the situation cool down in the Nalbari side and then you can go.'

But there were no signs of abatement of tension and violence, as yet. Sarin was trying to make the laggardly administration come alive and be spirited and impartial—but that required solid hard work; it could not happen within a short span of time. There were no positive signs of a meeting being arranged to discuss the matter with the Centre. Irrespective of whether there was any concrete working schedule of the movement, everyday news of fresh atrocities by the agitators in the Brahmaputra Valley reached people's ears; as a result the people from Barak Valley didn't want to go there. After coming here, Mahendra received only one letter, a brief one from Arati. Arati had sent this letter to the house of a Communist worker in Nalbari. She wrote that she was doing well. The agitators occasionally threw stones at their house, one day they even tried putting the house on fire, but considering that Mahendra had left his home for good, such attacks had lessened. Arati further wrote, 'If you can manage a source of income in Cachar, then I shall come to you immediately after the child's birth; it's impossible staying here.'

Mahendra smiled at Arati's naiveté. How could he manage a source of income here? Moreover in Cachar, the cost of living was so exorbitant that Mahendra did not know how the labourers and other working classes survived here. Actually, Arati had become impatient because of her long separation from Mahendra—and that was perfectly normal.

One and a half months passed in this manner. In the meantime, Mahendra along with others of the Association went to Dharmanagar and Kailashar in Tripura and came back. In that state also, the environment was steadily becoming poisonous; the difference between the Bengalis and the tribals rose. Mahendra did not like Tripura—there would be no peace anywhere, with so much anger prevailing everywhere.

Immediately after reaching Cachar, Mahendra received a telegram; it had come from Gauhati to Bhuluda's address. He had been blessed with a baby boy; the previous one was a girl. But how was Arati? This was not mentioned. Bhuluda's wife reasoned that his wife should be fine, otherwise, they would have informed him. Bhuluda also said, 'Don't worry, have these sweets now, here'. Mahendra had no inkling about when Bhuluda managed to get the sweets for this joyous occasion.

Mahendra could not bear it anymore, he simply had to go home this time, if only for a brief while. Wouldn't he see his son's face? He was willing to risk his life just to see his son's face. Mahendra started for Gauhati in two days' time. The money for his journey was arranged by Bhuluda and the others, who pooled in their resources for him.

Mahendra reached Samsul's house from Nalbari with a strong and powerful farmer-friend in the afternoon, when the scorching heat of the sun roasted Samsul's green fields. If Mahendra wanted, he could enter his own village in the afternoon itself, but did not do so. The Samsuls also stopped him. It was better to enter under the cover of darkness at night they reasoned, and then leave home one morning before the crack of dawn.

It was ten o'clock at night, the whole village was quiet, and almost everybody was fast asleep. Arati, after feeding her son, had turned off the lantern since nowadays there was a shortage of kerosene. The baby cried loudly—it was very hot tonight—and the baby shrieked with such intensity that it seemed that he was angry with the whole universe. The baby resembled his father; his face and his tiny frame indicated that he would be very sturdy, just like his father. At one point, the baby fell asleep after crying for a long while. Arati continued fanning while her eyes went drowsy with sleep. There were at least a hundred odd frogs croaking outside. And the croaking intensified. In the courtyard of the house, a pack of foxes roamed about. One fox yelped, then they all began to yelp together. By now, the dog in the house had woken up and, standing at a safe distance, it began to bark. Arati hugged her fifteen-day-old son. The window was near her feet, near the window was the custard-apple tree. Someone had opened the bamboo gate, the sound of footsteps could be heard; someone broke a branch off the custard-apple tree, and there was a knock on the window. Arati lit the lantern quickly with the matchstick.

'Who is it?'

'Arati, it's me, Mahendra.'

'You? How did you come here?'

'Open the door, don't make any sound.' Mahendra's father also woke up. Immediately after opening the door, Arati burst into tears while resting her head on Mahendra's chest. Hugging her, Mahendra walked towards his own room. In the steady light of the lantern Mahendra saw his son's face. His eyes became veiled with tears, he could not see the boy clearly.

Kamakhya Barman, an octogenarian, who lived in the house opposite Mahendra's, didn't sleep well at night. He had been observing for a while now that there were lamps burning in Mahendra's house and that all the family members were awake or slowly waking up. Kamakhya came out on the road and observed the house closely for a long time. So his suspicion was right! That base-born Communist had come. Kamakhya could clearly see Mahendra, wearing a towel, coming out of the privy with a lamp in one hand and a *lota*[iii] in his other hand, and walking towards the wharf of the pond. Kamakhya was the advisor of the local Ganasangram Parishad, and so he could not hide the news of Mahendra's arrival. Going inside his house, Kamakhya immediately woke up his grandson, who was a tout of the Students' Organisation.

In a short while, the hullabaloo began. 'A Communist has entered the village. Come wherever you may be! Come out! Communist Mahendra has come to his house in the dark—Come, come, come out!'

Within a few minutes, a huge crowd congregated in front of Mahendra's house. There was a scythe in somebody's hand, whereas someone else wielded a stick. Someone said, 'Go around to the rear entrance. Last time he escaped from there.'

But Mahendra had already escaped from the side door adjoining the pond, after fondling his infant son a little. Arati enquired whether she could also go with him. 'Are you mad?' Mahendra had exclaimed.

Mahendra ran with an empty belly and high fever. When he reached Samsul's house after walking across the field and wading and swimming across the pool, canal and swamp, he did not have the strength to speak. Samsul was awake since he knew that something like this might happen. He took Mahendra in his arms and led him inside. He washed Mahendra's hands and legs and then made him lie down on the bed. Samsul asked only one question, 'Did you see your son?' Mahendra somehow mumbled, 'Yes!' and then dropped off into a deep slumber.

After helping Mahendra to recline on the bed, Samsul came outside to light his *bidi* and noticed that, far away, on the side of Mahendra's village, there were rising flames of fire just like the diadem of mosques. Screams rent the air, but the words were not audible. Four boys of the village came on their bicycles with the news that Mahendra Das' house was on fire and those who have started the fire are shouting in excitement and also raising slogans against the Communist, Mahendra Das.

Samsul debated whether he should give this news to Mahendra, but coming inside, he found Mahendra in deep slumber. Samsul decided against waking him up—at least let him sleep for this night. Samsul did not know what news awaited Mahendra next morning. Was it only his house that had been burnt down? Was the son, whom Mahendra had gone to see, risking everything, safe and unharmed? Samsul came outside and lit another *bidi*—he wouldn't be able to sleep tonight. Rather, let Mahendra sleep.

It took a long time for the flames to subside. People later discussed that it took a long time for Mahendra Das' house to burn down.

Once again Samsul went inside to check on Mahendra and saw that he was murmuring in his sleep. The expression on his face suggested that he was kissing someone with a smile on his face. Mahendra was dreaming, perhaps of his son.

Translated by Rumi Rani Laskar

(Endnotes)

[i] Ethnic tribe of Assam and eastern India.

[ii] Infantry.

[iii] A small water vessel made of brass or copper.

Parbati's Household

Kajal Demta

In the early hours of the morning, when sunlight gently smeared the sky – glistening through the winter dawn – and the mynahs raised a chorus along the leafless branch of a mango tree, Parbati tied a few *roti*s to her *gamoccha* (thin cotton towel). Her one-year-old daughter clung to her breast, getting a last quick feed for the day.

Even at that tender age she had fallen into the habit of getting milk only very early in the morning or well into the night and once in the evening. Sometimes she rebelled by constant howling but it bore her no result. So little Budhni used all the energy she had in her one-year-old tiny frame to feed as much as she could, on her mother's milk. Parbati suddenly tore Budhni away from her breast and, looking at the road, called out loudly, 'Hey Somri, listen will you! Wait a bit; I too will go to the jungle! To collect firewood.'

Hastily she wrapped her sari tight around herself, placed the *gamoccha* packed with *roti*s on her head, collected the scythe under her armpit and called out to her son, 'Hey Sonichora, take care of Budhni! I've hung the *roti*s above the hearth to keep them warm. You can finish them, okay?'

Parbati's two grown-up daughters washed, cleaned and swept at the babus' large households. These two daughters had no time to help with the housework at home but they contributed valuable portions to the family income. The son, Sonichora therefore, was the one left to take care of all the basic important and unimportant chores in Parbati's household. As it so happened now, the one intended for Parbati's crisp and hurried instructions was this young soul – well-seasoned with ten long years of air and sunshine on this earth – who wandered carefree till this moment, deeply engaged in the serious business of shaping a bow out of a strip of bamboo. No matter what, he had no work in the mornings. This left him free to wander, though the soles of his feet froze from the cold and damp earth. And a pair of thin shorts and shirt were scanty protection against the icy cold blasts.

Still, Sonichora played during the day, making catapults and tiny balls of clay, drying and hardening them in the sun, laying traps with the help of home-made glue to catch small birds like the *runiya* and the magpie robins squatting on the branches of the Indian coral tree. Hunting down a bird finally, was all fun and excitement! Roasted bird meat was an enjoyable and tasty meal but his sister refused to eat the meat. Budhni was perhaps too young to really enjoy it. She was best fed with pieces of *roti* soaked and softened in salted tea liquor. Sometimes her incessant crying for her mother proved to be too much for young Sonichora to handle; he dumped her in a fit of rage and ran off to the field, playing blindman's buff with Pawan, Ratan, Kandra and Rama among the low hillocks. And yet again, following a sudden craving for Budhni, he would run back, scoop her up and lay her gently in his lap.

So Parbati left in a huff, murmuring to herself. 'You aren't listening, I can see!' she said. 'I'm fed up with you people…and the problems you create.' Parbati walked out, briskly rubbing tobacco leaves in the palm of her left hand. These women travelled far into the jungle to collect firewood.

Parbatis' husband Dasharath was a casual labourer at the tea estate. He got a temporary job at the estate only during the plucking season; otherwise he earned his living by running errands and working in the households of babus who arrived and set up new homes in the neighbourhood. He did not manage to get work every day and consequently, the daily household grocery of rice, flour, salt and vegetables remained undone. The family often went hungry with the children. Parbati complained in frustration and quarrelled. Dasharath never answered back. Drunk on homebrewn hooch, he forgot the hunger pangs and fell asleep on a torn sack in a drunken stupor.

Dasharath's forefathers had also spent their entire lives at the Barasingha Tea Estate but nobody had ever got a 'perment' job at the estate. Neither did Dasharath. And how would Parbati even try– hailing from a different tea garden altogether?

As a newly-married young couple, the times and circumstances had been quite different. They were then, in the prime of their youth; their inner worlds were touched by the radiance of spring and their spirits were as buoyant and carefree as the flitting yellow wings of the tiny 'iora'. Once, when he had been accompanying Parbati – his new bride – to her parent's home for the first time after marriage, a deer had suddenly flashed like lightning across the narrow, long-winding red-earth track lined with tea bushes. Delighted, Parbati couldn't stop giggling. Her veil had dropped; so had her bridal shyness. And the flush of crimson on her exposed face had drawn Dasharath to stare awe-struck at the flood of lustrous beauty for a long while.

Parbati had managed a halting, shy whisper – 'I simply love plucking tea leaves. I often helped my mother pluck leaves at the Chandighat tea garden.' His voice choking with emotion, Dasharath had replied, 'Ee…I love doing it too. If we work together in the garden, we'll build a beautiful home and a world together, won't we darling?'

He exclaimed in joy, drawing Parbati's attention, 'Look, look at the old tree! We used to come here to cut wood as children and used to swing on its branches. One day Madan was caught by a ghost and he turned mad. Ever since that day I never played here again.'

Dasharath's words flowed with a gurgling sound just like the water of an overflowing stream. Parbati walked along silently, sometimes wearing the tea flower on her hair, and then sometimes making jingling sounds with the *kharu* (anklet) on her feet. She exuded an air of happiness.

These memories faded away into the gloom just as the sky darkened the sun went down. Dasharath was disappointed with his dreams shattered. A cow somehow entered and started chewing the tuft of the kidney-bean plant. Dasharath drove away the cow. He sat in the courtyard and continued making fences for the hen house. Sonichora had found a hen from somewhere. He always took care of such creatures.

Long before dusk, Parbati returned with some rice tied in a *gamochha*. She flopped down on the ground and stretched her legs. She pulled down the loose end of her sari and kept it in a heap on her lap. Looking at Dasharath, she said in a frustrated tone, 'You look relaxed. Since you don't keep yourself abreast of any information why would you feel anxious?'

Now Dasharath became anxious. In a hesitant tone he asked, 'Guni's mother, what happened? What sort of anxiety?'

Parbati replied, 'This time neither your name nor mine is on the voter list. The *panchayat* said that if our names are not there on the list, we will have to face much trouble.'

'Would we be driven away? Is the fact that our forefathers lived and voted here not proof enough? Then why are our names not there on the list? They will ask for money to include our names on the list again,' Dasharath spoke slowly, almost to his own sad heart. 'We find it so difficult to just earn our daily bread. How will we ensure that our names are up on the voter list?' Parbati said, 'Now we have to take care of so many things. Earlier, there were no such problems.' Dasharath, trying to give the impression of putting up a brave front, told Parbati, 'The government will take care of us. Are we not their people?'

Parbati replied in an impatient tone, 'We have our children and if anything happens to them, where will we go then?'

Dasharath was not aware of the consequences of not having their names on the voter list. His thoughts veered towards the most grave misgivings. Would they be really turned out? Wouldn't they be given jobs? Would they not get rice, flour, kerosene and salt from the store? Could they be stopped from bringing wood from the jungle? Then what would happen?

Dusk descended on the horizon. And darkness gathered.

Translated by Rumi Rani Laskar

Notebook

Swapna Bhattacharjee

The place where the Shani[i] temple stands now—there under a huge banyan tree, he had his shop. The banyan tree no longer exists. Neither does his shop. It was not a shop in the true sense; just a temporary, impoverished shed erected out of bamboo mats for business transactions. Every morning, he sat in his shop. In the evening, he disappeared. And so, he carried on his trade in the shade of the ancient banyan tree. The passersby and the gathering of the young juvenile boys on the tri-road junction would form his customers. No one could tell what his age was. A sectarian vermilion mark on the forehead, eyes full of mystery—people used to remark that he hailed from Kamrup Kamakhya,[ii] and possessed great powers of incantation. Nobody knew how such stories spread about him. Under the banyan tree, there were a stone shrine of Lord Shiva, a *trishul*[iii] and a donation box. The money collected belonged to him. He possessed materials for exorcism and black magic. While extracting worms out of people's teeth, he mysteriously chanted the mantras: '*Kamrup Kamakhyar Kripaa*' (The blessings of Kamrup Kamakhya). Nothing remains now—the shop, the mysterious banyan tree, the stone shrine of Lord Shiva, the *trishul*—all disappeared one day. Manu'r baba[iv] too vanished one day. One morning it was found that someone had pulled down the roof of his shop. Ever since Manu'r baba disappeared altogether.

Now, in the midst of the bustling tri-junction stood the Shani temple. A different type of business. It was near this Shani temple that Amal found the diary one day. A small diary, which cannot be called a proper diary; it was actually a notebook. Even the very discovery of this notebook was fraught with mystery. One day, on his way back from the newspaper office, Amal got down near 'Shoroshi' *paan* shop after paying the rickshaw-puller his fare. He entered the *paan* shop. After chewing the *paan*, as he was about to make the payment, he suddenly discovered that his purse was missing. There were about five hundred rupees there and a tiny phonebook. Someone among the devotees of Shani might have … otherwise what else could have happened to the purse? He searched at length. How could it disappear in this manner from his pocket in so short a time? All of a sudden, for no apparent reason, the thought of Manu'r baba, the man of incantation, came to his mind. What magic he used to display! The way he used to lay traps for ensnaring people—throwing fake currency notes and frogs tied inside paper packets on the road for pedestrians to come and step on! *paan* shop Amal found this particular notebook at the remote corner of that *paan* shop, near the old post office, while looking for his wallet. Hesitantly he picked up the notebook. An unusually crowded street, blinding smoke, deafening noise of the automobiles, ringing of brass bells from the Shani temple, and the endless shouting of the auto-rickshaw drivers—amidst all the din it suddenly occurred to Amal as if he heard the cackling laughter of Manu'r baba. The blessings of Kamrup Kamakhya … Vermilion streak on the forehead, the shed of bamboo mats, the make-believe shop, the alluring smell of fried *papads*[v]—the lost days. The naphthalene-permeated smell of bygone days seemed to seep inside Amal and subdue all his consciousness.

The two girls, who just stepped out of Sen Beauty Parlour, offer *pranam*[vi] to Shani, while trying to shield their faces fresh after the facial treatment from the sun's rays. The place where the girl in jeans and half-sleeved top stood, anointing her head with the holy flame of the lamp, was once Manu'r baba's chosen venue for the marriage of frogs. Where was he now? How old was he?

The notebook held no special attraction for him. It was a simple, inexpensive diary. Untidy. Even then Amal could not throw it away. He put it inside the pocket where his wallet used to be and carried it home. 'I no longer see many old men now. Has the number of elderly people dwindled?' Amal turned the pages. No, nothing else was written anywhere.

Amal remembered clearly that the pages of the notebook were blank then. Nothing was written anywhere. But now strangely, on the page of 1st January (the year not visible), there was an address: '35/75, Mahanagar Sarani / *Dharitri,* Kolkata-51, "Sarojini Devi".' Near the address, there was a phone number: '2531078.' He feels tempted. Should he make a call? But why? How was this Sarojini Devi connected to him? Alive or dead? Old or young? Most probably old. He must somewhere have some connection with the owner of the notebook. Amal turned the pages once again. No, the owner's name did not figure anywhere. Amal closed the diary and wondered why he felt so anxious to know more about it. After all, there was nothing special in the notebook. Suddenly he noticed five more words at the bottom of the first page:

'Today the sky is cloudy

'I am four-legged now. But I also had my heydays, the days of my youth. Those days are gone. In the early hours of the morning, as I would sit washing utensils by the pool side and my brother-in-law would be about to leave for Kharagpur by the morning train, my husband would pluck flowers from the cluster of jasmine plants sprouting up amidst the bricks in the dim light of the moon. He would hum a song:

"*Come my queen, be my beloved*

I will decorate your bun with starry flowers."

With the stars shining in the sky, he would suddenly come in my way in the moonlit night and say:

"You are more beautiful than the queen of Babylon."

'My husband had been to Babylon during the Second World War. He had been to the wars in Iraq. And you will not believe how handsome he was! Seeing him in the military outfit, Renu's mother had once screamed, "A white soldier!" He had taught me—C-A-T = CAT; B-A-T = BAT. I also had my heydays.

'I am four-legged now. Four years ago, I broke my hip bones. My son does not get my operation done. My daughter-in-law has not consented to it. The doctor says everything is all right—pressure, sugar. But I do not get any treatment. I cannot walk, cannot even stand at a stretch for long. For me now, sitting is as good as sleeping. But I am not the stone of *Shalgram*.[vii] My filthy bed smells of urine and faeces! I am given very little food. There are lice in my hair. My hair has been chopped off. This year the floors of the house were marbled with my pension money. I had to put my thumb impression on the necessary documents. When my son and daughter-in-law step in, I sit crouched in some corner like a frightened cat. I am a prisoner in a stone castle. Princess? No! No one steps into my room. I do not get to see anybody. I hear the shrill cry of the telephone the whole afternoon. An agonised cry comes out of my heart. "Anybody there? Help! Help!" The day never passes.

'The person who used to dream of pinning starry flowers in my bun has himself become a star long back. Sometimes I see him and hum inaudibly in my heart, "*Debo khopaye tarar phool*" (I will decorate your bun with starry flowers). From the sitting room downstairs, a variety of sounds emanate and rent the air. Floods of tinkling laughter fill the air. I remain seated, isolated in my small room on the third floor gazing at my own star. Am I an old person? No, I am Sarojini—'

Amal is stunned as he turns the pages of the notebook. What are all these strange occurrences! Wherefrom have all these sentences appeared in the notebook? Nothing was written there till yesterday. Was that an illusion then? Or had he not gone through the notebook properly? But how could all of this have escaped his eyes? Or had it become a habit with him to look at everything superficially? Amal turns the pages. No, nothing else is written anywhere. Even Sarojini's phone number, the number he had called up, is no longer there. Strange! He had clearly heard someone groaning over the phone. When did Sarojini come and quietly write down all these words? It is inexplicable. Ever since he had found the notebook strange things have been happening. Amal had kept the diary under his pillow. It was entirely his fault. He himself might not have noticed it carefully. And what after all was there to observe in that plain notebook? It was meaningless on his part to keep it with him. It would have been better if he could throw it away under the lamp post, just as the people living in apartments throw away their garbage everyday. But Amal was now unable to throw it away.

~

The gathering at 'Shoroshi' in the evening was enlivened with the stories about the ghost. Terror has gripped the whole town. The town is abuzz with the rumours of a ghost who, they say, had started scratching people in the dark. Amal sets there and listens to all this. For the last few days it had been raining incessantly accompanied by load shedding every now and then. There had been no supply of electricity for the last twenty-four hours. In such a condition, it was but natural that a ghost should go about scratching people. Preparations were on for a fierce wrestling battle between two leaders of the same political party. Amal listened to their heated exchanges as he thoughtfully stroked his salt-and-pepper beard. The thought of Sarojini had occupied his mind to the extent that it seemed that his mind was possessed. He did not have much memory of his mother. His mother was not an old woman. The photograph that he had of his mother was of her youth. She appeared exceedingly young beside his ageing father. Amal thought that if he had got married, his mother could also have turned into another Sarojini. Was it because he is not married that his thoughts were so inclined? From what he had read in the notebook, it could be assumed that Sarojini was exceedingly beautiful. Her husband had served in the British–Indian army. They must have been a happy couple. Today, on this cloudy afternoon, he could visualise Sarojini's face. Hair cropped very short. Crawling on four legs, the beautiful Sarojini is gazing at her own star in the far-off sky … Almost bald and yet the dreams of starry flowers in her bun!

Amal lived like a guest in his own house. He taught in a school and was still unmarried. He wandered here and there attending cultural functions. Rushed forward whenever anyone was in trouble. Mangal called him the conscience of Silchar town. Seeing him slightly distracted, his friends from 'Samakal' club try to conjure up some excitement in his life. Mangal has come to know about the notebook. With a smile he asks, '*Guru*,[viii] have you adopted the role of *Pheluda*[ix] now?'

Amal does not answer. Thoughts whirl in his mind—'What do old people do nowadays?'

Somewhere the microphone blares suddenly, '... the one who is in the midst ... at the end of the day's end ...'

The song ends ...

'Ramkrishna Vanaprastha Old Age Home will be inaugurated tomorrow. Guru Ramji will be present as the chief guest. Venue: Chengkuri. Time: Evening five o'clock. Your presence is solicited.' The words float in the air. People casually sip tea at the tea stall. Smoke from the cigarettes fill the air. Amal sits depressed. A few words haunt him time and again: 'Now the sky is cloudy.'

Amal had vivid dreams in his sleep all night. He was an outsider in the family. His elder sister was a widow. She lived with him; rather he lived with her! Forty years of his life had passed in the midst of the dreams of *bhatiali*[x] and *baul* songs. He has never written diaries. Nobody had ever presented him with a diary. Regular visits to musical gatherings had helped him store diverse thoughts and tunes in his heart. More and more young people were added to the list of his companions with the passage of each day. His grandmother used to say in her husky voice, 'Love human beings.' She often visited him at night in his dreams. In his terrible nightmares he heard the screams of hundreds of grandmothers. It seemed as if he was seated in Kanumama's salon. Mirrors on all sides, and there were myriad images in the mirrors. He could see his grandmother everywhere. In whichever direction he turned his head there were the horrible, blood-chilling visages of old people. All of them, leaning on their sticks, rushed towards Amal. They tried to catch him. Pale, shrivelled skin, sparse hair ... they screamed, 'Help! Help!' Amal ran; he kept on running.

His grandmother screamed, 'Help! Bhai, help!'

Amal kept running. At one point he became tired and fell down.

Amal's dream is interrupted. He mumbles unintelligible words.

His elder sister muttered, 'You keep on roaming here and there the whole day like a vagabond. You can't pass your days like a nomad. Your health will not permit that. Turn your thoughts towards home, Amal.'

Amal spoke to himself, 'Didi, are you at home now?'

~

Amal's elder sister knew nothing about the notebook. He had not said anything to her regarding this. In fact, there was nothing special about it to tell her. His bedroom was a mess of torn papers, books and magazines strewn here and there. His clothes and books were scattered everywhere. Sometimes, when she felt like it, his didi washed his clothes and arranged them properly. Sometimes she didn't. Amal had fashioned his life in this manner. Today Barak Valley Blood Donor Association had organised a blood donation camp. Amal had to go there. Last night's terrible dream, Sarojini's words in the diary—everything appeared so confusing. As if there was no real difference between remaining awake and dreaming in his sleep. The sky in the morning was quite cloudy today. He recalled the song by Kabir Suman: 'An evening that saddens the mind is cloudy.' Amal looked at the sky while brushing his teeth. He started at the drifting clouds to his heart's content and began humming a tune silently …

'I feel very lonely in this darkness.

Beyond the sky … the play of the clouds.'

It was going to rain. , It was going to rain heavily today. Amal kept staring at the sky absent-mindedly. Today, Sarojini will not be able to see her own star. How far would she be able to go crawling on her four legs? How far?

~

No, not exactly a diary. This was not a diary in the true sense of the term. A diary had a dignified, neat and methodical air about it. Had an organised specification of date and time. Income tax–Pin Code–STD code–N.S.C. Interest Rate Chart–facts and figures of the world–Travel Planner—so many things. All of this was absent in a notebook. Even then everything could be written in a notebook. An ordinary notebook—nowadays children called it a copy. What was not there in a notebook? Everything is available—from market calculations to *Rabindra Sangeet* (Rabindranath Tagore's songs), from addresses to bus numbers, occasionally self-composed poems, doctor's address, sorrows and grievances ... appointments ... secret, personal revelations. But nothing of this sort was there in the notebook he had found. Only a few words: 'Today the sky was cloudy.' Had the rain seeped in from these few words and wiped away everything else written in the notebook? Were there a lot of things written there, which could no longer be read now? Or was something new composed everyday? Amal felt the urge to laugh at his own crazy thoughts. The notebook drew him like a magnet. He brought out the ash-coloured, rexin-covered notebook from under his pillow. Nothing noteworthy. On the first page, there were only a few words. Amal turned the page. On the next page there was another phone number: 25212127. Gosh! This number was not there yesterday. Where did it come from? Was it Sarojini's number? Again Amal turned the pages. Even after a frantic search he failed to find Sarojini's earlier number! Strange. A bone-chilling shudder ran down Amal's spinal cord. What a strange and ghostly affair! The whole town was reeling under the rumours of the ghost. Today's newspaper reported that it was a rare breed of monkey that has been attacking and scratching people in the dark. Ghosts seemed to visit towns even in the year 2005! Whether any ghost lurked elsewhere or not, there is definitely one in Amal's notebook. Amal felt a tremendous urge to make a call to that phone number.

'Hello, Hello ...' the phone rang. It continued to ring. He dialled once again ... it rang again. No one picked up the phone. There was the sound of a whistle in the wind. It seemed that someone had just picked up the phone. Someone appeared to have been taking deep breaths for a long time. Amal disconnected the call. He seemed to have suddenly entered some dark recess of time. The notebook ... the phone number ... the prolonged silence ... his grandmother

… the peculiar feverish sensation—a pensive breeze blew through Amal's mind. Amidst the drizzle, Amal walked along the path in a reflective mood. Drenched like a scarecrow, he reached Chhotelal Seth Institute. A blood donation camp was underway there. He had not had any food before coming here. But he would be the first one to donate blood. Mrs Dutta entered the camp clutching her umbrella and holding the end of her sari. She grumbled, 'All this trouble because of the old folks; I can never reach on time.' Amal suddenly felt his temperature going up. His body started shivering. Mrs Dutta had short, cropped hair. She was the Vice-President of the association. Well, did Mrs Dutta ever pin flowers in her bun?

'Please don't call up like this. I don't know who you are. Do you know, both my knees are paralysed? I support myself on a walker. Can I pick up the phone every now and then? What do you all need me for? I don't even understand your language. I was a teacher of literature. I also had my hey days. I went to Oxford twice with my husband. We roamed from one library to another; life was full of happiness. He had a premature death. We had money to survive after him. My only son now lives in a foreign land. Maid servants come here by turns. The sun's rays linger slantingly on the small verandah. I cannot receive anyone's phone call when the cordless receiver is not charged. Despite being handicapped, I run my household on my own. Your television-era has sped ahead of us. I don't have the capacity to build bridges after all. In the small verandah buds have sprouted in the *sandhyamalati* plant. The plant is drying up because of lack of water. My knees are broken and bent. The books kept on the shelves cry to me, "Please look at us." I have turned time into a stone and emptiness is my sole companion. My son and daughter-in-law are far away—in a foreign land—at a place where time plays hide and seek with the wind. No, let me go; please don't ring me up like this. I am like the roadside flower which no one cares about. Still I won't go to the old age home. I am Monoroma.'

Who had once again come and written all these things in the notebook? Why was all this happening? Most probably someone was playing pranks on him. Mangal? Among his friends it was only Mangal who knew about the notebook. Amal had only told him about the incident of the phone call. But the notebook was always at home. Then who was responsible for these stories? Amal was never a writer. Yet he always had the flair and urge to write in him. Like the soul of the town he wandered from one programme to another. Through the eyes of a passerby he observed innumerable stories unfolding—visible and invisible. He might also have written a serial in the notebook based on what he heard Mrs Dutta utter, 'It's impossible to tolerate the old people any more.' Amal felt helpless. Certainly someone was taking advantage of his forgetful nature and making fun of him. But the nature of the prank … Could it be the handiwork of his sister?

'Didi! Didi!' Amal shrieked. Nirupama entered the room in slow measured steps. Amal stared. He kept staring. Nirupama's wet tresses were scattered over her back. Silver lines were prominent on both sides of her temple. She looks at him with a sad helpless expression.

'Why did you call me?'

Amal continued to stare. The marks of old age were clearly delineated on her face. Passive body. Weak limbs. Bare arms devoid of any ornament. Did his brother-in-law ever pin flowers in didi's hair?

'Why are you not saying anything?'

Amal came back to his senses.

'No, nothing. I want to have some tea.'

Nirupama walked away slowly. Amal looked at his reflection in the mirror of the Godrej almirah. Most of his hair had turned grey. The beard was almost white. Amal sighed. Autumn had arrived. Winter dawned bringing with it the chilling cold. Dark clouds gathered across the sky.

~

He had not eaten the whole day. Amal had left home without eating anything. Sitting at Shoroshi he went through newspapers and looked at the photograph of the mysterious ghost in the *Anukshan* (journal). A red-eyed monkey. It was this monkey that was spawning terror in the towns and villages. In the midst of gossips and hearsay the monkey gradually became transformed into a ghost. You could see anything you wished to, you might believe anything you wished to. But Amal found no answer to the mysteries that had befallen him. Should he tell Mangal about it? Tomorrow was 19th of May, the Language Martyrs' Day. From Shoroshi to District Library and Gandhi Bhavan—preparations were on for various programmes tomorrow. *Banga Sahitya Sammelan* (Bengali Literary Association) had organised a quiz on the Language Movement, and thus had, assumed the role of a history teacher. Children were busy trying their best to memorise the names of the eleven martyrs in order to win the first prize in the competition. After wandering from the cremation *ghat* (ground) through Tarapur to the railway station, and meeting different friends, when Amal finally returned home it was almost dusk. Today he had kept the notebook in his pocket. He felt it with his fingers. It seemed as if it had suddenly stirred up at the touch of his fingers. Amal loosend his grip. As he entered the lane that led to his house, he found the way blocked by some children playing cricket. Amal scolded them: 'Hey! Go! Go away from here! What a nuisance ...' Saying this he moved forward angrily. They stopped bowling for some time. 'The old man is such a nuisance,' said the boys when he turned his back towards them.

Amal's sister was lying like a cloud on a cloudy day in her room. There were patches of darkness all over the room. His dark-complexioned sister's dark, dishevelled hair was scattered over the pillow. She lay with her knees bent. Load shedding.

It was dark everywhere. Didi's hair, the ash-coloured sari—everything together seemeed to have made the evening quite morbid and suffocating.

He was hungry. Even then Amal did not pay much heed to his hunger. He subsistsed on only four or five cups of tea the whole day. Remaining without any food or having food after long intervals had almost become a habit with him. While taking out the notebook from his pocket it suddenly slipped out of his hand and fell on the ground. Its cover had come off and a few pages fell on the floor. Amal groped about the room in the dark. He would arrange the pages in order when the light came back. But what is there to arrange after all? Unknowingly he had developed an intimate relationship with the notebook. He kept the notebook alongside his important papers and documents. Gradually, it dawned on him that the notebook itself was writing everything! The thought appeared like an enigma to him. Amal pinched himself—was he becoming a ghost too!

After dinner Amal leaned on his cot. As he tried to arrange the scattered loose pages of the notebook, he suddenly noticed innumerable numbers written on them! An endless assemblage of numbers. A procession of numbers before his eyes—all phone numbers. What were all these? Had he picked up some other papers in the dark and kept them here? Or pages from some other phonebook or perhaps the phones themselves had come and entered these pages! Amal turned page after page— numbers! An unending line of numbers spread in the pages till the last page. The first page of the notebook now no longer carried the reference to the cloudy sky. But clouds had spread all around, in the room, in the sky. Amal sat perplexed. The phone numbers started moving before his eyes. They called him … beckoned him …

In the adjacent room, his sister was busy conversing with her son who lived away from home. The day's arduousness found reflection in her voice. 'Must be very cold in Manipal … take care … old people … daily food …, etc. The conversation over the phone kept lingering on.

'Hello, who is it?'

'I am Shantilata … I am in my son's house in Mumbai … You know my daughter-in law is a working woman? … I look after my grandson. But I don't look at the sky.'

270900

'Hello …'

'I am Anathbandhu … I stay at Irongmara … Nibaran is my son … My wife is no more. Let me sing a song for you:

'If my son throws me out, where do I go?'

2509324

'Hello …'

'I am Sudharani. I had come to Agartala after selling my house. Baba, where are you? Please take me back. Who am I in the midst of a crowd? A bird in a cage. Who will provide me food and water?'

24137135

No. No more. No more. This notebook was very destructive. This game had to be stopped. Amal threw the notebook away. He had to forsake his food, sleep and peace of mind because of this notebook. Who were these people? Why did they all speak in the same monotonous tone? He looked at the picture of his mother on the wall.

Sunlight reflected from his young mother's eyes and seems to completely bathe him in it.

2711976 had said, 'Day and night, my son … yes, my own son, prays for my death.'

No, today Amal would drive all such thoughts away from his mind. This diary, no, rather this notebook, was ominous, like an eclipse. Tomorrow he would go and throw it away near the Shani temple. Let the person it belongs to find it there.

Amal fell asleep with the notebook on his chest. He seemed to be floating in the air accompanied by innumerable numbers in the thick clouds accumulated in his room. The stars were playing hide-and-seek behind the white clouds in the sky. Amal wished to pluck the starry flowers. Instantly the stars got transformed into numbers. Everywhere there was the echo of the 'kring-kring' sound of the telephone. Figures–stars–cradle and the whistle of the wind!

Hello-Hello …

Amal floated in the air like a bird. The stars bade him, 'Come, Come.' The cradle beckoned, 'Come …!' The notebook dropped from Amal's hand. Numerous pages had come out from the dangling cover and had floated out with the breeze to the sky. Words and figures started dropping out separately from the pages. Amal failed to grab them. They fell rapidly and rushed towards the human habitations.

The notebook vanished gradually. Only the endless number of words and letters jumped about in the breeze. Then they got crushed into tiny particles and formed clouds to enter every house of the human habitat through the windows … doors … ventilators …

Translated by Devashree Bhattacharjee

(Endnotes)

i Hindu God worshipped on Saturdays.

ii Sacred temple of Hindu Goddess Kamakhya situated in the Kamrup district of Assam.

iii Trident.

iv Manu's father.

v A kind of thin crisp flatbread.

vi Bowing down to the ground as a mark of reverence for God.

vii A black stone considered sacred, representing the Hindu God Vishnu.

viii Casual manner of addressing someone.

ix A popular fictional private investigator in Satyajit Ray's detective stories.

x Folk songs sung by boatmen.

xi Brother.

The Treasury

Shekhar Das

Isn't the AK-47 a Russian gun? Russia is a friendly country. How did a friend's gun kill my dada?

Eight kilometres away from the hilly railway station where a bridge touches the end of a tunnel, the dead body was found, after eight days. Eight days after they took him away from Siding camp on the third of the month at ten past something.

Dada was busy drawing the survey map, we are told. The report had to reach Dehradun within the fifteenth of that month. Someone would be sent to Gauhati with data sheets. Then all the information layout would have to be e-mailed.

There were six in all at the camp. Two cooks, two casual labourers, one overseer. Altogether six including dada. Others were camped three kilometres away from Siding camp.

Four grey poly-rexin tents were pitched there. Behind the tents lay a long slope. At the end of which were the falls of Didamchara, that finally flow into the river. The water of the falls was being used for drinking, cleaning–bathing, washing–scrubbing and cooking for all. All this was told later by the overseer. He too was in the group that brought dada's body.

They came after ten and were four in all: hats on their heads, camouflage dungarees on their bodies, making them untraceable in the jungle from a distance of a mere five feet. There was a clever mixture of colour in their attire. They all held in their hands the pinnacle of the art of technology, the fatal automatic weapons. Made to belch out burning leads in no time. After ransacking official papers they took dada away with them. Nobody could say anything. Neither the cooks, nor the labourers, not even the overseer. What they really could do was to inform the base camp, later. Who took him away? 'They took him away'—they said only this much. They mean 'they' who are present in the bloodstream of this subcontinent with different nomenclatures, with different identities.

At any time they can effortlessly and irrespectively slit the throat of a nation's leader or a daily labourer.

A few days back they slit the throat of a cabinet minister down South. On a Christmas Eve they hijacked a plane and forced it to fly from one country to another while demanding sky-high ransom. They were almost successful in blowing up Shrimati[i] Kumaratunga some time back.

They have their weapon-wielding presence in different geographical locations, in different colours.

Why have they taken dada away? Why have they pumped seventeen bullets into his body? It's a riddle.

The day before yesterday at seven in the evening dada's body, no longer a body, rather a dead body, was brought home. Two long days passed by in legalities—morgue, ice, etc.

Dada, that is Bikash my elder brother. He became an engineer with the help of the meagre earnings saved by baba in life insurance. How glossy is the word 'engineer'! Anyway, an engineer is an engineer after all. Unemployed for four years and suppressing his qualifications he took to tuitions. Mother's family pension provided for the whole family including Aditi's college and Bijan's—that's my—university education.

Althusser, Derrida, Roland Barthes are crystal clear in my brain. I write prose and poetry. Almost every two months I get an offer to read meaningless radio talk shows. Aditi's elocution class—*Jano na ki chand; Neel kasturi abhar chand*—procures some money. The poet Jibananda, who wrote these lines, has become a craze now.

By now, it will be wise to introduce my mother Bakulbala. Ma is a widow and a family pensioner.

We have a small two-storied house—our only asset. I was always cheerful by nature and all of five feet eleven. They say I have got sparks in me. My fingers can move very fast on the computer keyboard. Cigarettes, *adda*s, black tea, friends and books—I have an abundance of them in my life. I don't drink. Have a girlfriend; no complaints. All hardships are over. There's nothing more that I can wish for.

I know many things. Chemical formula of poetry and nuclear bombs. Publications on how to make a nuclear bomb are to be found in abundance nowadays.

Why just me, many are aware of these things. Why is a Taliban a Taliban? Which world does Osama Bin Laden belong to? What is the source of strength for Ranveer Sena and Sunlight Sena? I know why and whose hæmoglobin is being shed in Jehanabad, Palamou and Nalbari. I know almost everything.

But since the last couple of days, I simply cannot understand how an Indian Bikash has been killed by a Russian gun—what secret politics underlies the situation! Has the sober rose on Nehru's chest faded so soon?

He was my elder brother. Serene, self-restrained, quiet and composed. One who didn't even kill a mosquito inside a mosquito net and argued—'They too deserve to live.'

One who was deeply concerned for the lives which are carriers of diseases. How could he die in the bushes and creepers with bullets puncturing his body? The overseer said that wild animals did not touch my dada's body.

No marks of jaws or claws on the body, except the seventeen holes in his abdomen and chest made by the men.

Yes, it was the day before yesterday; the body was brought and unloaded from a mini truck. We were not asked to pay. We still don't know who made the payment. The government might have borne the expenses.

As we were informed beforehand, dada's lifeless home-coming was expected anytime. Dada's lifeless body caused an uproar. It was more out of curiosity than genuine grief. Only two people cried in chorus—Bakulbala and Aditi.

The house was crowded with relatives. The fragrance from the burning incense sticks could not dispel the faint yet distinct odour of mortuary lotion and rotten flesh. *Rigor mortis.* Aditi wanted to give dada a last hug, but was dragged back.

What a world-renowned name—AK-47! It does not merely belch out burning lead, it belches out the futile wailing of women like Bakulbala, or the screams of nineteen-year-old young girls like Aditi. Nothing happens to me. Neither do I cry nor do I wail. But what about the restlessness within me?

I am dumb-founded! It is strange! What can this world accomplish by the killing of a youth in his prime named Bikash?

I can hear an audio album playing on the second floor of a building two buildings always from ours. The house has been fondly named *Shantineer.*[ii]

It has been proven beyond doubt that grief is not contagious.

Ma's wails gradually disintegrate. On the one hand, the loss of the child, on the other, which is more acute, the ceasing of a fourteen-month-old source of income from dada. Two parallel griefs keep burning inside my mother.

Every death and death's causal relation make us feel—*Being is spontaneity*! First father, now dada. Bakhtin is a catalyst.

I can't cry like Bakulbala. Neither can I wail like Aditi. My failure to perceive those unanswered riddles makes me inconsolable. I too feel like a youth of early-adolescent period, full of ignorant rage. The unexpected death has made me change.

Once again we're back to only the money from family pension. Dada's fourteen-month-old job bought us a 165-litre fridge. Two sets of gold ornaments for Aditi's marriage. A foam-filled divan in the drawing room as Aditi desired—that too was fulfilled. And two thousand rupees for me. While giving it to me, dada said, 'Keep it. Buy whatever you like. Don't smoke too much. Change your hard brand. Are you going to the book fair? Take Ruchika (my girlfriend) to a decent restaurant and check out if books are available on Hawking's radiation theory, cosmology or archæology.'

I replied with a smile 'Why does a survey engineer need books on cosmic archaeology? I will get you trace paper. Will that be all right?'

Dada replied, 'Why? Why do you want to stop me?'

'Look, your field is survey-measurement; what is the need for Hawking?'

'So what? Now numerous areas of knowledge are considered as subjects of anthropological study. You write poetry yet you don't realise this?'

When a man like dada dies drenched in blood, how can anybody remain calm?

Bone marrow deficiency was detected in baba's bones, while dada was completing his last semester; Aditi and I were in school and college respectively.

Baba was an officer cadre of a government department where there was easy access to a lot of money.

Baba used to stick to an ideology of strict honesty. I have gone through the copies of a few unpublished poems written by him in his youth! The only published work of baba, which I had a chance to read, is a collection of poems in paperback. Many successful poets have never tasted success in their lifetime. Baba did not have any regrets.

Poets and poetry don't exist anymore. That what is left is merely pretension. Baba used to say, 'The journey of poetry has ceased. You people are writing, that is fine. Try finding a new language.'

I still remember the day when we went to watch Ritwik Ghatak's *Subarnarekha*. Both dada and I returned home walking quietly. It was a matinee show. On any other day, at that time of the day, returning home was a no-no for us, but *Subarnarekha* dragged us back home at that odd hour of the day.

While serving tea, Aditi asked, 'Have you seen the movie?' Dada replied, 'Yes. You are right Biltu.'

That day he did not feel like saying anything else. Only Aditi said, 'The film makes you feel depressed about everything. I was very disturbed for a couple of days. Baba and I have seen the film together.'

Aditi feels very strongly about films. After seeing the renowned Moroccan film *Amok*, directed by Souheil Benbarka, she said, 'Believe me Chhorda,[iii] among millions of films such a film is made only once. It is as though the film has brought out the inner soul of South Africa.'

Baba had a different opinion. In those days Aditi or I hardly had any grasp over the medium. Our knowledge was confined only to *Sonar Kella* or to *Close Encounters of the Third Kind*. Baba initiated us into an understanding of cinema but never tried to explain the film to us. In our family, things weren't explicitly spelt out.

Baba used to say, 'Look Bikash, even if you wish to differ with me, cinema suffers from tremendous limitations,' and we used to listen. Dada used to reply, 'Baba, you know, no other medium can provide such synchronisation of audio-visuals.'

Baba would shoot back, 'Let it be. One can only see that which the camera shows you. Only what is recorded on the sound track is listened to. But what about books? Numerous unseen visuals, sounds, drama—one can even smell the atmosphere evoked. Print medium extends your sensibilities. Of course the works of Kurosawa are quite exceptional.'

Listening to such conversations, Aditi would intervene, 'Chhorda did you get the point? Or did it fly past your head?' I would say, 'Yes, but only a fraction of it. Let the rest be for you my little Marie Seton.'

Unperturbed Aditi would reply, 'Place your ultra high frequency antennae at a higher elevation. Look there is a long bamboo stick to help you out.'

On evenings when dada would come home from his hostel, baba would return early from office. Aditi would not attend her elocution class. Those would be Saturdays. Ma would cook plenty of food for us and say, 'Don't go anywhere. We shall all be sitting together in the evening.' All meant the five of us: ma, baba, dada, Aditi and I. Our little council. 'Shrimatiji, let us inaugurate the session with your song,' baba would say to ma.

Ma, after initially objecting to the proposal, would start singing oldies from a Shantideb Ghose or a Kanandevi album. At one point Aditi would join in the singing. If load shedding occurred in the middle, Aditi would light coloured candles. Aditi prefers things to be neat and tidy.

Baba would light his cigarette. Sensing my discomfort caused by the smoke of tobacco, ma would complain, 'Stub out your cigarette. Look at Biju; do you know that he has started smoking already?

'—Really? But don't smoke a lot. I also started smoking when I was your age.'

Turning to Dada and Aditi, ma would say, 'What is going on? Is this how one disciplines one's son?' Everybody would start laughing after that.

Baba used to recite poetry by Premendra Mitra and Bishnu De. And Aditi would recite poems of Jibanananda and Shankho Ghose. I used to recite 'Lands of Grass', 'Ash Wednesday'. Dada would recite parts of *Gulag Archipelago*. Most of the time he used to read *A Farewell to Arms*.

Aditi was reluctant about reading 'Banalata Sen' and used to say, 'An excellent piece of poetry has been destroyed by mindless and whimsical singing and recitation by all the Toms, Dicks and Harrys.'

'How?' Baba would shoot back.

'You know the other day at a function a girl was reciting the poem—she intoned the words "*Etodin kothai chillen*" in such a manner that it sounded, as if, while getting off a city bus, Banalata Sen suddenly met the poet Jibanananda Das on the footboard; all the while the conductor was hurrying her to get off the bus.'

Baba burst into laughter and said 'Let each recite it in his or her own way. What is important is, how you recite. Why don't you take this girl to your classes?'

I would tease her, saying, 'Do you think, she really has anything to say, baba? Look how she sports her hair, like Jibanananda's dark night of Vidisha. Come on, pass me the bottle of sauce.'

Aditi would snarl at me, 'Chhorda!'

Dada would intervene saying, 'So you have started again. Please Biju. Now tell me Biltu, how would you like to recite the poem?' I would interrupt their conversation, 'Labangalata Sen, you have not told me yet where you had been all these years.'

'Look Chhorda, you again ...,' Aditi would complain.

Dada would side with her, 'Biju stop it. Biltu, I know that though Biju happens to be a poet, your sense of poetry is far stronger than his.'

Preening in her victory she would zealously reply, 'First thing—throughout this poem there lies an undercurrent of morbidity, right? So, "*Etodin kothai chillen*" carries a tone of melancholy. So is it correct to utter this line in an utterly casual manner? Not a single word written by Jibanananda is casual.'

Baba would say, 'Wonderful! Our Biltu has become an authority on recitation. Why don't you jot it down on paper?'

Aditi had never ventured into writing. She only used to recite in a sophisticated, well-modulated voice.

Suddenly, one day, detection of bone marrow deficiency in baba's body destroyed our evening *addas*. Aditi is right, when she says I have got ultra high frequency antennae. Still, I can't understand why TV and radio broadcasts of plane hijacking and related concerns of the leaders are invariably rounded off by Melbourne cricket news. I fail to understand whether a national crisis is considered any more universal by the media.

The news of dada's killing duely appeared on the third page of newspapers.

Many people were present at the cremation ground—about hundred and fifty of them. Some of them were indulging in drunken revelry.

Everything was over by dawn. Fire engulfed the bullet-ridden body of a man who loved to read *A Farewell to Arms* and reduced it to ashes. Somebody asked us to take the remains of the bones for immersion to Gaya or Allahabad.

I objected as it seemed meaningless. What could be sadder than the ceremony of grief?

Though we are abundantly gifted with humane qualities, our financial position is weak. Anyway, even with this constraint we took baba to Chennai for treatment. Dust accumulated in ma's emptied-out jewellery box as though the empty space were the depths of the Grand Canyon. With deep despair baba returned from Chennai. Dada and pishemoshai, accompanied baba to Chennai. The effort proved futile.

Playing with the bangles on ma's wrist, baba said to ma, 'Bakul, enough is enough now.'

'What is that?'

'You are pouring water into a leaking pitcher. We have already lost your ornaments. There is nothing left for Biltu.'

Ma rushed away to another room in her futile effort to resist the tears welling up in her eyes. Strained eyes blurred with tears; damp cheeks resulting from incessant tears; vain attempts to wipe away the sorrow from her face with the end of her sari—will all these minutest of details of those good and bad days be ever known to the AK-47-wielding hands?

Gently wiping away the beads of perspiration from baba's forehead, Aditi would ask, 'Shall I get you some water to drink?'

'No dear.'

'Tell me, what would you wish to eat.'

'No more desire either to drink or to sleep, dear Biltu.'

'I am sure you will get well soon.'

'How long can you keep filling a leaking pitcher, dear?'

'You write poems and yet you feel so frustrated?'

'What makes you say that?'

'Poetry has to be associated with dreams. Poetry born out of frustration cannot really be poetry. Chhorda and I have read all your poems secretly.'

'Really? And what is your opinion about my poetry?'

'A poet such as you, who weaves dreams into poetry—using the metaphor of a leaking pitcher does not really fit into your world.'

'Dreams are not everlasting, Biltu!'

Baba and dada used to call her Biltu, her pet name.

'No, baba, dreams are unending.'

Aditi's efforts to bring the 'golden-winged eagle' or 'Dhansiri river' (of Jibanananda's poetry) to baba's deathbed, would only bring tears to his eyes.

Aditi would wipe the tears with the end of her sari. She continued nursing him and at times his faint voice would utter just one word, 'Biltu.'

'Yes, baba.'

'Tell Biju—'

'What?'

'To recite "*Mir-Taki-Mir*" to me sometimes. No, let it be Khalil Gibran. I sometimes wonder where he has picked up such excellent enunciation from.'

'Okay. He would love to recite to you.'

In the next room, I stood speechless.

That night we were all in the same room. At eleven past ten the heart announced its inability to go on anymore. Baba started gasping ten onwards. Our family doctor said, 'Sorry,' as he let go of baba's lifeless wrist. Baba left us all behind.

Ever since, no one in this house has heard Bakulbala sing.

Time went by. Things would have continued in the same vein. Dada's job reduced the incessant gloom to some extent.

A matrimonial alliance came from Siliguri for Aditi. Only one who would see her devoid of any ability of real insight would reject her. No demand for dowry. It was almost finalised; the groom himself gave his word to dada.

He was five feet seven inches tall; with attractive physical features. The face had a calm but firm grace. The complexion had the burning glow of a candlelight. I am not bragging about my sister's beauty. Whoever sees her likes her.

I used to often indulge in leg-pulling, 'Forget your recitation. Without a proper understanding of poetry you just whimper on. Better try to be a supermodel.'

'What model?'

'Supermodel, you know, I mean catwalk on a ramp. You will have your photographs published in popular magazines with stupid smiles on your face.'

'Photographs?'

'Yes, undoubtedly. Maybe, flashing your teeth, you will smile for chilli powder, turmeric powder, hot spices or maybe even for a washing powder which makes clothes fade after a single wash.'

'Chhorda, you are really intelligent. Let me check whether it is still there or not. It seems one more has sprouted.' She would pretend to check my posterior for a tail.

She was a very smart girl and wanted to study a course in mass media. She had a masters degree in English. Our ma was also beautiful. But Aditi had surpassed ma's beauty. We felt proud of her. I don't hesitate to tell you that since she was a daughter of our family, having such a beautiful young girl at home was a matter of both pride and concern. We used to have a lot of fun teasing her. At that time, baba was alive and full of life. Dada had one more year left to become an engineer.

~

Bakulbala used to sing in those days—'*Emni kore jai jodi din jaak na …*' (If the days roll on in the same manner let them …)

But the days did not pass in the same manner. It never does. Dada's fourteen-month-old job didn't yield savings. Was it really possible to have some savings?

Baba's earnings and savings, ma's gold ornaments had all been spent till the last penny for baba's bone marrow deficiency treatment and dada's technical education.

Ma's monthly pension remained as our only source of sustenance. How much do I really earn from tuitions? The earnings from Aditi's recitation class? Will Aditi ever get back the spontaneity of her voice, choked by her wailing for dada?

It took only a day to rub off the beauty of my supermodel. Layers of dust are accumulating on her favourite divan. Nobody cares to clean it.

I have to bring back the Biltu who was baba's and dada's favourite. I must rekindle in her the desire to live and dream. But how? We have forgotten to take care of each other.

Has our treasure trove of humanity started depleting then? Have cracks appeared here too?

Aditi has become completely cold and detached. Yesterday I found her with dada's coat, sniffing at it. On the collar of the coat, she found a strand of one-and-a-half inch length of hair. Aditi carefully picked it out. Where did she keep the strand of hair?

Two kinds of misery roll down ma's eyes—losing a child and financial insecurity. A moderate standard of living is not possible with such a meagre income. This could not have been unknown even to the camouflaged men.

Showing us the star studded night's sky, the man who used to teach us 'paradox of information' had to carry seventeen bullets in his abdomen!

Often he would say, 'Whatever you say, Biju—'

'What?'

'I have seen many hills and ranges—Sahyadri, Aravalli, Vindhya, Mahakal—but Borail is without a parallel. It is unique.'

Where did my dada go while undertaking survey works in Borail?

Just a short while back, he had said, 'Next month I will go on a tour to Kolkata. I shall get some good books then—prepare a list.'

~

I thought of a list of books: *The Stone Raft, Cancer Ward, Rabindranath* in Joe Winter's translation. Getting a Benarasi sari for Aditi was also decided upon. Our sejo kakima,[iv] who resided at Kankurgachi, would select the sari.

But everything remained unaccomplished. No weapon ever knows that with its firing, innumerable unfulfilled hopes vanish like bubbles.

A debate erupted at the *samsan ghat*[v] over the ritual related to the burning—which part of the body was to be lighted first. I objected. Why should there be such a tug of war. Any random part of the body can be lighted. Or the body may even be returned to them—those who are responsible for it. Let them bear on their shoulders the burden of the souvenir of their own deed.

Four or five of dada's friends visit us twice a day. They sit beside ma and exchange a few words. Everybody seems to be all right, except one. Resting his hand on Aditi's shoulder he was trying to say something to her. Was it sympathy? Aditi, shattered, stared at him fiercely. Dada's grief-stricken friend immediately recoiled like a scared cat. I would have reduced him to a bundle of broken bones and mangled flesh. But I did not have to intervene. Aditi alone was enough.

Again altercations cropped up over dada's last rites. Everyone among our relatives had an opinion. Each of them seemed to be a great scholar of the *shastras*.[vi] One opined that the last rites of accidental deaths are performed on the fourth day after death. But the fourth day after dada's death was long over. Once again there was a lot of running around from pillar to post for an expert opinion. No one could offer a clear opinion. Unexpectedly and surprisingly Bakulbala put an end to this cacophony and said, 'I have a small amount of his money with me. Biju, distribute these to whoever you consider best. Nothing else is required.'

An elderly lady, our relative, objected to Bakulbala's decision, 'What are you saying? How will the spirit rest in peace without the last rites?'

Bakulbala shot back in a voice full of conviction but filled with grief, 'I know better than anybody else how Bikash would find peace.'

Ours is a small double-storied house. Slightly tucked away from the town. Till date there is an expanse of empty land left here. Baba built our house in a piecemeal fashion. It took quite a long time to be completed. On the first floor there are two adjacent rooms with a balcony. Dada's and mine.

The day after *grihaprabesh*,[vii] Aditi held out a piece of paper to baba, having written something on it. 'Get it engraved on a rectangular steel plate. I have noted down what is to be written on the plate.'

'What is this?'

'Nothing special. The name of our house. Won't you give it a name?'

'What name, let me see?' Baba was curious.

Aditi read aloud, '*Sindhu Saras.*'

Baba got the name plate made. Aditi stuck the plate on the pillar adjacent to the first step leading to the elevated verandah. Baba said, 'I don't think Jibanananda has another fan like her.'

Non-stop remixed songs of olden days are being played on a CD player in the stylishly-designed building which stands three houses away from ours.

I am sitting in the balcony all by myself. Dada's room is locked up. Grief has a short span. Fades fast. Food has been cooked today. We three sat down for dinner finally. I picked at some food. Ma took very little of it. Aditi's fingers toyed with the rice all along and she hardly ate anything.

Will Aditi drown? Depression is like a bog. Once you get trapped, it is difficult to come out. She must be rescued. Without fail.

Walking towards her room, I call out to her, 'Aditi?'

She is sitting on her bed. The window in front is wide open. Cold breeze is blowing in. As the house is a little secluded from the town there is a silence prevailing all around. A wide, open field stretches across the garden. Complete darkness. The highway lies far away. The headlights of fast-moving trucks twinkle in the distance; faint sounds reach our ears.

She turns her face and looks at me, 'Come in, Chhorda. Come.'

I enter her room and sit beside her. She gazes listlessly through the window.

I ask, 'What are you doing, Aditi. There is a nip in the air, close the window. What are you thinking about?'

Aditi shakes her head, 'Nothing.'

'Why didn't you have dinner, Biltu?'

And immediately I'm aware that I have made a mistake. For her, 'Biltu' is reserved for baba and dada.

Her eyes well up with tears. She cries, 'Chhorda!'

'Yes?'

'There is a smell.'

'Where?'

'From the coat. That one.'

'Smells like what?'

'Dada! It is still there. Just smell it!'

Wailing chokes the voice of my supermodel, dada and baba's Biltu. She sinks her face on my chest.

Does an AK-47 understand all this?

On the night of Lakshmi *puja*, there used to be a real celebration in our house. Ma's long-practised tradition was to fast all day long while preparing different kinds of food. Late in the evening the priest would recite from the *Panchali* (long verse written about the deities). The smell of incense sticks and the loud blowing of the conchshell from the *puja* room would spread across every corner of our house.

Our house would be full of life. Baba would invite friends and relatives. Aditi would help out ma all along. Though fasting like ma, she would not mind serving tea frequently and as many times as requested.

I would tease, 'Silly girl, fasting will rob you of your glamour. Break your fast. I won't tell Bakulbala.'

There would be a full moon glowing in the autumn sky. I would be in the balcony with a cigarette in my hand. Downstairs everybody would be in a jovial mood. Baba would bring a pair of *hilsa* fish and say, 'In our Naihati home, chhoto jethu[viii] would bring three to four pairs of *hilsa*. You people have not seen those days.'

Lakshmi *puja* nights were joyous carnivals in supermodel's *Sindhu Saras*.'

There would be a festival at dawn on *Mahalaya*.[ix] Ma would get sweets the day before *Mahalaya*. Next day whoever came to our house would not leave without having sweets. Almost every year during Durga *puja* we used to go on holiday trips to different places. By August end we would have the railway reservations confirmed. We would travel to different parts of India: Palamou, Ranchi, Nasik, Pune or Mumbai. Once we went deep into the coast of Bay of Bengal beyond Rameshwaram. They say it is the cape point of the mainland from where the clouds over the Sri Lankan sky are visible.

Aditi was in a *salwar kameez*.[x] The *chunri*[xi] was draped around her neck. She had a Bermuda cap on her head while her hair flew wild because of the strong winds. Ma's sari was about to fly away.

Bakulbala pretended to complain, 'Where did you people bring me? If I stay here all afternoon I will turn into a wisp of straw.'

Aditi's jubilance on the sandy beach and her collection of shells was a treat for the eyes!

Did they ever try learning about the daily schedule of our holidays from dada? Did they allow dada to tell them how Biltu's *Sindhu Saras* would turn into a splash of lights and colours on Lakshmi *puja* nights?

No, they did not. Now nobody cares to pay heed to others. Even the trees, shrubs and creepers of the jungle seem to have turned into barrels of guns. All humane expressions have become obsolete long back. The strength of the wild smell of gunpowder and blasts have obliterated everything else.

While trying to drag Aditi out of her mourning, I have made a mistake. The scent of the coat and the tiny strand of hair are cherished possessions for her now. Baba's death seemed to dry up everything inside her. Now after dada's death nothing is left inside her to dry up further.

Aditi moans without shedding tears. Will she lose all direction? Or will she be further sucked into the emotional quagmire? No, my dear Biltu, I will not allow this to happen to you. I will get you out of this. I will make you strong and resilient like me. I cannot let it happen.

No word of solace can rescue you now. I want to make you angry, in fact, I want you to seethe with fury. And perhaps your rage will draw the grief out. You have to be angry.

I throw the cigarette out of the room. Bakulbala and Aditi are downstairs—I don't know what they are upto. I don't get any sleep.

Some simple questions hound me—where are we? What is the role that people like us are supposed to play out? Who is there to ensure a safe and trouble-free life for us? Who has gained anything by killing unarmed people like us?

Why is our sorrow not felt universally? Why could our neighbours not desist from playing Baba Sehgal non-stop on the day of dada's last rites? Why was there a show of grief on the countenance of one of our close middle-aged female relatives? My ultra high frequency antennae could perceive many things except the answers to these straightforward questions.

I light another cigarette. The tip of the burning cigarette looks like a large drop of blood in the dark. The sticky nicotine-filled fumes enter my lungs. My nerves get restless and ache further. A determination to fight back haunts me incessantly. I need to stand erect. Standing with my legs apart, hands resting on my waist, I need to draw myself up to my full height—all of six feet—and that too alone. There is no one to assist me. But who would sponsor my rebellious resistance? Now every act or event is dependant on sponsors.

Time passes by. Neither does the rotation of the earth, at the rate of sixteen hundred kilometres per hour stop, nor does the rate of rotation lessen.

An erroneous calculation of the countdown to the millennium has started throughout the world. The media is indulging in the ridiculous act of counting a century of ninety-nine years. Everything is rolling by. Even our lives—the three left behind. At last Aditi has started eating a little. I can no longer say, 'Eat more. You're losing your glamour.' The days of cracking such jokes are long over.

Aditi does not recite poems anymore. The grace in her voice has disappeared. Some of her students come to her for guidance. She has appeared for her final year examination. Will she try for the university later?

She has become too grave. When at home, she serves tea, as part of a routine. I need not ask her for tea anymore. I have failed to provoke her into anger or rage. I have failed to do anything for her. She is sinking deeper and deeper into the quicksand of despair. It has been a long time since I have seen her perfectly arranged teeth. She has stopped smiling altogether. She has even stopped talking. While replying to anything she confines herself to one or two words only.

Ma gets irritated easily. She has started forgetting things. Sometimes she remembers them later on. The other day when I returned from the bazaar after buying vegetables she took the bag and brought out the vegetables. Suddenly she shouted, 'Biju, come here.'

'Yes, Ma.'

'Who has asked you to get so much green peas?'

'You yourself asked me to.'

'Me? Impossible! Never!'

I tried to pacify her, 'I bought whatever you asked me to get. You asked me to get green peas too.'

'—I see! Is it so? Maybe. I might have told you. Listen, in future never get peas. This peas-*paneer*[xii] curry with potato was a favourite of Bikash as well as your father. Never get green peas in future, mind you.' Bakulbala's voice was nostalgic with the afternoon's soft morbidity. But she suddenly started shouting in a hoarse voice, 'Aditi! Aditi! Where are you?'

Aditi came rushing to her, 'Yes, Ma, what happened?'

'To hell with your concern. Throw away that stuff. I say throw it away. Don't you hear me? Biju didn't know, and so bought them.'

At last I threw all those peas out of the house. Then we all sank into grief.

I don't go to university any more. Seven students come to me for tuitions. I instruct them in computer education. Enhancement in the rate of Dearness Allowance has added a few more rupees to ma's pension. Our days drag on. I wonder how Aditi learnt the technique of sewing. She has acquired the art of managing the kitchen as well.

I have cut down on my smoking to a great extent. Have restricted the habit of drinking tea. We don't turn on the switches of lights and fans too often. Never make a phone call. When it rings we just pick up the receiver and listen to the voice calling. Baba got the connection for just one thousand rupees. Nowadays it rings only if somebody calls us; we don't ring up anyone at all.

Ma's looks are becoming more and more expressionless. Aditi too has observed it and begun keeping a close watch on her. Every night Bakulbala is given high doses of Alpazolam. Ma might have gone to sleep by now.

Aditi does not get sound sleep anymore. I can observe everything from my upstairs room. Helplessly I nurture my rage in despair.

Dada's friends do not call upon us anymore. Once that 'friend' of dada's had wanted to come again. I gravely turned him away from the gate. Ever since he has not shown his face.

At times, mother is normal and at times she is slightly different. But not exactly abnormal.

Back home, late this evening, I sit in my room now. The fourth cigarette of the day is between my fingers.

Aditi has served tea already. She is now in her room teaching four students.

My room is dark. Lights from the neighbouring house and the neon lamp post on the street has partially lit up my room. Footsteps can be heard on the concrete staircase. Somebody is coming up the stairs barefoot.

A guest? Who could it be at this hour? Aditi? No. She is busy teaching downstairs.

A shadow appears at the door. Ma. Why is ma here?

'Why are you sitting in the dark, Biju? Why is there no light?'

'Let it be. It is comfortable.'

'What are you saying! Why sit in such darkness like a ghost?'

Ma turns on the light. Two decorated lamps light up the room—Aditi's effort at interior decoration. I enquire, 'Why did you suddenly climb up the stairs? Is there anything that you wish to tell me?'

'—Yes. That's why I came to you. See this.'

'What?'

'A letter.'

'A letter? Whose letter?'

'Theirs.'

'Theirs!'

Yes, from them. From Bikash's office.'

'From dada's office? What have they written?'

'Just go through it. Aditi has already read it.'

Bakulbala's weak voice evokes a hint of hope. Ma again says, 'Delivered at noon under registered post. It seems some documents need to be sent expeditiously. Then they will send a draft. Quite a handsome amount. Compensation, isn't it?'

Soft light gradually seeps into Bakulbala's voice. I look at her. The palpable excitement within her has driven her to the edge between normality and abnormality.

Bakulbala's bright voice continues, 'This money would help Aditi. What do you say, Biju?'

'Last week a reminder came from Siliguri. We should not let go of the offer. After all, how long can they wait for us? Write to them today itself that we are ready. We are almost ready. Biju, write a reply tonight itself.'

Ma retires downstairs. A deep, long-lasting grief died abruptly just a while back. Will the smell of gunpowder-permeated earth ever know this ruthlessness?

Aditi—baba and dada's Biltu—has not heard what Bakulbala, who used to sing, 'Bring us goodness, make us pure oh Lord,' uttered a while back.

If she had heard, who knows what she would have said?

Translated by Biswajit Sheel

(Endnotes)

i Formal term for addressing a lady.

ii Peaceful abode.

iii A brother who is older but not the eldest.

iv Aunt; father's younger brother's wife.

v Cremation ground.

vi Sacred scriptures of Hinduism.

vii Ceremonial inauguration of a house.

viii Uncle; father's elder brother.

ix Auspicious day, seven days prior to Durga *puja*.

x Traditional outfit worn by Indian women.

xi Veil; it is worn with *salwar kameez*.

xii Cottage cheese.

The Chronicle of Vyomkesh Kavyatirtha

Amalendu Bhattacharya

Vyomkesh Kavyatirtha paced along the huge jungle on the bank of the river Langai. A song sung while collecting water in the pitchers, by some country lass travelled from a far-off place breaking the silence of the fading night of the month of *Agrahayan*:

'*O friend! Your flute is calling at dawn.*'

Vyomkesh was now on his way back from the house of Mathuranath Chakraborty after performing the rites of *adhivaas* preceding the marriage of the latter's son. The day was about to dawn. He hoped to relax a bit and rest his weary spirit and body before the saffron rays spread out and lit up Langai reserve forest area. Tomorrow he would again have to toil about all day. Mathuranath did not want to leave any stone unturned for the wedding ceremony of his son. Vyomkesh had been entrusted with the chores of the priest for the wedding because he hailed from the birthplace of Mathuranath Chakraborty. Otherwise, Mathuranath, being the *bara* sahib (chief manager) of Baithakhal Tea Estate, was rich enough to hire a renowned pundit (brahman priest) from the town. Mathuranath still remembered his old ties with Vyomkesh. Both had their ancestral home at Panchakhanda, the hub of learning and culture in old Srihatta (in East Pakistan after partition and in present Bangladesh after the independence of the country in 1971). It was a sad fact that his native place now belonged to a foreign country.

Maheshwar Tarkalankar, Vyomkesh's ancestor, was a pioneer and a leading soul among the society of learned men—indeed a legendary figure. He had composed *Astabingsati Pradip*, a satire on the *Smrititatva* of Raghunandan. His eulogy for his own soil, his own land Panchakhanda was:

'Where there is an assemblage of learned men, there is Panchakhanda.'

The same familial blood throbbed in the veins of Vyomkesh. Mathuranath's home too was in Panchakhanda. He still respected the great family legacy of learning that Vyomkesh had inherited. The partition of the nation had suddenly removed Vyomkesh from his native place. They had to take shelter in the refugee camp at Dohalia. No one knew him there. He was utterly helpless, confused and at a loss. Small cabinets were curved out of the long bamboo-built structure raised on a hilly terrain. They had to pass days, have food and sleep huddled together in the same bamboo micro-cabinets. There were strange and diverse people around. Day and night he felt extremely depressed. At times he remembered the song that Mahesh Vairagi used to sing, which further added to his depression: 'We've become immigrants in our own land. 'Futile today seems the glory of Sita, Lakshmi, Gaya, Ganga, Kashi.' The great Mahesh Vairagi of Maulavi Bazaar. Who knew where he was now! Like all other refugees, Vyomkesh too had to stand in queue and collect daily rations. And every moment he, the descendant of Maheshwar Tarkalankar, felt like saying: 'Oh mother earth! Open up and take me inside thy bosom.' What a disgrace! In their family no one had ever done any work other than imparting knowledge. To compare with today! And today!

The sudden barking of a dog breaks the silence of the night. Vyomkesh has almost reached the backyard of Rasamay's house. The river Langai flows in front of him. Winter has set in, and very little water is left in the river. Still he hesitates before dipping his feet in the water in the chilly closing hour of the passing night. But he has no option. He has to paddle across the ford first and then cross two knolls to reach his own home—Pingchhara—a new colony for the refugees.

Quite unexpectedly, one day he met Mathuranath at Patharkandi, after the latter had joined as the *bara* sahib at Baithakhal Tea Estate. Slightly senior to him, Mathuranath could at once recognise Vyomkesh. He became very emotional upon meeting him. Vyomkesh too felt the same. After all both of them were sons of the same soil! It was Mathuranath who managed to procure some hilly land for him at Pingchhara. Fifteen to twenty years of hard toil made the small strip of land somewhat habitable. His efforts led to a few fruit trees, one exuberant bushy growth of bamboos, and a small pond as well, wherein he has reared some ducks. After one turn the knoll becomes indistinctly visible. It is a moonlit fortnight! The passing night is the fifth of the fourteen nights. The fog in the closing hours of the night has mingled with the bright moonlight.

Alaka must be sleeping now. He realises his mistake the moment he thumps on the door. Alaka responds in a clear tone from within, 'Wait a bit, I'm coming.' She opens the door and lights the lantern, 'How did you get so late in coming back?' Vyomkesh replies to his wife's query, 'Mathuradada did not let me leave. He kept saying, "No, Vyomkesh I can't let you go now; you should perform with your own hands the rites of *tika* (holy mark on the forehead) and chant the hymn for peace."'

'No sleep last night?'

'What could I do? It's the wedding ceremony of their eldest son. I didn't think it right to disrespect Mathuradada's wishes. How can I forget the favours he has done us?'

'Oh, that's true! But did you have your food?'

'No, it wasn't possible! How could I touch the food? He is the *bara* sahib of the garden. People of different castes were hovering about there. They might have touched the eatables. At my age I don't think transgressing sanctity would be right.'

'Binu and Oghu expected that you'd bring *sandesh* (sweetmeat) from that house.'

'Oh!' Vyomkesh utters a brief sigh and looks at the faces of his son and daughter who are fast asleep. He takes his wooden sandals in his hand and comes out under the jackfruit tree to wash his feet. Binu and Oghu—Vinayak and Oghavati. He named them thus with a lot of hope. He had his first son ten years after crossing the border. He was then passing his days in abject poverty. Vinayak was named with the hope that the boy would one day grow up to attain blissful success in life. Vyomkesh remembered the story of the *Vamana Purana*. Lord Ganesha was born from the refuses of Goddess Uma, the wife of Lord Mahadev. As he was born without the aid of any *nayak* (father), Ganesha was also named Vinayak. Vinayak is the deity of *siddhi* or success. Vyomkesh hoped that if the deity himself resides at his home, his life would also be blessed with prosperity. But he could never become wealthy. He heaves a deep sigh.

In the eastern sky *dhalphar* has begun appearing slowly. He utters the word and feels like laughing out bitterly. It seems strange that with the loss of their ancestral land they have experienced a sea change in the way they talk and interact with others. *Dhalphar*—what an exquisite word! When the white patchy line appears in the dark sky to indicate that sunrise is at hand, it is called *dhalphar*. Today's youths know nothing of such terms and usages. Vyomkesh dips his bucket into the well. He pulls up a bucketful of water and then sprinkles some on his eyes and face with his hand. The cool touch of water feels soothing at dawn even in the month of Agrahayan. It takes away the tiredness and the fatigue. Pulling out the second bucketful of water he suddenly recalls how Oghavati has been nourishing and rearing people in the form of a river with half her body. Having passed the test by Lord Dharma in the guise of a brahman, she was blessed with the capacity of protecting herself with her own powers. As a father Vyomkesh only wishes to see his daughter able to protect herself and get established in life. He realises that he is getting old and at his present age he cannot do anything more for her.

'What's the matter, dear? You've been standing so long by the well?'

'Yes, coming.' His wife's words brought him back to reality. In a little while from now he would once again go to *bara* sahib's bungalow. He has so many things to do today, so many rituals to perform! He goes inside the house, wipes his hands and feet and then relaxes his fatigued body on the bed. The sleepless night has really worn him out.

'You will have to accompany the party of the groom as their priest?'

'Oh, yes! There's no other way to it.'

'I've heard that the bride's family is also very rich.'

'That's only very obvious and natural!' Vyomkesh gives a very short reply. Such tedious talk only vexes him more.

'Er, I mean, there'd be bountiful varieties of delicacies for you all to sup and eat. You know how the guests in the houses of the rich men are served. I mean ... if you could bring some of the sweets—the children have never tasted such delicacies.'

What Alaka said is indeed, not untrue. How can you think of providing your little ones with nice food and decent clothes when you live in a colony of refugees amidst a reserve forest and depend on the performance of *puja*s and other ceremonies for your meagre earnings? Even if you sometimes wish to, where would you get palatable food from? There is hardly anything else sold other than *jilapi*[i], *gaja*[ii] and *danadar*[iii] at the market at the nearby Baithakhal Tea Estate. Moreover, there's only one market day in the whole week. Vyomkesh seems to accept his wife's suggestion, 'Well, let's see!' With a brief reply he eludes the topic.

After so many years Vyomkesh is going to Silchar again. After crossing the border as a refugee long ago, only once did he visit the office of the Deputy Commissioner at Silchar. Since then this is the second time he would visit the town. He's heard that Silchar is now the heart and centre of Barak Valley! It is an expanding town, with large houses, buildings and plenty of vehicles running on smooth roads. Sylhet, the birthplace he had left forever, too must have expanded to become a large town by now. Vyomkesh was thinking about all this while sitting inside the vehicle. Their car rushes past a varying countryside. The *lagna* (auspicious time for ceremony) for the marriage that night is thirty-four minutes past nine onwards. The party of the groom, therefore, has taken some time to set off. There is, however, another reason for this delay. *Bara* sahib does not want any disturbance in the routine work of the estate owing to the marriage ceremony of his son. Therefore all the officials could join the wedding party quite late only after the completion of the day's scheduled work. Most of the members of the groom's party would return tonight. Vyomkesh also would come back. Next day, when the bride and groom come home, Vyomkesh will have to perform the sacred rites of *badhuvaran* (ceremonial reception of the bride). He wonders where in Silchar the home of the bride would be. Surely it must be a lavishly-decorated mansion. Who is going to be the priest from the other party? It would be wonderful if the person turns out to be someone from his birthplace. One feels great to meet someone from one's own native place.

Vyomkesh has been dwelling on all such things sitting in the fast-moving bus. A truly comfortable bus to travel by; splendid colours, big windows! Such vehicles are usually not to be seen on the roads of Baithakhal. One has to accept that Mathuranath has left nothing more to be desired in the arrangements. Everybody has been equally provided for. Travelling along the meandering roads, crossing two successive railway gates, they all at once get a glimpse of Silchar—splendid and well-lit. After another ten minutes' ride along different streets all the vehicles halt in a single line before the house of the bride's family. What gorgeous and opulent arrangements! Electric lights of dazzling colours spread forth their radiance. The huge mansion is glowing and sparkling wondrously. In front of it a large entrance has been built decorated with diverse coloured papers cut in dainty shapes. Some Western music is playing in the background. Amidst *uludhvani* (uluating sound uttered by women on ceremonial occasions), blowing of conch-shells and scattering of puffed rice flakes, the groom is received and taken into a big hall to sit down and relax. Being the priest from the groom's party, Vyomkesh too receives a warm reception. The priest from the other party now comes and takes him aside. Mathuranath is very busy in trying to ensure that all the proceedings occur smoothly and on time. So the ceremonial performance of *dadhimangal* (a ritual in marriage) has already commenced.

The bride has completed her seven rounds around the groom. Garlands have been exchanged and *sampradaan* (ceremonial handing over of the bride to the groom by the bride's father) has begun.

The bride and groom are now seated side by side on flat wooden seats. The girl has a very pretty face, shaped like a betel leaf like that of

Goddess Lakshmi. In her bridal attire she looks like a goddess. Now the groom is pouring puffed rice into the sacred *yagna* (oblation) fire and chanting a hymn as uttered by the priest,

Aun iyang naajyaruparutey laajaanaapantikaa
Aayusmaanstu mey patih e dhastung jnaatayoman.

A prayer to the deity of fire, asking for life and prosperity. A chant from one of the Vedas, passed down to Indians by the ancient sages. How wonderful and exquisite! How gracefully poetic! But do they have any relevance today? Vyomkesh too once chanted the same sacred verse while marrying Alaka. But till today he is yet to become prosperous.

Aum idam laajaan aaba paavyagnou samriddhikaranang taba.

This verse also asks for prosperity. How destiny differs from one person to another! Otherwise, why would the same chanting act differently in the lives of different people?

Meanwhile preparations for the sumptuous repast are on. It is difficult to get a large space for any function in an urban locality. Therefore a tarpaulin shed has been erected just beside the place for the marriage and *yagna*. Flocks of gorgeously dressed young men and women are moving in and out and strolling around. Light giggles, scattered speeches add to the bustle. All the choicest delicacies are exuding their aroma and making the air all around very alluring. Vyomkesh's mind suddenly gets diverted from the chanting. He is reminded of a particular episode from *Naishadha Charita*. It is a description of Damayantee's wedding feast:

Abhilasadvaspamakhanditakhilang
bijuktamanyonyammuktamardabam.

(Delicate streams of smoke are coming up from the served rice, each grain of it is well-cooked, delicious, unbroken, pure white and fragrant.)

Oghavati and Vinayak must be waiting for him. Alaka, too, surely would be expecting sweets brought from the town. Vyomkesh has never been able to get them good food and sweets to relish. The host of people scattered over places like Pingchhara, Baithakhal, Nalgai and Asaighat, in whose houses he carries out his profession of priesthood, are not all that solvent. Some preparations comprising of fish and green vegetables seem to be sufficient among them. It is sheer good luck that Mathuranath has chosen him as the priest for his son's wedding. At least he'd be able to see broad smiles on the faces of his son and daughter.

Aum praanaistey pranaan sundadhaami, asthibhisastheening, maangsairmaang saani tvachaa tvamey.

The groom is repeating the last verse of the *yagna*. The verse means: 'Let my soul, bone, flesh, skin be united completely with your soul, bone, flesh and skin.' From now on it is a bond, a union for the rest of their lives; its effect will persist even in the life after death.

The scriptural rites being over, bride and groom are taken inside. It is now time for another round of dining. It is very late in the night. Mirth and merry-making have somewhat subsided. Drumbeats too have faded and died out. Vyomkesh is arranging and packing his sacred books. At once, after *uludhvani*, women inside the house sing in unison:

'Lo lo oh ladies
All minds filled with jollities,
The new groom is now about to eat.
Bring curd, milk and other sweet dishes,
Kheer,[iv] curd and *mistaanna*.'[v]

Vyomkesh is surprised by the fact that such songs are still sung in towns! Although there are songs for almost all occasions in Sylhet and Cachar, nobody really sings them nowadays. Perhaps they feel ashamed of it! But no! Not Mathuranath's new relatives. Like Mathuranath they too have not forgotten tradition.

This is a good sign. Vyomkesh feels really glad. Mathuranath has formed an alliance with the right family. He has not made any mistake in recognising people. Perhaps that is why he could scale such heights in life.

It is very chilly now. Vyomkesh comes out of the marriage bower and goes to a deserted spot at the other side of the *pandal*. He feels slightly uncomfortable under the glare of dazzling lights in his rustic attire. He drags a chair into a darkened corner to avoid the attention of the gathering. The priest of the bridal party has gone inside, perhaps to hasten the preparations for their supper. He too is a knowledgeable man—the principal of Surya Kumar Chatushpaathee (Sanskrit school). From the bits of conversations he had with the man in between the proceedings, he has come to know that nowadays pupils do not come to Chatushpaathee anymore. It is indeed something to worry about. Will the rich tradition of Sanskrit completely vanish in independent India one day? Should our nation continue to remain besotted with the West and be oblivious of itself? Oghu and Binu will never know anything about Maheshwar Tarkalankar!

Vyomkesh yawns. The whole day has been so tiring. He has travelled such a long distance after many years. He feels fatigued and sleepy.

'My Goodness! You're here! And we have been searching for you throughout the house?' Vyomkesh is startled by the loud voice of the young Tila babu. How shameful! He's been sleeping!

'Me? Why?' Vyomkesh replies like a culprit.

'What do you mean "why"? Do you have any idea about the time? It's only because of you that we haven't started on our return journey. *Bara* Sahib's order is that there should be no delay in commencement of work in the garden tomorrow morning. Unless we start now we can't reach before six in the morning!'

'No … I mean … er …' Vyomkesh can only mumble feebly. The drowsiness induced by sleep having passed, he feels a twitch in his stomach. He is extremely hungry. But feels shy to say so to the young babu.

'No! No! Let's go.' Without giving Vyomkesh a chance to speak, the babu picks up Vyomkesh's bag lying beside the chair and almost pushes the latter towards the door.

Vyomkesh, helpless, starts descending down the stairs towards the main door. As he comes near the bus waiting on the road, the passengers in the bus, who are on their way back to the garden, start screaming and squabbling. Many express their annoyance, some even disgust.

'You should opt for short-cut methods on such occasions.'

'What nonsense! These long-winded chantings! Couldn't they have been shortened slightly?'

Bits and pieces of such remarks come floating to Vyomkesh's ears. He feels like merging with the earth below in shame. With much effort and restraint he boards the bus and then takes the rearmost seat and collapses in confusion. Within a few seconds the vehicle starts on its course with a low sound. All the marriage party members, well-fed and contented, now rest their heads on the slanting comfortable seats and enjoy the mild swinging rhythm of the moving bus. Vyomkesh is seated with his eyes wide open; he is looking ahead. He is not getting any sleep. Hunger almost consumes his stomach. He only had some fruits at noon. Alaka must be sitting up at home waiting for him. Oghu-Binu too must be sleeping hoping that their father would bring *sandesh* and other sweets for them.

The bus is heading fast towards Baithakhal Tea Estate as the strong yellow beams of its headlights light up the surroundings. The paddy fields lie on both sides of the road. The paddies have bent with the heavy weight of corns. Looking at such abundance around him provided by mother earth, Vyomkesh suddenly thinks—what sins committed in his past life, have deprived him of the grace of Annapurna, the goddess of fruitfulness, and turned him into a homeless refugee?

Translated by Udayshankar Chakraborty

(Endnotes)

[i, ii, iii] Fried sweet crispies soaked in a thick sugar syrup. A kind of fried sweetmeat.

[iv] A sweet preparation made with milk.

[v] Sweets.

Ashraf Ali's Homeland

Moloy Kanti Dey

The sky is dark. The wind too seems dark. The fields, marshy lands, woods and the habitation on both sides seem engulfed in gloom. Darkness is ahead and behind those fast asleep in every hut. Two sharp headlights pierce through the deep gloom like a couple of spears. The tar on the road, melting in the heat all day, now dazzles in the light. The grating roar of the heavy engine spreads through the layers of the atmosphere. A sub-inspector is seated beside the driver in the police van. At the rear on the wooden deck of the van are eleven people squatting together like a flock of lambs or cows sent to the wholesale market. They have no expression or emotion in their eyes; only the surrounding gloom is reflected in their eyes. The two constables on guard doze as their batons lie idle on their sides.

Ashraf sits pushing his head between his knees like a beast tied for sacrifice at the altar. Both his hands are tied over the shoulder and his fingers are in chains. His ankles dangle on either side. Often his head or ankles dash against the hard wall of the rushing van. It hurts him and there are scratches all over his body. Ashraf does not raise his head, nor does he open his eyes. He does not even groan in pain. That does not necessarily mean that he is asleep. In fact, he is seething like a broiler inside.

Amina is seated beside Ashraf. No one might have seen her face behind the veil or noticed the dried up tears on her cheeks. But Ashraf can feel the fire in both her eyes without even opening his eyelids. The dumb sharp look pierces Ashraf's conscience like a needle. He has nothing to say. Abdul was hungry and was crying in the evening. Now he sleeps near his mother like a curled-up puppy. They comprise three in the group of eleven. We know nothing about the remaining eight. We can only guess about their plight on the basis of Ashraf and his family.

The talks, the pleading, grabbing of feet, the reasoning are all over. At this moment they have resigned themselves to their fate. They have no strength left to ponder over their future. Now they are tossing about on the crest of the waves of events.

Two years ago Kader Mian had glanced at Ashraf's small piece of land. Kader Mian was a very powerful man then. His land was expanding in the twinkling of an eye and so was his rice mill. The sow mill was established. It was a bit difficult to devour Ashraf's land, because Ashraf had never borrowed any money from Kader by putting his thumb impression on a piece of paper. Even then Kader Mian lodged a case. Surprisingly Ashraf won the case at the Karimganj court six months ago. And that victory proved fatal. Having lost the case Kader now employed some other means. The 'foreigner' issue had spread throughout the state by then. Events followed one another in quick succession and Ashraf was proved and declared to be a citizen of Bangladesh. Ashraf's Bajan[i] had created the habitat out of a jungle. He has been thrown out of that land through several contrivances and now in the middle of the night is imprisoned in the fast-running police van. They are fast approaching the Indo-Bangladesh border check-post.

Ashraf is not asleep. But he is completely lost in his thoughts. He is hungry and exhausted. His brain is restless. Endless scenes flash before his eyes in quick succession. His senses fail to keep pace with the time and it is difficult to trace their destination. From his long-lost past a known voice swims into his ears 'Ashraf! Dear Ashraf! O Ashraf!'

Tossing on the waves, the words from the depths of slumber dash against the screen of his ears. And the knock brings Ashraf back to consciousness. Tearing through the layer of sleep the face of his mother takes shape in the yellowish twilight of the country lamp. Ashraf gets back to his senses through this ever-familiar picture frame.

'Get up, we need to go.'

'Where are we going, ma?'

A very stupid question. Now Ashraf realises that. This simple question was so tough for his mother then. Where are they to go? Where? Why does one have to give up the land of seven ancestral generations? Why does one have to leave the near and dear ones behind? Why does one have to escape under the cover of darkness? His mother could not give him an answer that night. Rather she asked him to hurry, 'Get up! Get up!'

Ashraf got up from bed. He recalled that they had been secretly getting ready for some days to go somewhere. No one told him anything, yet Ashraf could sense that. He heard his father's voice from the verandah.

'Don't know what is in store for us. But it can't be worse than the way we are living now. We shall have to start begging here within a few days.'

'Your bad luck. Otherwise, you see, Irfan is your relative; why should he throw you out from your land?'

Ashraf could identify the voice of his neighbour, the white-bearded Nanaji. 'What relative! There can be no kinship with a landlord. This son of a bitch is no human being.'

'Go since you have decided to. But will you be happy in Hindustan? So many have gone there ...'

... Even though the legs had become stiff from continuous walking, there was no scope for rest. There was a sack on his father's head and a tin box in his hand. There was another bundle in his mother's hand. Ashraf by then was ten or eleven years old. It was impossible to walk carrying him. Ma was following Bajan. Bajan halted at last. The sky overhead was dark. He looked around and then said, 'We have arrived in Hindustan.'

Ashraf felt a strange joy. It was as if they had reached *beheste*[ii], walking on foot—from Pakistan to Hindustan. When? When did they cross the border? Why was there no wall anywhere? It was merely like a stroll from one street to another. Is this how the two countries were divided then? Ashraf seemed to be in a trance. Hindustan, Bharatbarsha. It's not a separate country—rather an assurance that promises supply of food ...

… Ashraf couldn't see his Bajan in the jungle. Only the sound of the axe striking a tree could be heard. He wiped the sweat on his forehead and lighted a *bidi* sitting on a piece of wood, which he had cut just then. Suddenly a piercing cry filled the air, 'O Ashraf, I am undone!' Bajan's eyeballs were protruding out of his sockets. A few men assembled upon hearing the cry. Two drops of blackish blood on his foot. The poison never subsided. Bajan was cremated near the jungle …

'Is Ashraf at home?'

'Who is that?'

'Open the door.'

Ashraf moves to the door and looks back. Amina lifts the mosquitoe net and stares with fear in her eyes. Before opening the door he asks once again, 'Who is it?'

'We are from the police station. Open the door.'

Ashraf begins to sweat. He has been apprehending such an eventuality. Kader Mian is full of vile tricks. Ashraf opens the door with trembling hands. It is getting clear outside. A few men stand outside in brown (khaki) uniform. Someone standing behind them suddenly runs away. Isn't it Farjan Ali, one of Kader Mian's family members? He came to identify the house?

'Are you Ashraf Ali?'

'Yes sir.'

'You're a Bangladeshi. When have you come here?'

Ashraf feels the earth under his feet slipping. His lot is burnt. He can't recall the questions that followed. A few unintelligible words crowd his brain: citizenship, migration, etc. Ashraf mumbles something in response to what the police officer asks. He is instantly greeted with a strong rebuff, 'Shut up bloody immigrant!'

One more comes forward …'Move, you'll have to go to the police station …'

The van halts with a big jolt. Once again Ashraf's head is dashed against the wooden frame. He is freed from the chains but does not open his eyes. The jolt has awakened the two constables as well. They look around. The sub-inspector emerges from the open field and orders them to hurry.

'Hey, get all of them down from the van.'

Though all the eleven creatures, except Abdul and a baby girl of his age, are awake, no one responds. They have probably forgotten how to respond to a human voice. Two constables push them with their batons. They get down from the van like a herd of sheep. Gloom all around. The headlight is turned off. The concrete structure of the check-post building can be seen in the dim light of the stars. The sub-inspector walks towards it. A few minutes later a lamp is lit in one of the rooms. A few gun-toting border security personnel can be seen around. The sub-inspector comes out after some time and the light goes out. Their stealthy movements in the darkness make it seem as if a war is on. There is an iron gate across the road. Vehicles are allowed to move in by lifting one side of the gate.

Following the order of the sub-inspector, two constables along with two armed guards begin to move with the eleven-member group. They walk like creatures possessed by the spirits. Their feet seem tied to a heavy rock. Even then they have to move on. They are led from the metalled road to another road. A few steps ahead lies a dense forest. The policemen stop. One orders in a hushed voice, 'Move! Go ahead.'

No one moves. The utterance doesn't seem to have any meaning for them; or they do not seem to be aware of human language. One is struck at the back with an iron ruler. He moves a few steps ahead. Falters. Stands up and keeps standing. Now one by one each of them is beaten with rulers or struck by rifles accompanied by curses and abuses. When the policeman shoves a young married woman but it is impossible to realise what happens in the dark, and the woman instantly shudders and moves aside. It becomes impossible to withstand repeated beatings. They move slowly and then suddenly one of them lets out a piercing cry; like a death lament. The loud cry floats through the forest. They move, falter, fall, stand and proceed. Where? Who knows?

Dear readers! Hope you understand. I don't know exactly where the story began or came to an end. It becomes incoherent as I attempt to write it. Who are those who install check-posts on earth's breast, making her two lungs two different nations? You must have noticed the word 'deportation' in the newspapers. You might have also witnessed rigorous checking in the railway compartments of trains for illegal immigrants.

Ashraf and his family are sent back to their homeland in this way. I am not supposed to know what happened afterwards. I can only imagine. They are at a loss in the midst of the forest. Where can they go? Can they go back to the land they left amidst much agony one generation ago? I can visualise all too well the fact that they have received no warm welcome on the other side of the border. They have lost whatever money and possession they had with them. I get occasional reports from different people and my doubts get shape. One day a person, back from Mahisashan, narrated an incident to me, 'You can't believe it, you know! We go to the forest to collect firewood! Scattered here and there are torn pieces of cloth stained with blood. One day I even saw the dead body of a completely naked woman. Some foxes had torn out flesh from her breasts ...'

A police constable told me once at a tea stall, 'You'll probably beat me up if you come to know all that actually happens there ...' I could not resist the temptation and asked, 'Where do they go ultimately?'

'Who knows? They may come back to this country secretly, add to the gathering at railway platforms or footpaths; and dream of their homeland, their homes, their land, their paddy fields ...!'

I can only imagine ... Ashraf is standing in the forest in distress. Abdul asks him, 'O father, won't we go to our country?' Ashraf does not reply. The place where he now stands at is a no man's land. As he stands here Ashraf realises that he does not have a homeland anywhere in the world. He has lost his homeland in Pakistan to Irfan *chacha* and in Hindustan to Kader Mian. Homelands are now in their control. And Ashraf? Standing on the strip of no man's land, Asraf, in fact, now is no man—a nonentity.

Translated by Dipendu Das

(Endnotes)

[i] Father in the Bengali-Muslim lingo.

[ii] Heaven.

The Elevation

Bijoya Deb

Though the subject demands contemplation, till date Ujjaini has never seriously wondered whether her long married life lacks something. Suchibroto is heavily suspicious about this nonchalant stance of Ujjaini's. Since a woman is a housewife and the house is her prime retreat, her thoughts should be centering round the house; and if it doesn't, then it is certainly something to worry about. What Ujjaini does throughout the day and what she broods over or what dreams distract her mind that make her remain standing by the window till the dead of night—all these are matters of anxiety for Suchibroto. Nowadays he feels exhausted and doesn't think about Ujjaini anymore. He has stopped trying to draw her towards him since he has realised that she is whimsical, fanciful and prone to day-dreaming. There is no point in trying to form an opinion about the lack of concern for the present and the sense of reality of the person who surrenders herself to poetry, immerses herself in Manik (Manik Banerjee, a distinguished Bengali fiction writer) and Jibanananda (Jibanananda Das, an outstanding exponent of Bengali poetry) as if they were holy scriptures. Shomi is the only son of Suchibroto and Ujjaini. Suchibroto had always apprehended that his son might be indifferent like the mother, and so he reserves a lot of time for his son. The child is so smart! At the age of five, he speaks English fluently, has picked up a good hand-writing, has memorised thoroughly at least three books of rhymes, can crack jokes in English and has developed an intimate familiarity with Phantom and Archie. Yet Suchibroto is sad today. Despite such potential and much training, Shomi could not get admitted to South Brabourne School. The heavy heart is further bogged down by irritation. He considers Ujjaini to be at the root of this failure. She works secretly like the radicals. Surely she holds the key to this fiasco and plays a diabolical role. Her veiled influence behind the deviation of Shomi cannot be ruled out. Thus he creates a huge tree of suspicion by watering its roots regularly. Ujjaini stumbles while serving rice and writhes in pain. Suchibroto gets irritated and says, 'Why do you walk keeping your eyes fixed upon the sky? One has to use one's eyes to watch the ground!' The sting in the words lessens the intensity of the pain. Ujjaini knows that Suchibroto does not want their child to be close to her. It's a queer demand of Suchibroto. But despite so much effort, has he been able to recognise his own failure? If he had, he would not have been so angry!

Morning, noon and afternoon; it is always the hour of crisis. Ujjaini feels anxious in the evenings. Suchibroto's heart wails and pines as the evening moves on. The night seems so beautiful. So charming. At such moments only the fairies descend from the sky. They jot down so much in dazzling letters in Ujjaini's blue notebook. Each single syllable helps to create loving words. The words in unison give birth to poems. The words never seem to visit her in the daylight. They get lost somewhere. Nights are splendid. Be it the starlit sky, the gloomy cloud-ridden pitch-black darkness or the moonlit backdrop … 'Ujjaini!' 'Haven't you slept yet, Broto?' 'No. No sleep at all. Feel so disturbed. You are blessed. Free of worries. At peace with yourself. Bah! Splendid! So now, will you please teach me the magic trick of remaining free of worries?' Ujjaini feels alarmed and looks around. 'You know, in fact, you are rather selfish. Shomi is bright. Simply a lack of proper guidance has made him lag behind. Now I shall have to look for other schools where he may get admission. You are indeed at peace with yourself. But I get so frustrated!' Ujjaini does not respond to such taunts and complaints. Doesn't involve herself in verbal duels. She never says, 'You know it well, Broto; I am not a part of your rat race. My first identity is my Self. I am not ready to part with it at any cost. I would have nurtured Shomi the way I would have wanted to. Why do you accuse me in spite of knowing that?' These retorts have credence, but Ujjaini doesn't say anything. She remains silent since it is not in her nature to get entangled in conflicts. And she feels a sense of guilt as a consequence of her inability to speak out. This facet of her personality is indeed a weakness. Why is she so apathetic to fights? Is she afraid of Suchibroto? Why fear him? Is it because of his male identity? Ujjaini gets very irritated with herself. She and Suchibroto had fallen in love with each other. How on earth could that have happened? Love and marriage—these were very strange affairs. There are numerous reasons why a female is attracted to a male. Such instances are a regular feature. Suchibroto has always been ambitious, clever and smart. On the contrary she is whimsical and a dreamer. Even then they had fallen in love. That was quite an intense love affair. These intense relationships often end in marriage. She had never paused to think whether this love would last. She has always been so indifferent. She was earnestly angry with herself. Heaving a long and deep sigh, Suchibroto goes downstairs. Leaving everything to the blind inevitability of middle-class drudgery, Ujjaini yawns out of exhaustion. The family for her has turned into a bundle of habits only, a skeletal frame devoid of flesh, blood and fat. Still she lives. She longs for profound love, lives in deep search of a concerned lover. Both of them suffer from utter discontentment. But the reasons behind their discontentment are very different. Everyone seems to have joined this fast-paced race to reach the top. Who knows how all of this will end! Ujjaini shudders when she thinks of the terrible consequences of such an obsession. Today Suchibroto couldn't get a wink of sleep because Shomi failed to get admission into South Brabourne. Thus renowned English medium schools like South Brabourne have either caused loss of sleep for some harassed parents or ushered in wonderful contentment for many others.

Today is nineteenth May. On the nineteenth of May, 1962 eleven agitators, leading a strike, demanding special status for the Bengali language in Assam, died in police firing. Since then every year that day is observed as Language Martyr's Day. Like every year, Ujjaini participates in the procession this time too. 'Remembering the martyrs, dedicating Self, repay your debt of blood,' the procession proceeds step by step. The town wakes up slowly, watching the procession in silence. 'Break the iron door of the prison, destroy it …' How many doors are yet to be broken down! Prison within prison. She feels sad for Suchibroto. How much pain must he be going through! The cruel demands of life have been making him somewhat lose his balance. Gradually Shomi too would turn into another Suchibroto. Why was she like this? Why does she not possess the capacity to influence others and have only a shadowy existence even after being a part of the family for so many years? Her only child too has drifted away in this mighty flow. Has she been able to prevent it? She has not been able to fight it out. Everyone doesn't have the ability to fight. She thought that the philosophy of her life would indirectly exert influence over her husband and son. Things might have been different then. Shomi might have asked his mother, 'Mummy, please tell me a story—the story by Upendra Kishore, where a tiger faces a lot of ordeals in his effort to marry a girl in the guise of a human being.' Or he might have recited Bengali nursery rhymes running about the room, 'Oh mother, who tripped on your father's nose …' But that never happened. Suchibroto has always created a wall around his son.

There is a play at the railway station. Standing in the midst of people a queer sense of guilt makes Ujjaini recoil within herself. She is a culprit of the language martyrs of nineteenth May. She could not spread the love for her mother tongue in her own family. She herself was in love with Bibhuti Bhusan, Jibanananda and Manik. She had her first taste of Jibanananda at the age of twelve—

> At the hint of the night, as the river flows far in the distance—
> The lamp burns in my boat too
> With the identity of Self.
> I feel I've got the mythical myrobalan
> In my closed palm;
> All kerosene-lit fire has died out; leaving the water aglow,
> As if by the force of magic.
> The soldiers of the world sleep at the gesture of King Bimbisar,
> After performing many remote roles;

> Running all day on a golden bull,
> Truth has now turned into stone.
> has now turned into a statue.'

At the age of twelve, Ujjaini had infiltrated into the golden bower created by the enchanting words of the poet. The essence of poetry kept her immersed throughout her life in a different sort of love. It was as though she inhabited a different planet. Today Ujjaini has suddenly realised afresh the significance of the martyrs' great sacrifice. It is the love for the mother tongue—whose magical touch kindles light in the gloom, harbours love within love—for which people sacrificed their lives! She understood nothing then, but even at the age of twelve she was in possession of that prized property—popularly known as *amloki* (myrobalan) in her palm. Tears fill her eyes. She feels sad for Suchibroto and at the way he runs about breathlessly. True, he has not achieved much in life! Aniruddha delivers an inflammatory speech not very far away, 'We all know that the main prerequisite for protecting one's mother tongue is regular practice of speaking and writing in the mother tongue. There were many people here present today, who are publicly shedding tears in the name of martyrs, but send their children to English medium schools. What is this hypocrisy? Do you know what crime you are indulging in? The children reading in English medium schools are losing their originality under the heavy burden of studies. In this manner, their creativity will gradually get blocked. Have you ever thought of how the continuous disregard for the mother tongue has led to this pathetic state at present? Has the observance of the Martyrs' Day on the nineteenth of May survived merely as a ritual? ...' Ujjaini comes out of the gathering. Someone closer to her speaks out, 'Aniruddha is simply splendid. The hypocrites must be made aware of their faults in this manner.'

Ujjaini walks under the scorching May sun. 'Have some sugarcane juice, didi.' The dark man under the tree places a stool in the shadow and wipes it with the napkin on his shoulder. He fills the glass with the juice. It's so cool and sweet. It refreshes her body. 'How do you feel now, didi?' Deep indifference makes Ujjaini languid. The familiar town, familiar people vanish from before her eyes.

> 'At noon, you may sail to another ocean
> Baishali to Alexandria.
> Light from the candles remain strewn at a distance,
> Dim signals on the beach,
> Yet you are not content.
> Your heart is set upon
> Winning a haze of the horizon
> Which mirtures boundless youth.'

Ujjaini is submerged in grief.

'Are you back home, boudi[i]?'

The excitement evident in the question makes Ujjaini look up instantly.

'You know what happened!'

'What? What's the matter, Siddhartha?'

'Manu has committed suicide.'

'What are you saying? Manu?'

'Yes *boudi*, go and see the situation for yourself.'

Manu was twelve years old. A timid lad. Every day he went to board the school bus at seven-thirty sharp. He was a student of South Brabourne. His mother was all praises for her son. Suchibroto quite often used to visit Manu's mother to gather information about Manu's coaching and preparation while seeking admission for Shomi at South Brabourne. Ujjaini hires a *rickshaw*.

There's a crowd in front of Manu's house. An anxious silence. Every face is frozen and panic-stricken. Manu's body has been laid down. A boy of only twelve. Ujjaini was acquainted with poetry, the language of verse and her mother tongue at the age of twelve. And in his twelfth year, Manu lost his faith in life! They calculated a successful career for their son and in the process lost their son! Surely Manu didn't dream the same dream that his mother did. He didn't know how to dream. Schools like South Brabourne did not know how to instil a dream in a child. It could only shatter dreams.

Otherwise Manu wouldn't have been so keen to cut short his twelve-year-old life. What irony, resulting from the ruthless attempt to wrench a child from the world of his dreams, and thrust him in the direction of a career!

Like the declining afternoon, Suchibroto comes out with a haggard look. A neighbour, Abhirup Choudhary accompanies him. Manu failed in the race and left the world. They say that Manu's mother had been suffering from depression in the recent past. The son had been lagging behind. A picture lost forever flashes in front of the eyes. Manu used to alight from the school bus where the road turns. He always carried a heavy load of books on his shoulder. Exhaustion writ large in his eyes. Walking wearily, step by step. One hand would be in his mother's hand. Waving with the other hand he used to say, 'Hi Auntie.' The twelve-year-old boy consumed the sleeping pills of his grandmother. How many did he have? A handful? After consuming a handful of medicines he slept in peace.

At the advent of evening, Ujjaini lights a lamp in the name of the martyrs. Kamala Bhattacharya, Sachindra Paul, Kanailal Niyogi, Kumud Das, Tarani Debnath, Hitesh Biswas, Chandicharan Sutradhar, Sunil Sarkar, Sukomol Purokayastha … 'Ujjaini?' Suchibroto approaches her with Shomi by his side. 'Give me the match-box.' Ujjaini hands over the match-box without realising anything. Suchibroto lights the lamp. Handing over the match-box to Shomi he says, 'Please light it, Shomi.' … Birendra Sutradhar, Satyendra Deb. Eleven lamps are lighted. The flame is steady and motionless. And very bright.

Translated by Ashok Kumar Nandy

(Endnotes)

i Sister-in-law.

Whirlpool

Debabrata Choudhury

Lying supine on the slender strip-like deck of their boat, Neelkantha inhales from the butt end of his *bidi*[i], gulps down a big lump of smoke, and then releases dark twirled puffs of smoke towards the sky looming overhead. The sky is overcast with a dark pall of clouds, with sudden lightning flashes cutting it up into shredded uneven strips. Surely there is a storm brewing up today.

There are three people in the boat. Neelkantha, Dudhnath and old Haazim Mian. They are now rowing up the river to the large expanse of the backwater area of Chatla, to fish with their cross-net. It was not overcast when they set out from home; only heaps of cotton wool-like white clouds were strewn here and there against the blue sky. Hoping that such a day would hold bright prospects for fishing, they set off in their boat. But their intentions have perhaps made the scattered clouds jealous and prompted them to conspire and league together to form dark plans.

'Pugh ... ...'

Neelkantha blurts out broken words of disconcertedness as he fails to light up his extinguished *bidi* after repeatedly puffing at it. Disgusted, he throws it away. The overcast sky fills his mind with dejection.

'Fuckin' foul masses ...' Neelkantha hurls abuses at the clan of clouds. The gust of wind coming from the other direction pelts the slangs into the river water. The two men sitting at the tapering far end of the boat have not heard the abusive words.

'Oh Neelu, what are you thinking of?' asks old Haazim as he rows, seated at one end of the boat.

Neelkantha does not reply. He simply stares at the sky and continues to lie in a reclining posture. The hissing gurgling sound of water-bubbles, lapping by the side of the boat, keep ringing inside his head. Thoughts come up like bubbles upon bubbles, and crowd the flux of his mind.

At home his little son has been suffering, God knows, from what ... the boy is turning skinnier by the day. A stony lump of flesh has developed on his sunken stomach; day by day, grain by grain it is turning into a hard, solid mass.

Neelkantha knows pretty well that his Nayaan's days are numbered. Even some name was whispered by the doctor. And to cure it one complex and costly operation has to be performed. Sympathising with Neelkantha's plight, the doctor has however asked for a lower fee. But how will he arrange for even five hundred rupees!

Kamali, Nayaan's mother, too was taken to the medical college for a check-up. She is left with no hope or chance of another baby in future. Only a grief-torn mother's heart gasps helplessly in her bosom.

Neelkantha and his men work at Harin Tilaa with Kshirode Das's fish net. They wander about and ransack all the submerged and watery expanses around and catch fish, while Kshirode supplies them to Silchar market at wholesale rates. He is not a bad man; rather has a sympathetic air about him. But he is tough when the work does not match his expectations.

Earlier, they worked with Mohim's fish net. Mohim was malicious and mean-minded; he would take into account even the smallest fractions of transaction; he would call them names, often hurl abuses at their forefathers. Thus they were almost compelled to leave him.

About a year ago, one day Kshirode called in Neelkantha and gave him a fish net costing two-and-a-half-thousand rupees and told him, 'Neelu, the day you finish repaying me for this net at an interest of ten paisa per day, you know for sure that it is yours.'

Neelkantha was delighted beyond words. It was as if Kshirode had pushed him into a do-or-die, a must-win game that day. Even today he is a tireless fighter of that game. Compound interest is like a galloping horse with one snapped rein. Yet, Neelkantha is desperate. Till now two hundred rupees have been paid as interest alone. One day the game will have been won when the rest of the amount is paid.

'It looks so bleak, Neelu.' Haazim's drawling words snap him out of his slumberous meanderings. For the past few minutes his thoughts had been spinning webs inside his head like a spider. He looks at the sky: the canopy overhead is already dank with the besmeared gloom of the imminent warfare.

Dudhnath is just past the threshold of eighteen. Already orphaned by his father's demise, he is trying to do his father's job. He is still a novice tottering and struggling to get through the giant billows of experience in a fisherman's life. Haazim's words make his heart beat faster. Somehow he mumbles, 'Indir da would have been a great support today. The water is full of hidden currents; it'd be difficult to keep the boat from turning over.'

Indra, the fourth member of their crew, has not come today. It has been several days since a gripping stabbing pain in his bowel rendered him bedridden. When the pain starts gnawing, the helpless man goes tossing about, heaving and rocking in his bed, like the beheaded torso of a goat. The pain is accompanied by bouts of nausea when he throws up sour liquid.

'The lad is so young and yet suffering from such a foul disease!' moans Haazim.

'That's nothing but the doings of his age. That's disease from hunger, as you know; even a stout young elephant collapses if it goes on working without eating.'

Neelkantha's voice echoes a muffled discontentment. He sits up on the deck now. A sudden strong twirl in the water rocks the boat vehemently.

'Oh father!' blurts out Dudhnath in sudden terror. Haazim, who has always been deft with his oars, however, controls the boat. It once again starts sailing with the pull of the current.

Neelkantha glances at Dudhnath whose tender face has paled in fear and anxiety. Looking at the poor, luck-lorn lad, he is reminded, who knows why, of his own innocent youthful face. Something stirs in his bosom, choking with anguish. He heaves a heavy sigh out of the depths of his breast. Taking some water in his palm, he sprinkles it upon the bosom of the river and says, 'This is but the beginning, Dudhnath. There'll be many more gales to see and face … No way can you become crippled with fear!'

Dudhnath feels surprised and speechless as he stares at Neelkantha's grave expression.

'We're all fishermen … all our meat and dole, our household dreams, our life and death … all flow and dance with the river. Can you stay away from it?'

Neelkantha's philosophical strain wrings out a loud laughter from Haazim at the oars.

The bosom of the sky is cut to the quick with lightning flashes. Clouds huddled together rumble and roar. The low gushing sound of water from the backwater marsh is heard at a distance on the river. Dudhnath watches the restless opacity of water under the hooded black sky and feels vacuous inside his heart. Breaking the silence suddenly Haazim sings:

'*Had I known, my boatman, beforehand,*
I'd not have come in your leaky boat,
Away from that land …'

The song then comes to an end. Neelkantha praises in delight, 'You've such a touching sweet voice! Why've you given up singing regularly?'

'Oh Neelu! It was always my heart's desire to sing songs. But the hunger burning in this stomach has made me forget all my songs.'

Even as he says this, Haazim feels heavy within his heart. Realising that the conversation has taken a grave turn, Neelkantha tries to change the context, 'There's a foul gust scudding through the wind, Haazu bhai …'

From the distant backwater the noise of water breaking into the river gradually becomes louder. Chatting away about this and that they reach their destination.

Reaching this bend the river turns perilous. Twirling all about, open gushes of water are sliding down with a babbling roar. The force of the current is much stronger here. With very cautious moves Haazim is trying to moor the boat at the bank. Dudhnath also works with a *logi*[ii] in his hand. His chest is thumping rapidly. But Neelkantha is unruffled. Now he snatches the *gamochha*[iii] lying across his shoulders and ties it like a belt around his waist.

Tying the boat at the bank they step on to the ground. They are hurriedly folding the fish net when rain leaps down with torrential gusts of wind. It becomes difficult for them to stand exposed to the lashes of wind. They scamper through pelting silver drops and take shelter under a big *kalohuja* tree, a kind of tree found in southern Assam. But they fail to save their skins; the raging wind seems to drive them aloft. At last they lie down prone on their backs on the sand at the base of the tree trunk. Moist puffs of wind come howling, carrying clammy dust particles and sand that cling to their bodies. In such hostile circumstances Neelkantha tries hard to keep his eyes open.

The trees on the other bank are all dancing to the whim of the wind. There is a rushing, rustling, maddening and deafening sound all around. The storm, churning the bosom of the river, is making python waves toss up their hoods as though they would juggle with the boat tied at the bank and break it.

'The vulture-like eyes! ... Always on the lookout for a chance to hunt us down! … Thrash dead us poors!' mutters Neelkantha calling names to the unseen adversary.

The storm takes a breather after an hour of relentless *taandav.*[iv] The black lumps of clouds have now become pale and washy. The big round drops are now followed by fine drizzling droplets.

Neelkantha and his men shake off their languor and spring up. Now, on their rain-washed bare bodies, glimpses of bright rays are visible as though playing hide-and-seek. Through every nerve, every vein runs a charged-up pulsation. Dragging the dripping heavy net they move towards the *haaor.*[v]

Toiling with the net unceasingly amidst the dirty waters of the *haaor* they feel exhausted. Till now not many fish have been netted.

Barring a few *boaals*[vi] and *mrigels*,[vii] the rest of the catch consists of small fish.

Old Haazim regrets, 'Pooh! Had I known, I'd not have come out of home today.'

Neelkantha is also regretful, but he is not without all hope. Keeping his eyes on the water he says reassuringly, 'Wait a bit, Haazu bhai, I will catch big fish today; only we've to take the boat upto the mouth of the *haaor*.'

Dudhnath, however, has not got over his fear yet. 'The current is much stronger there, Neeluda,' he mumbles.

Neelkantha loses his temper, 'Why on earth have you come with us when life's so dear to you? Go home and suckle at your mother's breasts!'

Dudhnath, transfixed, shamed, sinks his head. He knows Neelkanthada is a short-tempered man, who would otherwise jump to the rescue of anyone in trouble, but when enraged, would care the least about what he is saying to whom.

Neelkantha realises that Dudhnath has been hurt. At once he pats him on the back and says, 'What? Angry?'

Scolded by his own loving leader, Dudhnath is on the verge of weeping. To hide his tears he turns his face away.

'Come boy …,' Neelkantha laughs out serenely. 'You're a stout lad; so be a man and not a poor sissy.'

After that Neelkantha's voice turns dim. 'Do you understand, Dudhnath? I'm gripped by a passion: I've to catch real big fish; there're loads of debts sitting heavy on my head … and that of you …'

Dudhnath looks at Neelkantha. The latter's sad tranquil look has by then swum across the teeming flow of the Ghagraa (a river in southern Assam) to a far-off region. Something stirs within Dudhnath: grasping the *logi* with his right hand, he jumps onto the deck and calls out, almost in a cry, 'I too need real big fish today, Neeluda!'

Pushing his *logi* with utmost care, Haazim brings the boat to the mouth of the *haaor*. Torrents of river water are breaking through the narrow duct at the mouth; turbulent waves are circling about in the open water. Around the boat, below the apparently tranquil surface, there lurks the devastating whirlpool ready to gorge the victim in.

Resting the balance on his *logi*, Haazim keeps the boat riveted at the slack muddy bank of the *haaor* and whirls it around. Neelkantha and Dudhnath cautiously spread the fish net on the water around the boat. The sinkers start floating in a round, on the water. Haazim then draws the boat into the *haaor*. With the pull working in the towline, the net comes closing in. When this process is repeated over and over again, catches start coming in fair numbers.

However, the haul till now is hardly satisfying for the desperate Neelkantha. He has sworn to catch a really big fish, and he has decided to strive for it till the very end. He must catch Kshirode a fish of considerable weight and enormous bulk and somewhat lessen the burden of interest.

Their eyes suddenly flare up. There is a heavy pull at the floating spread-out net this time. Pushing his *logi* Haazim tries to take the boat once more inside the *haaor*. But the rope-line does not come away. Neelkantha feels as though his blood has caught fire. His breathing becomes faster. He won't let this fish escape his snare; he won't, at any cost. He sits restless and anxious at the end of the tapering deck. Then, suddenly tightening the *gamochha* around his waist, he leaps into the river fraught with current. Estimating the depth of water there he takes a deep plunge.

An intense and endless waiting starts on the deck of the boat. Each passing moment is filled with excitement. Two thumping chests heave up and down with doubtful expectation. After some time, the fish net becomes loose. Dudhnath clutches the rope tightly. Haazim works with the *logi*, pushing the boat slowly further into the *haaor*.

At last the heavy net comes up to the boat. Haazim and Dudhnath pull it onto the deck. Good heavens! One real big fish! A *boaal* (a large sweet water fish available in eastern India) weighing almost twenty kilos. Their eyes are suffused with happiness and excitement. Overjoyed, Dudhnath embraces the net-wrapped fish.

'*Inshaah-Allaah*! Dudhnath! It has been many days since we have had such a big catch! ...' Old Haazim's cheeks glow as a smile spreads over them.

'O-h-m-o-t-h-e-r-s-a-v-e ...'

The sudden cry shatters their joy into pieces.

At the *haaor* mouth, Neelkantha has got sucked into the turbulent whirlpool. He looks like a morsel of grub for the hidden twirling monster. Still he fights tooth and nail to survive. With the pull of the hidden current, he keeps vanishing by inches.

A few feet away, a man is sprawling, floundering helplessly on death's lap. The two men on the boat stare at him devoid of any hope. The man is their team leader. The man, though overburdened with debt, has been a constant companion in their day-to-day life full of joy and sorrow. Thoughts stagnate in boatman Haazim's head. Dudhnath pushes the *logi* with all his might. With lightning speed the boat rushes to the *haaor* mouth. Old Haazim summons all his strength to shake the fish off the net on to the deck and throw the twisted net full length at the mouth of the whirlpool.

At the very last moment before drowning, Neelkantha grabs the net. And the other two pull with all their strength and manage to get man and net back on the boat.

They take the boat to the edge of the water, take up the senseless man in their arms, and lay him down on the ground. The body lies there, flat and befuddled with exhaustion. His breath is shallow and uneven. Haazim gently massages his chest.

Dusk closes in when Neelkantha comes back to his senses. His body is fatigued. Once again, clouds accumulate in layers across the sky. Darkness descends from all around. Slowly, by degrees, Neelkantha sits up. Resting his weight on Haazim and Dudhnath's shoulders, he languidly strolls back to the boat.

The wind starts blowing with the tide. The boat sails homeward with fair pace. Haazim is seated, rowing now and then, at one end of the boat; at the other end, Dudhnath silently sits with his head resting on his knees.

The darkness congeals to become even darker. On the boat the corporeal loom as shadows. None can see the others' faces. The only perceptible thing is the audible breathing. Neelkantha is lying supine on the deck. Beside him lies the stupefied *boaal* wrapped in the fish net. At times the tail of the fish touches Neelkantha's wretched body.

Kshirode will extract, like on previous occasions, a large sum for the *boaal.* The first lorry at dawn will take the fish to Silchar market. The fish-loving, fish-crazy babus of the town will swarm around to gloat over and examine such a big fish. Kshirode will place a steep price on each kilo, since aged, full-grown *boaal* tastes even more delicious.

But then he'd return as usual with a sulking face and say, 'Can't help it! The rate is so low for *boaal*!' That is quite understandable: at particular times, rates of all fish do go down!

But Neelkantha knows better than to fall for that. In two months time, Kshirode's wish is going to materialise: his kitchen compound shall be decked up with glistening tin sheets, Dashahara *puja* shall be celebrated with much pomp and splendour. As Neelkantha thinks of all this, embers seem to glow and singe in his head. His head resounds with the sound of horses' hooves to the point where it is ready to burst.

Neelkantha realises that somewhere beneath his numbness, a fire is being fanned. That ball of fire heats up his entire body. Unaware, he continually clenches, opens and clenches his fists. Slowly he sits up on the deck.

Dudhnath is lying drowsily coiled up at one end of the boat. Holding the oars, Haazim at the other end is lost in his thoughts and moping on his own. Neelkantha stoops down and silently takes up with both hands the half-conscious *boaal.* Then, still stooping, he quietly releases the fish in the bosom of the river. Glob-glob … the Ghagraa chuckles. Nobody has seen or realised anything. Neelkantha resumes his supine posture.

Translated by Udayshankar Chakraborty

(Endnotes)

[i] Tobacco leaf stuffed with tobacco, rolled up and tied with a thin string to form a variety of the Indian cigarette.

[ii] Bamboo pole for pushing boats.

[iii] Thin home-spun length of cotton cloth used to dry the body.

[iv] Formidable destructive dance.

[v] A wide-stretched watery swamp.

[vi] Kind of fish available in eastern and north-eastern India.

[vii] Kind of fish available in eastern and north-eastern India.

WAKE UP CALL

Amitabha Dev Choudhury

Come morning, the impatient knocks rain on the door. It has become an everyday affair. A new irritant one can hardly ignore. It will not stop till I leave my bed to respond to it. If allowed to continue, it will spoil the last vestiges of slumber of the neighbourhood. It's better instead to open the door. As you open the door, a human figure would emerge before you. Hair twisted like a rope, wrinkles lining the face, shrivelled skin—all suggest that the hey days of this person are gone. Wilderness haunts her open eyes. It is hard to figure out whether it's a male or a female figure. The white piece of cloth wrapped around is the only testimony to her bygone femininity. Neither masculine nor feminine, she is beyond such attributes. Just *Homo sapiens*. Merely a human being. We call her 'Masi', the elderly aunt. Even the kids in the neighbourhood, who should be her grandsons or granddaughters, call her Masi. I told her umpteen number of times to not wake me up so early. Everyone at home is utterly annoyed with her. But who cares? Our Masi is oblivious of the world around her. She belongs to a completely different world altogether.

At the slightest provocation, she would start narrating the forgotten history of this urban Silchar—a period, when the horse races used to be held on the vast green stretch beside Trunk road. The ground was much larger then. The cluster of buildings and other signs of urbanity around the ground were non-existent. In winter, the Europeans used to erect tents at this place. Bathing in the soft sunshine, the ladies would join in the revelry. Dancing, drinking and wild merry-making were interspersed by wet nostalgia for the homeland they had left behind. Needless to mention, Masi can hardly be expected to be coherent in her narration. This story is basically cobbled in my imagination, in the confluence of Masi's disorderly dialogue and my acquaintance with the history of this town. Masi says that once she saw a horse-riding ghost of a European who was beheaded. That happened on one moonlit night. I wonder whether what is revealed of this frontier town's past, of the British era, did really exist in reality. How old could she be? Her wrinkled skin, her outward appearance generally attribute her to be around seventy-five, which means it could be a story from 1936–37. Moreover, how could she have been in Silchar at that period? Then, when was she on the other side, that is in East Bengal? Was it Bangladesh or precisely, Sylhet?—the soil she is determined to be on when she breathes her last. It may be a possibility that those two different times live together in Masi's memory. Somehow two different histories are juxtaposed in Masi's imagination. Did she witness those events during the British era with her own eyes? Or is it that she actually heard those stories somewhere? All those stories were reborn in her reminiscences as first person accounts.

Waking up in utter disgust, I discover that it is just five according to the clock. I was busy correcting answer scripts and preparing a lecture for my class, till late last night. It was half past midnight when I went to bed. However, these things don't figure among Masi's priorities. She went to sleep very early, just at the stroke of dusk on the previous day, after having her meal, comprising of food doled out in the Kali temple of the locality, unfolding a worn-out wrapper and a mosquitoe net, kept bundled up in daytime, in the prayer hall of the temple. Now waking up to her call, I would discover that all her morning preoccupations—washing, bathing and managing a breakfast—were already over. The Kali temple of the locality has a sprawling campus with outhouse, guesthouse, pond and tube well and a host of other amenities. Everyone in this neighbourhood has a strong faith in the divine power of the idol in the temple. During the annual worshipping, there is a huge congregation of devotees every year. Seven months ago, when Masi, bereft of any belonging and without a destination to go to, came down drifting along the turbulence of her life, to this locality, we took the initiative of convincing the priest and the members of the managing committee to arrange her night stay and food at the temple. A large section of the residents of this locality are basically destitute refugees from East Bengal who settled here in the wake of the great exodus of 1947 that followed the Partition. The past generations of many of these residents had reached this town of Silchar after they were rendered hapless in East Bengal. This is history. To many, it was attainment of independence of their motherland. To most, it was synonymous with the withering of their ancestral homes. It's no wonder that the siblings of the once-destitute would empathise with another hapless soul. Therefore, with hardly any difficulty, we could arrange for old pillows and worn-out mattresses and mosquitoe nets for her as alms from every household. For her food, there was the customary daily offering at the temple. Whatever was available as offering was enough to fulfil her meagre requirements. Most of the days, the temple provided rice offerings. In the evening, occasionally, it would be semolina cakes or sago pastes; or else it would be the traditional preparation of a fruit mix. The door of the temple shut down immediately after the evening prayer and accordingly Masi's hour of sleep would approach. 'Early to bed and early to rise,' characterised her daily life.

Ultimately, I open the door everyday. 'What's up, Masi?' I attempt to frown as usual, and fail. The Kali temple facing my door or the field beside or Dwiju's tiny shop—all seem to be still immersed in deep slumber. The reluctant rays of the monsoon sun might shine today. The sky above is more or less clear. Manish uncle, Soumen sir, Jaganmoy uncle—the retired seniors of the locality are busy with their daily schedule of morning walk. No one ventures too far. The junction at a little distance, where this lane meets the main thoroughfare, is their limit. Just three or four rounds along this stretch suffice as their daily quota of morning stroll. The neighbours wake up by the time their walk is over. Dwiju's employee, who sleeps in the shop, does his morning washing and prepares to light the stove.

I stare at Masi's vacant eyes. I find a mirror there. Is it in her eyes or in my imagination? 'Did anything progress, my son, regarding my journey across the border? For God's sake, please let me have a glimpse of my homeland. Once, at least. It keeps haunting me all the time.' As if a mirror emerges in her eyes. Images fade in. That of lush green fields; vast horizons, endless expanse of water, full-grown crops of corn bending downwards in the vast open golden fields; the archetypal dwelling places of rural Bengal; the big ponds; the clamouring fish; the village barns spilling over with the overflowing reserve of harvest; the rostrum of the holy herb of basil; a village elder, wearing a pair of wooden sandals, strolls in the yard, hookah in hand. A village elder, or an old canopy of banyan tree living through the ages? A seamless spectacle of eternal Bengal. These are the imaginary sketches of my homeland piled up over a long period of time in the sublime interiors of my mind. I was born here. Long before my birth, in the fifties, my father's family had to flee their homeland with whatever little belongings they could gather along, and in order to survive, had to cross the border. Freedom, which partitions one's homeland and renders crores of innocents homeless, was gifted to our earlier generation. Masi's homeland thus became my own homeland too—the lost homeland which lurks beneath my consciousness for years.

I try to console her. 'I will take care of everything, Masi. But you need to give me a little time for that. Why do you become so impatient every morning?' Maybe her homeland beckons in her sleep. The irrepressible call of her own abode! Maybe the musings of nocturnal dreams chase her to our doorstep daily at the stroke of dawn. It makes her very emotional. Maybe, what night unfolds in her mind earlier fades out in the intensity of the daylight. Masi knocks at our door in the inertia of that spell. Maybe I don't understand her emotion, but the lifeless wooden doors of my house surely empathise with her and feel gratified.

What I say in meaningful words to her are nothing but empty promises. For the countries on either side of the barbed wire, she is merely a nonentity. Once she made an attempt to slip into the other side. It was an incident that happened three months back.

Actually, some of us raised money for her passage and for other meagre logistics. But Masi couldn't make the trip. The kingpin of the clandestine transportation racket denied her a passage without paying heed to her desperate prayer, not even considering the amount of money she was prepared to pay for the service. Perhaps they too considered her a rejected person, not qualified enough to be duped. All her mad cries fell on deaf ears. Can an old person, whose final jouney is so imminent, afford a dream of going back to his or her country?

Yes, it's hardly deniable that Masi is a rejected person. Even at this temple, she is not worthy of providing any service. She can somehow only wash her enamel tumbler, plate and clothes. Masi is a rejected person. One who can no longer deliver anything, either physically or mentally, is surely a spent human being, a rejected person, a useless entity—though her heart beats on. When the physical structure fails to drag forward, the heart spills out of life. It's true for our Masi too. Essentially, Masi is purely governed by her emotions. Her homeland, the indomitable obsession to go across the border, all reside within her heart.

Of late, Masi has developed a new mania. She has procured an old, black leather bag. It's rusty and the zip fastener doesn't work. Masi collects all varieties of torn papers and keeps them in the bag with a lot of care. Her interest mainly centres on those torn papers which bear some kind of resemblance to official documents. For example, receipts or bills with faint impressions of official stamps. Needless to say, all of them are rejected and trash but Masi collects them as her treasured belonging from the dusty roads, backyards of school and from the lawns of the houses of this locality. For me, it has become almost a habit to follow Masi's trail very closely. I noticed with an eye of a sleuth that Masi never picks up shrivelled up papers. This mania has developed in Masi after her vain attempt of crossing the border stealthily. Necessity of possessing a passport or visa might have reached her ears during those days. She cannot make out what exactly those words meant, but the faint memory haunts her. On her return from Karimganj, the neighbouring town of Silchar, Masi asked me, 'My son, everyone says, I shall have to procure some papers to go to my homeland. Why don't you get those for me?' Though I take all the trouble to calm her down with a variety of fictitious excuses, the rest of the people get annoyed with her impatient pleas. 'It's not fair, Masi. We shouldered responsibility of your food and shelter. What else do you want? We are not interested in getting involved in more trouble because of you.' Yet, many laugh at her instead. Why not? Everyone cannot be assumed to be living in the realm of emotions. The obsessive habit of Masi, which we were discussing earlier, began since then. Does that mean that Masi assumes all these torn papers to be her passport and visa, the usual documents to go across the border? Does Masi, a rejected person, regard these piles of waste papers to be her testimonials?

It doesn't evoke laughter in me. Doesn't cause any anger either. I feel deeply sad. I don't know why it stirs up memories of my mother. My mother too, during the last years of her life, used to yearn for her homeland all the time. 'For God's sake, please take me to my native land. Just once. I just want one glimpse of my ancestral abode.' In reply, I had only false promises to offer as consolation. Reminiscences of her childhood kept flashing before her eyes. Though my mother spent half of her life on this side of the border. I wonder, after all these years, why couldn't this land become her own? The search for one's homeland eventually becomes synonymous with the longing for one's childhood. Isn't it a familiar adage that in old age a man enters his second childhood?

Often, I feel that as a person I too have been rejected. I can't keep pace with the jet speed of our times. The whole world races forward leaving me limping far behind. I too, like to revisit the memories of my childhood days. I want to escape from the present, which hinges on television, satellite channels, internet, hi-tech advertisements, STDs, PCOs, nonsensical notions of hotel management and business management—all a never-ending rat race. I like to delve into my past—my childhood. To the lantern-lit nights of fables and fairy tales. To the lush greens and the thick of child-like adventures. I long to go back to the days when we used to flee our stuffy and enclosed classrooms and run towards the freedom of football and cricket matches. Can one go back to the past? Can mere change of place accomplish that? What Masi is searching for is essentially a magic key that can take her back to her past. But the time that she is obsessing over, has withered away from the face of this planet long ago.

I ask, 'Do you have acquaintances there, Masi?' A self-assured Masi replies, 'All my relations live there! My father, my mother, my son.' It's yet another riddle in Masi's conversation. She has lost track of time. Maybe outliving others, or being destitute from her own self over the years, she turned away from her memory as well. What was her past has become her present. The dead seem to have come alive again in her life. Once she said that she was never married. On another occasion she said she was married here, on this side of the border. Yet at other times, she shifts her venue of marriage to the other side of the border too. She had a son who now lives across the border, she claims. During the partition of this country (Masi refers to it as holocaust), she lost her mother. Another version of her tale is that, consequent to that, all of them had crossed over to this country. In a different version, she claims she had been smuggled into this country by two persons along with hordes of others to work as contract labourers. Elsewhere I had heard of similar incidents earlier. There are seven assembly constituencies in the district of Cachar, namely, Silchar, Sonai, Dholai, Katigorah, Barkhola, Lakhipur, Udharbond. Even in the remote areas of these segments, cheap labourers were made available by smuggling in poor people from Bangladesh. Masons, labour employed in brick kilns, and work force used in other kinds of construction work—all belonged to the same group of smuggled labourers. These have-nots who escaped from the other side in search of a little happiness or were allured into this land, were employed for meagre wages. I don't know whether the legacy continues or not.

Masi probably had come to this land much before partition. She had been engaged in a variety of work or maybe she was pushed into different occupations. She might even have had to sell her chastity. She never speaks of her youth. In her old age, she was employed for household work in a well-to-do family. It's a remote village on the other bank of Barak, far from Silchar. After she became too old to work, the master turned her out. Treading the rough terrains of life since then, Masi finally reached our locality, at the temporary shelter of our Kali temple. But Masi still cherishes a dream of having a permanent shelter—which is why she wants to be on the move further.

Finally a morning dawned without a knock on my door. On that fateful morning no one in our locality could trace her. For a few days more, she figured in all the chitchats and conversations. Over cups of tea in the tea stalls, in the usual pleasantries exchanged at the grocery shops, in the gossips of the young people, in the intermittent small-talk during the card-playing sessions, in the liquor dens after dusk —everywhere Masi's sudden disappearance was the only news. Like everything else, all the speculation surrounding Masi had a natural demise. Everyone eventually went back to their own engagements. The young ones to their schools and colleges. The grown-ups to their usual race at their offices and establishments. The women-folk went into their kitchens or out to their offices. And the elders to their cards and chess sessions. There were preoccupations like morning walk, noontime nap, gastric troubles, coughs, spondylitis or spasms, diabetes or blood pressure to keep the others occupied. All these anxieties pushed the case of Masi's disappearance into oblivion. Initially, I felt pity. I had a strange feeling for a different reason too. She, who used to spoil my early morning slumber and therefore was an utterly annoying existence as far I was concerned, filled me with a sense of bereavement instead of relief, after suddenly vanishing, along with her small bundle of meagre belongings. For the next two days, I woke up early on my own. As if I was desperately awaiting Masi's call in my sleep. As Masi was no longer there to wake me up, I overslept and consequently woke up late-almost at nine o'clock. My wife was terribly upset as I hardly found any time to go to the market. So, in effect, the dishes served at lunch and dinner tasted less than savoury. On one or two occasions, I arrived late at school for which I had to swallow the mild admonishment of my vice-principal. All these events repeatedly reminded me of Masi.

Nowadays my wife has taken the responsibility of waking me up at seven in the morning. She does it by simply pushing me out of bed. As part of my daily itinerary, I go to the market with a bag in my hand. Spend time in idle chat with the neighbours. In this period we, the teachers, were on strike in our school. Later on, I spent some days helping my daughter prepare her project work as part of class assignment. In the same chain of events, I took part in a protest march against the communal carnage in Gujarat. There were some cultural events in the District Library Auditorium of the town. I took my wife and kids along to enjoy those. After a long, one-month gap, I spent considerable time in an extended chatting session at Dwiju's stall. That occurred one evening recently. There was a little booze as well. Time rolled by quite fast and along with that Masi slipped out of my mind.

All of a sudden, it was in the darkness of night yesterday, that I happened to see Masi again. She was in Karimganj, the neighbouring town of Silchar, where the river acts as the international border between the two countries. Masi stood alone with her old, torn, black, zip-less leather bag in hand, in front of the sentries of the border post. I saw her showing the torn waste papers one by one to the stoic sentries. A rejected person exhibiting all the waste papers as her testimonials. These consisted of her passport, her visa to go across. Piles of waste papers, slipping out of her hand cast a gloom over the entire surroundings. Soon, more and more waste papers started flying in from different directions to join their brethren. A huge avalanche of waste papers came down on the riverbank. A thunderstorm of waste papers enveloped the entire sky. Testimonials of a whole rejected population, from all the places, who are bereft of any identity or lineage, are roaring along the riverbank. In this whirlpool of waste papers, their dreams and memories of a time lost are swirling. From thousands to millions, from millions to crores, they spiral incomprehensibly. The incessant shower of rejected dreams and rejected memories is drowning the riverbank. The unending piles of waste papers have covered the riverbank in a numb white shroud. It seems as though there has been a snowfall.

It wakes me up. After many days, Masi knocks at my door again. How can I not respond to her? Struggling out of the inertia of deep slumber, I go out into the open. Sporadic clouds of late monsoon are hanging heavy in the sky. Residues of late-night showers are visible here and there. The leaves on the trees, the potholes on the street, the grass shoots in the green—all bear the memory of the downpour of last night. See how the raindrop on the tip of the grass is frozen like morning dew. I rush to catch a glimpse of the wonder. Yes! This is my homeland, my own soil. Eternal! Embodiment of my soul! My beloved nest of tranquility! My dream! My memory! My identity! I never had the opportunity to look at her properly. For years, for ages, it seems, I haven't seen my own soil. The greens beneath my feet, the sky over my head, the breeze murmuring in my ears, the heavy monsoon showers, the huge trees, the tender grass were nowhere in my vision. But today after ages, I can fully appreciate the natural canvas in front of me. Have I seen it on my own? Or Masi, our old beloved forgotten Masi—has she shown me the way?

Translated by Subha Prasad Nandi Majumdar

The Man of Geramthan and Duliya

Jhumur Pandey

Duliya suddenly tumbles down on the pile of bricks. She somehow gets up and puts her clothes back in order. Removing the straying hairs from her forehead she breathes heavily. It's irritating. Maybe there's a bigger scratch on her forehead. All this, while she was piling the bricks one by one. Initially she would pant while doing such work. Her mind would dance with joy as she would sow paddy in the fluffy soil of her own field. Duliya would, as it were, be intoxicated by the moist smell of the earth. Then the load of paddy on the head would make even her nose-ring smell of dry earth moistened with rain. Her nose-ring would somewhat break into a smile with the heavy load of paddy on her head.

'This is our land, it is our parent.' The man, so passionate and crazy about the soil, the man of Geramthan (the place of worship of god Gerambaba under a banyan tree) would not leave the field so easily. Duliya would also consider this a land of profound love. Oh land! Where are you? Duliya continues placing the bricks in order and, with every spasm in her heart, she sees in her mind's eyes the fluffy soil, the smell of earth nourished by rain.

'Bhouji,[i] have you finished?' Duliya looks up in surprise.

'Not finished yet?'

'No, quite a bit left.'

'Work fast; see how the cloud is gathering above.'

She finds clouds sailing across the sky and gathered up in dark patches in different corners.

'Won't you take the money?'

'We'll get payment tomorrow.'

'Tomorrow?'

'Yes. Singhji went to town today.'

'Then?'

'What then? I'll have to take credit from Basudev's shop.'

'Let me go now. You may come later. The children might be crying.'

Subal's wife leaves in a hurry.

Duliya now comes down from the hillock of bricks to her own house. She takes a bath at the well. The smell of bricks lingers on her body. She builds a fire to make tea. Then sits on the dark terrace stretching her legs. Now the rains come down heavily. It is almost five years since the man has gone to jail. Why did the man go to jail? Why did he go? Why? The clouds in the sky roar. Duliya's heart roars. It roars and goes on roaring.

Today Duliya leaves the bed quite early at dawn. The morning star hasn't disappeared yet. Duliya calls it the star of the morning. The man of the house has gone out long back with the plough. The morning star was still shining then. Her father used to say that men should leave bed when the stars are still in the sky. Otherwise one can't ever hope to earn more. Duliya nowadays has got used to this practice. She rises when the stars are still there in the sky. Duliya drives her sleep away by stretching her body. Then goes to the field for morning ablutions. She washes clean the utensils heaped in one corner of the kitchen. After plastering the floor with cowdung she sweeps the courtyard. Then she takes a bath and making a fire on the hearth, sits down to prepare roti. She would take tea and roti to the field when the sky became clearer. The man is incredible. He works like a buffalo!

'Has been murdered?'

'What do you say?'

'Who? Who got murdered?'

'Shambhu babu.'

'Who killed such a good man like him?' Duliya starts crying in a shrill voice. 'Possibly stabbed in the neck when he was deep in sleep.'

'Is it?' Duliya now starts running with her hands smeared with coarse flour. Satish, the mechanic was going to the marsh with a locally available twig to be used as toothbrush.

'Hey, have you heard anything? Oh, mechanic brother?' Satish, the mechanic stares with drowsy eyes. His eyes are still sleepy. The mechanic simply has to get drunk at night after working all day. That inebriation lingers till morning. The mechanic looks at Duliya with intoxicated eyes.

'What? What happened?'

'Shambhu babu got murdered.'

'What? What are you saying?'

The rustic toothbrush drops off the hand of the mechanic.

The old mid-wife was going to throw away some rubbish. Subal's wife has given birth to a son last night. She sees the police coming from the other side of the canal. Why the police? To seize liquor perhaps? Here almost every house is part of the illegal country liquor industry. The old woman too possesses a pitcher at home. Of course if it is seized, they get paid some amount of money for it. If people do not make liquor, they are again urged by the police to prepare it. The old woman throws away the rubbish and begins to run.

'Where are you going, Buri didi?'

'The police is coming to seize liquor.'

'Can't be liquor. Shambhu got killed.'

'Our Shambhu? What do you say, Duliya?'

'Yes, didi, yes.'

Suddenly the people of Geramthan are shocked by a death. Who knows where the boy had come from. But he used to call a spade a spade. All the charms and incantations, amulets and talismans had been driven out of this village. The poor and destitute people were taught to fight to survive. But who killed the boy? Such a good boy too!

There are patches of clouds over the sky of Geramthan. Duliya is cooking fish curry. The man has caught a big fish in the morning. So Duliya is cooking it with sufficient care. She has come out once to glance at the sky. The entire paddy would surely get wet if it rained this winter at the time of mowing. Duliya feels giddy. She enters the cottage with the dried clothes in a hurry. Duliya offers him water to drink. The man gulps it down eagerly. Then sits tucking his head between his knees.

'What do you think?'

'Nothing.'

'Could they catch Shambhu babu's murderer?'

'No.'

'You told me that you know who killed the man.'

'Yes. I know.' The man now sits up straight.

'Then why don't you tell them that?'

'I told them.'

'Yes, then why are the police not arresting the culprit?'

'They won't. How can they? They're close chums of powerful men.'

'Oh, God! All right, leave such topics alone. Go, take a bath. I have cooked fish curry today.'

'I don't feel like eating,' says the man with a deep sigh. 'I've lost the desire to eat. Such a spirited man like him got murdered. Moreover, you see the heavy clouds in the sky. We could not store paddy.' The man now sits on the terrace and fans himself with the *gamochha*. Duliya sweeps the floor and sits beside the man.

'Get up, go, hurry. See, once again the clouds are approaching. We never have dark clouds and heavy shower in this season.'

'You're right, Duliya.'

The rain comes lashing down on the stock of paddy piled over the courtyard caked with mud. They stand petrified looking at the rain.

Today the sun is shining fiercely since morning. Duliya spreads the roll of paddy, wet with rain water, to dry in the sun. The old midwife sits on the terrace with a big bundle in her hand.

'Hey, where did you go?'

'Subal's son had his bath (ceremonial first bath of a new-born baby) today.'

'Oh yes. I was invited. I completely forgot about it.'

'The entire paddy got soaked.'

'Yes. What could I do?'

'Well. Have the police arrested anyone?'

'No. Whom would they arrest?'

'Everyone knows who did it.'

'Yes, they know. The man in my house also knows. He has informed the police. He has told Bisweswar babu.'

'They won't arrest anyone. Even if they do, they would release them soon.'

'Why?'

'They're related to powerful men.'

'I-m-a-k-e-u-m-b-r-e-l-l-a. O-r-d-e-r-u-m-b-r-e-l-l-a.'

The old woman says, 'Isn't that Hussein Mian calling?'

'It has been many days since I last heard him calling out loudly.'

'I-m-a-k-e-u-m-b-r-e-l-l-a. O-r-d-e-r-u-m-b-r-e-l-l-a'—Hussein reaches Duliya's house.

'Come, come, oh, umbrella-*wallah*! Where were you all these days?'

'I wasn't here, sister. Are you well? I hear our Shambhu babu has been murdered. He was such a good man. The extent to which men can fall!'

Duliya spreads the paddy from one side to another in the courtyard. Then she brings some ripe bananas and offers them to Hussein Mian. 'These are from our banana trees. Brother, please eat, She says.'

The evening has just settled in. Satish, the mechanic has broken into a drunken totter on the elevated narrow ledge leading up to his front door. After the day-long hard toil of a daily labourer, he enters Shyamroti's hut to gulp down a few glasses of liquor. He then wears an altogether different expression. He curses everyone. His wife eloped a few months after marriage never to return again. The mechanic never harms anyone. But today he wants to know who murdered Shambhu. He has been shouting continuously. He is cursing the police; even Bisweswar babu hasn't been spared. Everyone passing by the road peeps and pries into the scene.

Duliya went to Basudev's shop to buy some essential commodities. Usually there is a heavy rush at Basudev's shop in the evening. He dozes all day. People here work throughout the day and come to buy goods in the evening.

'You have already bought a fair amount of goods on credit, Noni. You won't get any more credit.'

'Please brother. I'll pay the entire amount next week.'

'You too have a big amount to pay up, Shyam.'

'I'll pay; sure I'll pay the whole amount the coming month. I've got a good job.'

'Please pay or I'll be finished.'

Basudev is busy handling so many customers all at once. Duliya gets no chance to speak. The old mid-wife is also standing there.

'What do you want?'

'Pulses and salt.'

'You?'

'Pulses, chilli and garlic.'

Duliya and the old woman leave as soon as they collect their purchase. Probably some meeting is being held in the school building on the other side of the main road.

'Will you be going to the meeting?'

'No.'

The moon surfaces in the sky. The trees seem to shiver. All of a sudden a jackal howls in front of them.

'Oh! I'm gone.'

'Are you afraid?'

'Tut-tut! No.'

'The mechanic is off his head today, isn't he?'

'Yes.'

They reach Duliya's hut as they converse.

'I'm leaving, didi.'

'All right, go.'

It is past midnight; desolate all around. The owl hooting all this while has stopped just now. Duliya waits after making the bed. The man is smoking *bidi* while lost in his own thoughts.

'Won't you sleep?'

'I will.'

Duliya now rests her hand on the man. 'What has happened to you? Tell me. I have been watching you for quite some time now; you remain engrossed in thought.'

'Well, do you remember how Shambhu babu prevented them when they came to capture Subal's aunt's land?'

'Yes, I remember. They had struck him on his head.'

'See the way they roam freely after murdering him.'

'Are you sure you have seen them?'

'Yes, I saw them when I was going to the paddy field. There was the moon in the sky. Stars too.'

'Hush, don't say anymore. Could they see you?'

'I don't know.'

'If they know, they'll kill us.'

'I am wondering.'

'What are you wondering of?'

'Thinking of gathering people.'

'Nothing will happen.'

'Surely something will happen, I bet.'

'I heard your father, who was my father-in-law had died of a police bullet in his attempt to *gherao*[ii] the tea garden manager.'

'Yes. I was very small then.'

'That's why I say—no need for all that.'

The man only mumbles, 'Yes.'

'If you die, I have no one else. No mother, no father, no child.'

The man now turns Duliya's face towards him and looks on intently. A dark and greasy face; so dear to him. That greasy face now smiles at him.

'Think. Go on thinking. Think the whole day tomorrow. Now, let's sleep.' Duliya pulls the man towards the bed. Duliya falls asleep as soon as she lies down on the cot. But the man does not sleep. He keeps tossing and turning in bed. For a long, long time.

Today also Duliya wakes up quite early, sharp at dawn. The man is not in bed. The door of the house is wide open. She comes out of the house in search of the man. He seems to have changed a lot in these few days. Particularly after the murder of Shambhu babu. The paddies spread out on the front ledge have not yet been properly dried. This is their sustenance for the whole year. After cleaning the dirty utensils of the previous night, Duliya prepares tea and waits for him. The man doesn't return. The cows are tied up in the cowshed. The day progresses. Duliya takes the cows to the field. Finishes her kitchen work. She then comes out and looks at the sky. The flaming sun is right above her head. Duliya now steps out in search of the man.

'Where are you going, bhouji?' Subal's wife is going to the river to take a bath with clothes in her hand.

'Don't ask me. The man hasn't even had tea this morning. Where has he gone?'

'Oh. People have assembled there. Possibly some meeting has been arranged.'

'Meeting? What meeting?'

'Meeting in connection with Shambhu babu's murder.'

'Tut, he didn't tell me anything about it.' Duliya feels hurt. Tears almost trickle down her eyes.

'The man in my house also must have gone there. Don't you see Basudev's shop is also closed?'

'Where are they assembling? Do you have any idea?'

'There, near the Durga temple.'

Duliya now walks rapidly. She crosses the main road. Keeping Basudev's shop on her left, she walks through the middle of the premises where the banyan tree lies and reaches the temple of Goddess Durga. It is desolate all around. Nobody is there. Only a crow is pecking at a chicken. Where are the people assembled? Duliya suddenly notices someone crawling under the tree. Who can it be? Duliya proceeds a little. Ho! It's the old mid-wife. 'What happened?'

'What should I say? The police came and forbade everyone to assemble here. Some heated exchanges followed. Immediately the police arrested him.'

'Whom? The man?'

'Oh yes. The people went to *gherao* the police station. I've grown old. Health doesn't permit. How can I go?'

'So many things happened and I don't know anything?'

It is past evening. Darkness has crept in. Duliya sits quietly with a dejected expression. At a distance an owl hoots perched atop a tree. A mixed feeling of grief, humiliation and anguish throbs in the veins of her head. The police have beaten the people with sticks and burst tear-gas shells. Duliya has returned home just now after waiting at the gate of the police station the whole day. The man has been kept in the lock-up. The people of Geramthan are still crowding in front of Basudev's shop. The man has not eaten anything the whole day. Duliya too spent the day without food.

Why have they kept the man in the lock-up? The murderers of Shambhu are still at large; the police do not arrest them. On the other hand, the villagers have been kept in lock-up for seeking justice for the murder. Duliya feels like destroying everything in a fit of rage and anguish.

'Duliya?'

'What?'

'Do you have money at home? Bisweswar babu said bail may be procured if money is provided.'

Duliya ransacks the whole house to find one hundred rupees.

'One hundred rupees will be of no use.'

'Then?'

'Then what? Mortgage your land.'

'To whom?'

'Bisweswar.'

Duliya covers her face with her hands. She now remembers her father. Little Duliya, accompanied by her father, once got lost in the fair.

'Father. Where are you, father … Oh, father …'

Then a storm broke out. Duliya was running all alone in the midst of the storm. For how long? Today Duliya feels that she has again lost her way …

Morning arrives with its busy, humdrum activities. Duliya has remained sitting since last night with boiled rice at the gate of the police station. She could not even manage to have a glimpse of the man. The old mid-wife arrives.

'Why did you take the trouble of coming here? Could you feed him rice?'

'No. I've not been permitted entery.'

A constable takes the man out of the gate of the police station in front of their very eyes.

Duliya runs behind them.

'Where are you taking him?'

'To the headquarters.'

'Didi, yesterday I mortgaged my land for one thousand rupees. Still no bail. Why? Why?'

Duliya looks up at the clear sky pressing the bowl of rice to her bosom …

It has been five years since the man was sent to jail. Why was the man sent to jail? Duliya now gets caught in a spell of heavy rain. She continues to get drenched. She gets up once to discover that the boiling water for tea has dried up already. The fire has got extinguished. She doesn't feel like making the fire again. She again sits on the front ledge. The old mid-wife of Geramthan has grown older. Satish, the mechanic nowadays remains even more inebriated. Basudev's shop has extended and flourished. Subal has become the father of four more kids. Duliya nowadays presses her face close to the bricks to smell the scent of paddy and wet soil.

That night she mortgaged the land by putting her thumb impression on plain paper. Now Bisweswar tills the whole plot.

'The man was put behind bars for no fault of his own?'

'The man was put behind bars without any allegation of crime.'

'What do you mean?'

'I mean that there has been no trial till date. Nor was he produced in the court.'

'Did they arrest Shambhu babu's murderer?'

'Do the close chums of influential people ever get arrested?'

After the heavy shower the moon appears in the sky revealing a small portion of her frame. Darkness gathers on the clean front ledge. Duliya remains seated there. She inhales the smell all around her. The smell of profound love, rain-soaked, moist, earthy …

Appendix (1): The peasant's wife, Duliya, now carries bricks at the brickfield. With a sad look she wipes sweat from her forehead. She does some shopping at Basudev's shop. Then takes a deep breath inhaling the fragrance of the earth and paddy and goes on waiting for the man …

Appendix (2): The man of Geramthan at last returns home after spending six years in jail. But their paddy field no longer yields a golden harvest. Where is the land? The land of profound love, the smell of rain-soaked, moistened earth. The man too is now engaged in the work of breaking stones.

The two persons, who loved the soil and its smell, now lose themselves in grief and anguish in the lifeless world of bricks, concrete and stones ...

Translated by Ashok Kumar Nandy

(Endnotes)

[i] Sister-in-law.

[ii] Literally meaning encirclement, it is an indigenous word for a form of protest where the protestors encircle the person/persons in authority till their demands are met.

Our Home

Saumitra Baishya

My father and his elder brother came to this land in 1950. Three years after Independence. Bereft of any resource and means, two brothers, along with their widowed mother, crossed the border to reach this land. We didn't have any relatives or acquaintances here at that time. Initially, they possibly found shelter in one of the refugee camps. During those days of 1947, when there was a mass exodus of Hindu population to this country, my father's family decided to stay back clinging onto their ancestral dwelling in East Pakistan. They might have had a faint hope of somehow succeeding in staying back amidst all the adversities. Ultimately, they had to desert their own soil forever in the decade of the 1950s.

They might also have got a small amount in exchange for that property. Otherwise how could they buy land and build a house of their own on the outskirts of Hailakandi? At that time of course, the system of providing loans, to the displaced people for rehabilitation on behalf of the government, was still in operation. Later on, I came to know that their land was indeed purchased with the money from the loan. They had escaped from East Pakistan on a riot-stricken night without any belongings. Faint imprints of the words 'Sylhet, East Pakistan' on the citizenship certificate of my father, shown as ancestral home, still survives as the remains of that vanished past.

Our home in the village of Hailakandi was built of bamboo. There was a pond in front of that thatched house. I heard from my grandmother that, as they could hardly afford to hire labourers, my father and my eldest uncle themselves dug the pond and erected the structure of their house. My father and my eldest uncle were quite obsessed with their new house. My early memories of our home, date back to a time, by which our family had already tided over the initial phase of their intense difficulties.

With the passage of time, we eventually got integrated into the wage-earning class of society. Jyetha babu, our eldest uncle (we used to call him that since my father addressed him as Dada babu[i]), got the job of a clerk in the army and my father got a teaching job in a railway school. My father loved to collect flower plants of different kinds and Jyetha babu used to plant saplings of a variety of fruits around the fencing of our home. He used to drop different varieties of fish-seedlings into our pond. When those seedlings grew into fish, he used to hire fishing nets to catch them. Keeping one or two big fish only, the rest were left behind in the pond. In winter, after the pond dried up, *magur* and *cheng* fish used to be the catch of the season. In the rainy season, those fish, if caught, weren't left in the pond. Instead, the catch used to be preserved in an earthen pot filled with water for later consumption. Fish was not cooked in our kitchen. That was meant to be cooked in the kitchen of Sonapishi, a distantly related paternal aunt of our kin.

Sonapishi's family also had come here after losing all their belongings in East Pakistan. They lived in a hut constructed in the vacant space of our courtyard. My grandmother and Boropishima, my eldest aunt, were widows. That is the reason why fish was not cooked in our kitchen. We could have built a separate kitchen for non-vegetarian dishes but separate utensils needed to be arranged. However we didn't pursue the matter to that extent since we were never permanent residents of our home. Jyetha babu's job was transferable and my father was transferred from Maligaon Railway School to Badarpur. He wished to live in proximity to his home.

In case of Jyetha babu, there was hardly any scope to cherish a similar desire. He was transferred to different places across the country. In office, Jyetha babu had to wear military attire. Dressed in his office uniform, he looked like an unknown person to us in the black-and-white photographs. My father used to wear dhoti and shirt to school. The heavy rugs in our home in Hailakandi were all brought by Jyetha babu.

During my childhood we used to go to Hailakandi at intervals. After coming to Badarpur I was admitted to school and thereafter it became difficult to go home to Hailakandi frequently. It was possible only during summer and Durga Puja vacations. Also, it was possible to find time during recess after the annual examination in winter. We used to take the train from Badarpur for Katakhal. From there, time simply wouldn't pass. The train moved at a snail's pace in the countryside. The engine used to be placed in the opposite direction with the front side facing the compartments at the back. The train used to run beyond Lalabazar and Hailakandi.

I never liked to be in our home during the summer recess. Rains invited puddles here and there. We had to hire rickshaws to reach our home from the railway station. That was a wider road. But to cross the narrow lane from the main road to our home, we had to take off our shoes and carry them in our hands. Branches of betel nut trees were laid down across the lane to work as a bridge over the muddy soil. Even slipping slightly meant skidding down into the puddle along with the shoes. In the incessant rain, with water and puddles everywhere, my marooned life ensued.

In the meantime, some of our relations coming from East Pakistan also settled down in our locality. We could spend time by visiting their houses as well. Or else, with Nodada, my elder cousin (son of Sonapishi), I used to go to the house of the only weaver in our neighbourhood. I would stare at the weaver's loom, listening to its rattling noise, and would see various designs appearing gradually on the clothes. I never liked to go to our village during Durga Puja. We used to go after Lakshmi Puja too. It seemed best to me to go there in winter after our annual examinations. Our home used to be full of fun and merriment at that time of the year. Jyetha babu with Borda, his eldest son; Chhorda, younger son of Jyetha babu; Bordi, the eldest daughter of Jyetha babu, and Jethima, wife of Jyetha babu, came home at that time of the year. Fulda, Boropishima's son, too, used to be here at that time. He was employed in the engineering section of the Indian Air Force. His duty was to oversee the maintenance of the fighter aircrafts. They were called ground staff. Fulda used to take our photographs with his own camera. He used to send those photographs to us, after going back to his workplace. Once, Fulda sent one of his photographs in which he was seen standing beside a fighter aircraft. Fulda later told us that there was a strict prohibition on taking photographs of fighter aircrafts. Photographs sent, were taken clandestinely. Fulda's uniform seemed peculiar to me. Jyetha babu's attire resembled that of the police, but Fulda's shirt and trousers were stitched together. Fulda told us it was their customary attire.

Come winter and it was time for maintenance work at our home. Rooftops were prepared afresh with bamboo and thatches. Though my father and Jyetha babu did not stay in the village throughout the year, they nevertheless had many acquaintances around the village. But I did not know any of them. It seemed rather strange to me. Later I discovered that all of them were their acquaintances since the days in East Pakistan.

The annual event of maintenance work of our home used to be a noisy affair with a lot of drama. I saw a photograph where a bunch of thatches were being thrown from the ground to a labourer standing atop the roof. It was a photograph in black and white. That a home is built blending one's dream and sweat, was evident in the photo. What seemed odd to me was that Fulda captured all these events of annual maintenance of our home in such detail in his camera.

It was a busy time for Sonapishi because we all belonged to the club of fish-eaters. Fish was caught from our pond by hiring a fisherman. It was purchased from the market of Hailakandi as well. Occasionally, my father and Jyetha babu joined our club of fish-eaters. Fulda used to be the only vegetarian dining with our eldest aunt, Boropishima. Incidentally, there were two separate bathing platforms adjoining the pond. One especially for our grandmother and the other one was for Sonapishi. After having a non-vegetarian meal one would wash up on Sonapishi's platform. My grandmother's platform was out of bounds for such a purpose. We were made to believe that it would be a great sin to wash on our grandmother's platform after having non-vegetarian meals.

We used to be sad as the day of departure became imminent. We would eagerly wait for one long year to come home to Hailakandi. Jyetha babu's family used to be in the first batch that would leave, accompanied by Fulda. They had to undertake a longer journey, to Pathankot. That is how I first heard of that place. Jyetha babu was posted there at that time. Fulda accompanied them upto Calcutta before leaving on his own for his workplace. They used to take the rickshaw from the main road after crossing the lane leading out of our home. Nodada and I used to be sent to fetch rickshaws for them. My grandmother beside Jyetha babu, Fulda with Boropishima, followed by my mother and Jyethima, Borda, Chhorda, Bordi and we behind all of them—formed a column in the lane to bid each other goodbye. Even our relatives in the neighbourhood used to come out to see us off. My grandmother used to place a water-filled earthen pot on the doorstep before they set out for their destination. When Jyetha babu stepped out of home, my grandmother used to bite his little finger and would hand him a small packet containing tokens signifying blessings of *Mongolchondi*, the goddess of well-being. Each time Jyetha babu left with his family members, an atmosphere of gloom descended upon our home. We too used to leave within a couple of days of their departure.

On the day of our return trip, it was my little finger's turn to be bitten by my grandmother. Needless to say, it used to be no less painful. I remember that grandmother and my elder aunt used to weep at the time of our departure.

After having lunch including fish at Sonapishi's place, we used to catch the afternoon train from Hailakandi. According to my grandmother, commencing on a journey (she used to mention the word 'journey' to mean exactly that), after having a meal comprising of vegetarian dishes was a good omen. Our favourite *mug dal*, a soup of split peas of a particular variety prepared by Sonapishi, was included in the meal. Jyetha babu's family couldn't make it in the year Bangladesh attained freedom. Nor could Fulda's family. I learnt, since the war was on, they weren't entitled for leave. But I discovered two boys of my age and two girls, a little senior to us in our village home, that year. They were Fulda's first cousins from Bangladesh. The names of the girls were Laila and Moyna. Their real names were Lila and Monu. Laila's hair smelt of wild water hyacinth. At night, I could smell it while sleeping under the heavy rugs brought by Jyetha babu. Laila used to be in deep sleep. I never happened to meet them later. Two of their brothers, Dipu and Tipu, became my playmates. They stayed back after the war was over. Buying a plot in Ramkrishnanagar, Fulda's uncle settled down there. Once, my grandmother and my elder aunt had been to their place in Ramkrishnanagar for a month.

On one occasion Jyetha babu came alone. Fulda, also came along. None of our cousins came. Jyethima didn't come. Jyetha babu said that since Borda was studying in a senior class, he wouldn't come to our village home before his school-leaving examination. For the next three years, my elder cousins did not come home. They went to Darjeeling instead. Jyetha babu was transferred to Shillong. After passing Matriculation examination and completing college education, Borda got admitted into an engineering college in Kanpur. We met them after six years. That year we went to Darjeeling after my Matriculation examination was over. My grandmother and Boropishima were also with us.

After being promoted to the eighth standard I too couldn't go to our village home anymore. My father used to be the lone visitor. On one or two occasions, Jyetha babu also couldn't manage to go home. But he never forgot to intimate us about that well ahead through a letter. Normally, Jyetha babu's letters were a regular feature all round the year. Its contents included many important suggestions and advices to my father. Every letter had a word of advice—'Never ignore savings.' My father had a strong passion for reading. He had a passion for music too. He was fond of gardening too. One day he purchased a radio for us. Next, he procured a record player of the size of a rectangular box. Every month he brought recorded discs from Silchar. Those things were not available in Badarpur at that time. Jyetha babu was aware of these activities of my father, but to him all these passions were simply a waste of money!

Jyetha babu was later transferred to Pune. Winding up the establishment at Darjeeling, Jyethima too shifted to Pune taking Chhorda and Bordi along. Exactly two years later we were reunited again. The occasion was Fulda's marriage. After a year, Fulda took Boropishima to Chandigarh to stay with him. A year later, my grandmother breathed her last. By that time Borda had completed his engineering degree and had started working. On completion of his Ph.D., Chhorda too joined a college in Pune. And for Bordi, a search was on for a suitable match for her marriage. Jyetha babu had an intense desire to settle down in our village home in Hailakandi after retiring from his job. In the years in between, my father bought a plot of land in Silchar. Ultimately it was left to Sonapishi to be the custodian of our village home. She was living with Nodada in the village as Pishemosai,[ii] her husband, was still posted at his job in Lunglei. Sonada, our eldest cousin and eldest son of Sonapishi was employed in Itanagar. He too bought a plot of land in Hailakandi town, although he was still unable to erect any structure there. Thus no one was left to look after our village home since everyone decided to disperse elsewhere.

After retiring from his job, Jyetha babu returned to our village home and expressed his desire to settle down there after arranging a suitable match for Bordi. He held the view that, living in one's own home gives one a different feeling of liberty. One early morning suddenly, Nodada turned up at our place to inform us that Jyetha babu had suffered a massive heart attack on the previous day. We could reach our village home only after everything was over.

II

Fulda retired from the Air Force. I came to know that he had constructed a house of his own, purchasing a plot of land near Barasat. Jyethima at that time was staying with Chhorda in Pune while we were residing at Silchar. Sonada's plot was still lying vacant. Sonapishi, Nodada, his wife and their two children were staying in our village home. Pishemosai had expired by then. Jyethima, Borda, his wife and their son and daughter—all came down to Silchar. All of us decided to pay a visit to our village home. Boroboudi, Borda's wife, told us that Fulda had built a beautiful house in Barasat. He joined a job at the Calcutta Airport after retiring from the Air Force. Boroboudi showed us some photographs of Fulda's house. On the occasion of their house-warming ceremony, Fulda invited us through a letter, to attend the function. Once I got Fulda's phone number, I was in constant touch with Fulda and Boropishima over the phone. Ageing cast a shadow on Boropishima's voice. Fulda kept inviting me to visit his house every time I talked to him over the phone.

Finally, at long last, an opportunity came my way. Talking of distance, it's hardly a twenty to twenty-five-minute drive by taxi from the airport where Fulda received me. I observed that Fulda's language had undergone a change and colloquialisms from Calcutta had made inroads into his native dialect of Sylhet. He had been living here for at least five years.

I found Fulda's house to be nicer than what it had seemed from its photographs. The plot was merely two *kanthas*[iii] in area. There was a small flower garden in the front yard. It was a two-storied building. The gate in front of the house was under lock and key from within. I observed that the other houses in the locality were also under lock and key. It is the usual practice in the metropolis, I was told. Day in and day out, everything is under lock and key and hence you have a secured life!

But the same was not true for our place. Boudi, Fulda's wife opened the locked gate. My nephew was at office and my niece was attending college at that time. Boropishima had taken to stooping with old age. Her skin had shrivelled up. There was a garland of basil beads around her neck. She was wearing spectacles made of thick glasses and her eyes seemed bigger compared to her face. My father touched her feet. Boropishima said, 'I had lost all hope of seeing you again in my lifetime.' Reminiscences about Jyetha babu cropped up time and again in our conversations. Nostalgic memories of bygone years clouded in like the fading light of dusk.

Though Boroboudi was known for her effervescence in the matter of showering praises, after having seen the house, it seemed that she had not been exaggerating matters while praising Fulda's house. It had marble flooring on both the floors. Everything was neat and tidy. On our arrival, Fulda and Boudi immediately bustled about, offering us the best of their hospitality.

We wanted to take a tour of Calcutta. Therefore Fulda took leave from his office to take us for sightseeing. Wandering around, our days went past in a trice. On the day of our departure, Boropishima lamented, 'You won't see me next time. I don't hope to remain alive till your next visit.'

Exactly one year after our trip, I happened to go to Calcutta twice in succession on official work. Our previous penchant for travelling around was understandably absent. On the first occasion, I stayed at his house at a stretch for fifteen days. Fulda was insistent that I shouldn't stay at the guesthouse provided by my office. From the airport, he drove me straight to his house. I wasn't familiar with the roads and alleys of Calcutta. As a result, the whole city seemed like a jigsaw puzzle to me. Therefore, it was arranged that my nephew would drop me off at my office the first day. After completing my assigned tasks at office, I would give him a call to pick me up. I observed on that trip, that the aircrafts fly past over Fulda's house at a very low altitude. One can easily identify the logos and names of the airlines imprinted on the body of the aircrafts. In the evenings, Fulda used to sit with me in the balcony on the first floor. Red lights blinked beneath the planes. Fulda used to describe to me the various directions in which the flights were travelling. Boropishima went to bed at seven o'clock in the evening. But we used to sit idle till late at night in the balcony.

I found Fulda to be quite concerned about his house. Every corner of his household used to shine. No dust, no cobwebs to be found anywhere. On Sundays he would be doggedly busy in the cleaning of his household. Sometimes he worked single-handedly, sometimes he employed hired labourers. I used to spend time talking with Boropishima. Our conversations were mainly about

Boropishima's bygone years in her father's home or in her in-law's house, which she had lost long back in East Pakistan. Fulda's father died in the year my father and Jyetha babu arrived on this side of the border. A year later, my father went back again to bring Boropishima and Fulda to this land. Boropishima's in-law's' ancestral home was in Bagherkora, situated at a distance of sixteen miles from Chhatak, Boropishima's father's ancestral village. Boropishima often expressed the feeling that the houses here were too stuffy and small. The ones in Bagherkora and Chhatak were spacious. I had never heard Boropishima talking about Bagherkora or Chhatak during her years in the village of Hailakandi. But today, in her own house, she did not find anything enchanting. This house, according to her, did not possess any memory of her husband, my Pishemosai, whom I had never met. The only thing that evoked her husband's memory was Fulda's conspicuous resemblance to the facial features of Pishemosai.

On my second visit, I discovered that the exterior of Fulda's house was garbed in a new colour. Fulda said that he changed the paint of the exterior of the house every year. He employed a mason to construct a new bathroom. That was a time when the month of Kartik[iv] was giving way to the month of Aghrayan. Looking out from the balcony in the early morning one could see smoke-shrouded fog at the top of the trees at a distance. There was a public pond behind the house. A dusty road lead out beside it. It reminded me of our home in the village. During one of those days, Trinamool Congress called a strike. It was not possible for me to go to office. In the afternoon, Fulda brought out an album of photographs for me. He showed his treasured photographs one by one and this exhibition was interspersed with detailed queries on my part about the persons or objects seen in each of the photographs. It was all captured by Fulda himself with his own camera: Repair works of our village home; me, a kid clasping my mother with Jyetha babu and my grandmother in the cropped paddy field. Again I found Fulda's photograph where he stood beside the warplane. I remember, I had become Fulda's greatest admirer at that age when I first saw that photograph. Fulda standing beside the aircraft which hovers around in the sky and bombards targets below! Excitement gripped me whenever I thought of that. Flipping through the pages of the album on that afternoon, I discovered that Fulda had captured innumerable moments of our village days in his still camera. I also discovered that he had a brilliant flair for the art of photography. It was his passion. A new passion of household management had overtaken him of late.

He often bought books on interior decoration from College Street. Intermittently, Boudi expressed her displeasure about this new-found obsession. Fulda used to laugh at these admonishments. Had Jyetha babu been alive, he also would have advised him to mind his savings. Fulda now started capturing images of the rooms of his house with a costly camera. It seemed to me that, for Fulda, his own house seemed to be the embodiment of his lifelong dream that had come true.

Boropishima stayed downstairs. Often, I used to sit by her. It seemed that time was dragging by in leaden feet. In our conversations she used to travel back to her past life: to the days in East Pakistan, their ancestral home, the days of her lost acquaintances. She used to talk about my father and Jyetha babu's childhood; about the final hours of my grandfather's life. They used to call the ailment thrombosis then. Amidst our conversation, dusk used to draw closer. After having her meal, comprising of a cup of tea and some puffed rice, she used to go to bed.

Each time, just before my departure, she used to voice her fear that she didn't hope to see me again. Her apprehensions were proven wrong every time. But it seemed that an age had lapsed since I had heard the word 'journey' to refer to my departure. During her final days, Boropishima lost track of time and space. But her remembrance of things past had improved remarkably and she used to be under the delusion that she was staying in Bagherkora or Chhatok. She desperately wanted to return to Bagherkora from Chhatok. Again on another occasion, she wanted to go back to Chhatok. Fulda and Boudi attributed it to delirium. Only my father could understand from the telephonic conversations that Boropishima was living in the realm of her nostalgia.

Fulda's obsession with his house, seemed to me, to have been inherited from his maternal uncles. For minor repair works of our household, my father too, didn't depend on others. He personally used to shoulder every responsibility. Every time I went to Fulda's place, I used to observe the similarity between how my father managed things and how Fulda was going about his affairs. I could never understand their mindset. It seemed irritating to me at times. I considered them to be maniacs of a kind. Why should one be so obsessed about his household?

The year I retired from my job, I availed my last L.T.C. (Leave Travel Concession) to visit Fulda's place. At that time, he was in his eighties. My grandsons had got engaged in various jobs by then with the help of my nephews. Fulda's only regret was that no one had any time to look after his household. For two years the house did not have any facelift. On being exposed to rains and sunshine, the paint of the building faded over the years. The window-grilles of the toilets became rusty. Cobwebs gathered everywhere. He just didn't like staying in surroundings mired in dirt and filth. It was two years since the demise of Boudi. I tried to make him accept the fact that time had undergone a considerable change and that he too had become aged. But he was unrelenting in his obsession that, in order to live a normal life, one needs a clean and healthy dwelling place. Fulda used to live in Boropishima's room at that time. Sometimes he used to idle in an easy chair in the adjacent portico. Insomnia wreaked havoc with his sleep at night. Reclining in the easy chair, he used to gaze at the stars in the sky.

I also have developed the habit of sitting idly in an easy chair on the terrace after dusk. Staring at the stars. It is my feeling too that our house is falling to pieces with cobwebs in every corner of the rooms. The mosaic finish of the floors done during my father's time has worn out completely. Twice a year, I talk with Borda and Chhorda over phone: on *Poila Boishakh* (Bengali new year) and on *Bijoya Dashami* (last day of Durga Puja). Bordi has begun to show signs of deafness which is why I cannot maintain contact with her via phone.

Recently I discovered a huge banyan tree with its innumerable roots making their way down the edges of the terrace of my home. The darkness of inferno enveloped its surroundings. My desperate attempts to gauge the depth to which the roots have gone inside went in vain every time. Instead, my eyes got steeped in the depth of darkness. Gradually, the banyan and its serpentine roots are wrapping me under the dark blanket of its lengthening shadow.

Translated by Subha Prasad Nandi Majumdar

(Endnotes)

i Respectful form of address to an elder brother.

ii Uncle; paternal aunt's husband.

iii A unit of measurement of land.

iv Eighth month of the Hindu calendar: it roughly corresponds to a period between mid-October to mid-November.

Sucking Milk

Dipendu Das

Salema, alias Sarama, slaps herself on the cheek while half asleep. Without opening her eyes she rubs her two fingers to feel the squashed mosquito. She finds nothing. As she rubs her fingers, the collected dust on her cheek accumulates to a point. The sleep is gone. The dazzling light of the platform cannot drive away the dense darkness of the midnight completely.

A train has arrived at platform number three. Probably the Super. With his '*chai garam, chai garam,*' (hot tea) the busy hawker has suddenly leaped up. Most of the shutters of the compartment windows are closed. The tired passengers are deep in slumber.

Nena's body has crossed the periphery of Salema's sari spread under him, and is exposed to the cold platform. Salema did not realise when her son fell asleep with his mother's nipples in his mouth. She could not earn a single farthing as she has been unwell for the past two days. She did not have the strength to beg when the trains arrived. She shivered frequently as her temperature shot up.

Nena began to cry in the evening as there has been nothing to eat since noon. Even Salema's milk has dried up. She could not control him by pushing her nipples into his mouth. The loud cry gradually subsided into a moan. She lifted her sari to allow him to suck her nipples in the hope that the baby might extract something. In his unsuccessful attempt to suck the last drop from his mother's dry breast, Nena fell asleep.

Salema supports herself on her elbows, raises her head and drags Nena's legs onto the piece of cloth. She feels a pressure in her abdomen and then somehow stands up holding the pillar of the platform.

The Super Express will leave within a short while. Her eyes are fixed on the open window of a compartment. A man peeps through the lifted shutter. He is in fact looking at her. The sari covering her bosom has slipped from the shoulder leaving one of the two breasts exposed. Salema is about to pull it up, but does not do so finally. She moves towards the window with her breasts dangling like bait on the hook to trap fish.

A sudden terror now looms in the eyes of the first-class passenger, who till now has been relishing the midnight delight served on a platter. Salema pulls herself ahead. She stands before the window. Draws a twisted tin bowl from under the cover of her cloth; summons as tragic an expression on her face as possible and lifts the bowl before the terror-stricken eyes of the passenger. The man is taken aback. A female voice asks something from within the compartment. The man utters a few half audible words, '… not getting sleep.'

A fifty-paisa coin drops into the bowl. The shutter is drawn in a hurry. Salema ties the coin in one end of her sari and draws herself away from the window. The Super Express blows its whistle to indicate its departure.

Salema pulls herself to the other side of the track. She looks around and then squats in the dense darkness and relieves herself.

Two years have passed on this platform. Ismail had died in an episode of police firing while he was trying to burn down a Hindu household during the Babri Masjid–Ramjanam Bhumi riots. His house was burnt down that night. Salema fled to save herself and the baby in her womb. She was tossed on the waves of life and then cast ashore on Chaparmukh junction, where she lived for some time. Seething hunger compelled her to beg from door to door, and ultimately she reached Lumding junction. Nena was born in the deserted cabin of a condemned compartment in the railway yard.

For the purpose of having both ends meet, Muslim Salema one day gets transformed into Sarama in the Hindu-majority Lumding town.

Quite a few trains pass during the day and night through the junction. Begging remains her only source of earning. Gradually she discovers other means of income also. Often she entertains customers in the abandoned compartments near the shed. A few good saris are purchased and she can sometimes have a few sumptuous meals in the small hotels near the junction. Occasionally she can even watch a few shows in Jyoti and Radha cinema halls.

It haunted her initially. She felt guilty. She even considered herself fallen. Gradually she got used to it. Now she feels bad when there are no customers for the night.

Time passes. Her body fails to bear the burden anymore. Occasionally she has to share her income with *lathi*-[i]wielding constables, sometimes from the amount she earns, sometimes by spreading herself on the broken seat in an abandoned compartment.

Secretion from known and unknown bodies allow diseases to enter her. She always feels feverish. Sometimes her temperature shoots up. She often coughs loudly, nearly breaking her ribs. She develops a few pimple-like swellings here and there. She feels weak as well. Her knees totter as she tries to move. Earnings during the night almost come to a halt. The only means of income she is left with is begging in the railway compartments with her son in her arms.

Fear creeps in. Some terrible disease seems to have taken shelter in her body. In her attempt to save her child with her breast milk, Salema realises that she is pouring poison into his body. Nena too, nowadays, often shivers from cold and fever.

At dawn the rising sun slowly overwhelms the lights on the platforms. The junction wakes up from slumber gradually. Shop shutters are lifted one by one. The owner of the tea stall doses while washing the old and rusty kettle. The employee of the bookstall cleans the dust accumulated over the stacks of books with a dirty cloth.

The red-eyed station master slowly totters back home after completing his night duty. The huge bell strikes to announce the entry of Brahmaputra Mail. Setting aside the comfort of early morning sleep, the auto-rickshaws gather under the overbridge to earn some extra money. The coolies tie their turbans with the pieces of cloths they have been lying on, spring up and run after the train to catch passengers.

The Brahmaputra Mail roars in, shaking the junction out of drowsiness and slumber.

Nena opens his eyes. Salema rubs her son's forehead. Her body shivers a bit. She manages to get up supporting herself on her hands. In a couple of minutes her temperature shoots up as she begins to shiver severely. She feels dizzy. It is no longer possible to sit up any more. Salema lies down beside her son.

The Brahmaputra Mail gradually leaves the junction behind.

The day moves on. She feels better as the sun gets warmer. She sweats profusely and the temperature comes down. She buys half a cup of milk mixed with water in exchange for the coin she earned last night. Tap water transforms half a cup into a full bowl. Nena sips and finishes the bowl in a moment; he then begins to play by throwing his arms and legs about his mother. Salema lifts the bowl to drink the last drop of milk from it. Then she goes near the tap and drinks the flowing water clasping both her hands.

Only then does she hear the news.

Lord Ganesha in the temple has started drinking milk!

Salema drinks water and then sprinkles some on her face and eyes; she rubs her hands on one end of her torn sari and then lies down on the platform beside her son.

The young employee from the bookstall calls out to the nearby old sweet-stall owner, 'Dadu, haven't you heard of it! A miracle is taking place. It seems Lord Ganesha has started drinking milk today! Aren't you going to see that?'

The news soon spreads through the junction. Lord Ganesha is drinking milk in the big temple. There is no scheduled train in the afternoon. The platforms wear a deserted look in a short while. Many have downed shutters of their shops and rushed towards the temple.

The day rolls on. The station is almost empty now. The shutters of the stalls are down. The old on-duty station master, compelled to sit in his chair, holding his face between his palms, is the only person left behind because he simply cannot leave the station.

They will have to starve if she stays back at the platform. There is none here to whom she can go for help.

Salema too, with her son in her arms, drags herself along as she slowly leaves the station behind.

All the streets are unusually busy today. The hooting of scooters and auto-rickshaws result in cacophony. Freshly bathed girls and married women in red-bordered saris gather in long rows in front of the temple.

A scarecrow of a young rake, busy brushing his hair with four fingers, follows them. A large number of railway employees join the devotees bunking their office after lunch hour.

There are long queues in front of the big temple. Separate queues for male and female devotees. Every hand is carrying a bowl or a glass or a pot full of milk.. They have heard that the milk disappears as soon as the bowl touches the idol's lips. The Lord has been drinking milk with his holy trunk.

The crowd outside the temple boundary is quite charged up. The topic is obviously the miracle unfolding in front of their eyes. The news has reached them from different corners of the country of Lord Ganesha exhibiting the miracle of drinking milk everywhere.

Some are elated after feeding the lord. Some have a depressed demeanour. The lord has not accepted milk from them.

A man is selling milk near the temple gate. Half a cup for two rupees. The big cauldron becomes empty in a moment.

Milk is all around them now. Seeing that Nena suddenly cries out loudly. The loud cry of a hungry baby appears incongruous in this holy atmosphere. Salema slaps him to stop him from crying. The slap incites him to cry harder. Devotees get irritated.

Salema somehow stops her son's wails by pushing some cloth into his mouth. Then lifting her begging bowl she stands beside the queue. The devotees shout at her. They instantly move away from her unholy touch with the holy offerings in their hands.

No coins fly into her bowl, as coins will be offered to God today!

Volunteers engaged in maintaining discipline rush in furiously. They do everything else save assaulting her physically. Probably they hate touching this dirty woman.

Salema rushes out of the temple arena with her son in her arms.

The coins offered before the idol, accumulate into a huge pile. Lord Ganesha made of snow-white stone is immersed in *dakshina*[ii] and milk. Unsuccessful and exhausted, Salema drags herself back towards the station with her son in her arms.

She belches as some sour juice gushes up her throat and spreads through her mouth. On the left side of her chest she feels a severe pain resulting from starvation. Salema cannot move any more. She sits spreading her legs under a tree behind the temple. Nena weeps, leaning his head upon the base of the tree.

Salema feels darkness descending upon her eyes. She tries hard to keep her eyes open. She clutches the foot of the tree for support. The sound of Nena's weeping has subsided. Salema somehow reclines at the foot of the tree.

Suddenly her eyes encounter a strange vision. The narrow canal, through which the bathing waters of the idol passes, is now brimming with the stream of milk from the temple. All the milk poured on the idol of Ganesha now flows along the dirty water of the big canal.

A drop of tear hangs on Nena's eyelids. He has no strength left to even moan. Salema feels a strong surge of pain between her chest and stomach. She gathers all her remaining strength to move forward on her knees. She looks around, scanning the horizon, and then pushes the twisted bowl in front of the canal. There are no devotees around. In a moment the bowl is overflowing with milk. Salema holds up the bowl full of milk to her son's mouth. Nena grabs the bowl with his little fists and begins to sip the milk. He throws about his hands and legs in glee.

The flow of milk seems to have accentuated hunger. The pain is sharpened. Salema lies on the earth clutching her stomach. Then she begins to drink the milk from the canal joining her two hands together. The accumulated hunger of several days makes her drink in a frenzy. Her body gets drenched in milk and mud. Salema swallows milk. Her body begins to shiver; she continues drinking. Her body shakes and her temperature rises further. She drinks profusely and feels an unbearable pain below her chest. She goes on drinking.

Her eyes seem to protrude out. She drinks with the last reserves of strength that she possesses.

She fails to continue anymore. The pain below her chest gradually numbs her whole body. She wants to get up, but cannot.

Nena is busy playing with a piece of stone. She tries to move towards her son. Her body rolls into the drain. She almost drowns in muddy dirty water. The flow of white milk gradually turns blackish.

Salema tries to raise her head by grabbing the clay bank. Her head hangs down. Her body shivers uncontrollably. A terrible cold grips her. The body shivers for a while and then becomes still forever.

The stream of milk flowing down from the stone idol of the god pours down on the lifeless body of Salema.

Translated by the author

(Endnotes)

i Stick.

ii Holy offerings.

The Bamboo Bridge

Subrata Kumar Roy

He has to walk by this road every day. The river Longai is on the right; and on its immediate bank, a straight tarred road runs its course. Just after the turn on the Thana road, there is a huge silk cotton tree. It stands there resplendent in red.

As a child, he used to gather quite a number of tops on the way to school. The lunch break was the time for the boys to compete at playing with tops.

The cotton tree brought back memories of Saibal's school days as he passed by it today.

It is the same tedious road everyday—Azad Sagar road crossing, the turn at Thana road, Hospital road, the dam, one right turn to Banamali road, a full u-turn to reach the point parallel to his house. Only the fact is that his house and his office are on the opposite banks of the river.

Saibal does not want to pass by the hospital, painted in yellow. Whenever he comes in the vicinity of the hospital, an all too familiar nauseating smell seems to envelope his entire being.

A queue of rickshaws. A badly injured body, smeared in blood, is taken in from one of the rickshaws. Another rickshaw brings in an unconscious person.

One day a truck-load of bodies was brought in, some dead, a few on the verge of death, while the remaining being mere body parts.

There was an accident at the Puamara bridge. Saibal couldn't even go to office that day. He had to return from that place.

For Saibal, it is not much of a trouble to avoid that road.

Just after the turn on Thana road, on the right a dilapidated bamboo bridge on the Longai connects it to Banamali road. This bridge provides a shortcut to Saibal. It cuts down the distance almost by half.

Even though the bridge is in a deplorable state, people take this route.

It has been quite a few years since the bridge was mended.

The bamboo in the bridge has rotted in some places leaving huge gaps here and there. There is not even a railing to hold on to. A few places have just two or three bamboos sticks and to cross those places, one has to learn balancing tricks. At some other places, the bamboo has become hollow. One does not realise immediately by just looking at it, but a single foot on it would be enough to make that person fall through completely.

The long bamboo bridge looks like the famous Laxmanjhula bridge. If anyone tries to walk fast, the entire bridge swings dangerously. Its base has been built with only a few bamboo sticks.

The dry Longai river, some twenty feet under the bridge, can hardly be seen.

Saibal tried walking across that bridge once or twice. Walking a distance of just a few paces made him perspire. His heartbeat increased rapidly. With wobbly feet, he had to come back to the main road.

On such an occasion when Saibal turned back midway, an old man, who walked on the bridge like an expert, laughed and said, 'Afraid! You've to walk on, avoiding looking down. Look just in front.'

Saibal had smiled a superficial smile that day.

Whenever Saibal took the main road in order to avoid the bamboo bridge, the bridge seemed to throw up a challenge at him. The small boys and girls, middle-aged couples, old men and women, who walked on the bridge seemed to point their fingers at him and call him 'a coward'.

Saibal continues taking that longer route every day.

He gets tired in the heat. Very often he reaches office late by ten–twenty minutes.

Someone or the other at office always tells him, 'You've the option of taking a shortcut across the bamboo bridge.'

Saibal doesn't feel the need to reply.

One day he happens to meet one of his colleagues in front of the Telephone Exchange.

The man asks, 'What happened, why are you coming this way?'

In reply, Saibal has to tell a lie, 'I had come to meet someone at the hospital.'

He found no reasonable answer to the question: why he was compelled to lie.

Many a time, while on his way to office, he has to be cautious of not being spotted by someone, as if he were a criminal, who is afraid of being caught.

A strange inexplicable fear starts taking form as soon as he crosses the turn at the Thana road.

When the bridge seems to tease him by smirking at him, Saibal feels crabs and caterpillars crawling over his body and gets so agitated that he wants to settle the issue once and for all. At that precise moment the same fear starts taking hold of him all over again. He can feel the hammering in his heart quite clearly. It seems to him that each pedestrian is staring at him, as if he is all alone in a field with a hundred pair of eyes trained on him. If he is unable to cross the bridge and turns back to the main road after covering a few paces, then all those spectators will laugh out loud.

Saibal finds himself not up to it. He casts one glance at the bridge, lowers his head and walks past it at a rapid pace.

Last night, while lying very close to Saibal, whose body had almost with the deep darkness surrounding him, Moni said, 'You walk to your office everyday; but you still have a paunch.' Saibal lay like a piece of rock, devoid of the feeling that generates a reply.

'Do you walk across that bamboo bridge? I'm quite afraid of stepping on that bridge. Do you remember what happened once when we were going to the fair ...'

'Ah! Will you stop talking?'

Saibal's rough rebuke made Moni silent for a while and she changed the topic, 'When are you getting your salary?'

'I don't know if we shall get it this time,' Saibal's bitter reply jarred Moni. After a while, she again spoke while moving her fingers along Saibal's chest, 'Last month's electricity bill is still pending. This month dues for milk has to be paid again. I won't be able to manage with a thousand rupees this month.'

'There is no certainty whether I will be getting my salary this month and your long list of demands is already on display. Will you allow me a little bit of rest and sleep?'

Since the past couple of months, people at Saibal's workplace have not been getting their salaries. Moreover, there is a rumour that a few workers could be fired. Saibal considers himself to be at the top of the list of such people.

All the savings have almost been spent. Some amount of money had come into his account from his Peerless savings, which is still there.

Saibal could have spent a carefree life like his co-workers, only if he had mastered the art of transactions under the table.

Saibal can't do it. His hands tremble.

When Moni gets angry and shows instances of corrupt people like Anjan babu, Sikdar and such others, Saibal explains to her the satisfaction of having rice, bought with hard-earned money, that brings forth a belch of hollow self-contentment from his inner being.

Everyday Saibal has to fight with an invisible competitor. On returning home, he witnesses no electricity, no cooking gas, no kerosene—nothing—he doesn't even have his name on the voters' list.

Everyday Saibal loses this fight.

The spirit to survive makes every human being crave for life by holding onto a straw even as he is being swept away by a flood. In his deep slumber, Saibal hugs Moni as if she were that straw.

Today there is a strike.

The strike called by one of the political parties has disrupted the normal routine of the town.

Only a few bicycles are moving along the road. Sometimes the cadres of this political party can be seen driving their scooters pretty fast, holding the flags of the party. Most of the cadres are local hooligans, anti-socials.

Last night an urgent message was circulated with the strict order for all government employees to be present at office.

There is hardly anyone on the roads. Everyone is glued to their TV sets.

Every home has a cable connection. The cable antennae have spread overnight all over the town like an upside down umbrella.

Saibal hasn't been able to get a cable connection yet. Moni had once or twice thrown a tantrum demanding cable TV and Star TV. Saibal had pacified her by reasoning that it would hamper their children's education.

The sun is strong. The tar on the road has melted and is sticking to the sandals. Alternating between strong and mild earlier in the day, the sun's rays have become severe now.

The grocery list for the month is in Saibal's pocket, which also has the princely sum of twenty-five rupees in his pocket.

He has to buy household items from the market. He can't even buy on credit as his last month's dues at Pori's shop haven't been cleared yet.

Saibal snaps irritably on being asked the time by a passerby, 'Watch isn't working.' He looks at the silk cotton tree after crossing the turning at Thana road. The tree seems to be on fire. The red hue spread against the background of the clear blue sky appears very beautiful to Saibal.

The clanging sound of the school bell at lunch break rings loud in his ears.

From force of habit, his eyes travel towards the bamboo bridge after crossing the turn. Saibal appears to be unprepared in front of the challenge. The bridge seems to beckon him. Saibal is alone in the middle of the field, a hundred pairs of eyes look at him from within the dark stadium. There is pin-drop silence. For the first time, Saibal doesn't feel any fear. He inspects his surroundings. He is suddenly startled by the sound of a bicycle and crosses the road. The bamboo bridge is quite near now, just one or two steps down the road he is standing on.

Saibal's jawbones harden. A sudden surge in his blood pressure makes the nerve at the side of his head throb. His body bends in the shape of the arch of a bow on descending the steps.

A strange shiver runs down his spine as he places his right foot on the bridge. The bridge makes a cracking sound. His legs follow a perfect rhythm. Today there is no one on the bridge except Saibal. Beads of perspiration gather on his forehead, his heartbeat quicken its pace. His shirt has become completely wet as a result of profuse sweating. He walks a few steps slowly.

A glance at the sky gives him the impression that everything around him is shaking. The strong sun itself appears to be sweating under the scorching rays. He walks like a drunken man. Sweat runs down from his eyebrows and rolls down to his lips, Saibal gets a taste of his salty sweat.

A big gap yawns in front of him—there is just a huge bamboo stick. He will have to walk along that. The mat-like covering on the bamboo has become rotten and has fallen off. Saibal places his right foot on it carefully, without shifting his full weight, and with a single jump, crosses that portion. A weightless jump. For once, his eyes look downwards. It immediately makes his head spin and his heart about to jump out of his body. It is the same feeling which one gets at a fair, while sailing down from the top in a ferris wheel—a sudden emptiness in the stomach.

The bridge shakes horribly. Being unable to handle it, Saibal sits down. There is no railing on either side to get some support to stand up again.

There is more than half the distance left to be covered. He debates whether he should turn back. But the hundred pairs of eyes are still watching him. Will Saibal lose it all in this manner? At a distance, some people are walking down Banamali road. No one is looking at him. Saibal stands up slowly, shifting the weight on his knees.

The swinging motion of the bridge is under control now. In front of him, there are two pairs of bamboos. Saibal places his feet very carefully. Immediately one bamboo cracks and moves further downwards. Saibal's reflex action of transferring the weight onto the right foot is so fast that it surprises him. An unbelievable trap. It is turning out to be an interesting game. Saibal can feel the adrenaline flowing through his body. He glances ahead. A few more holes or traps and he would reach the touchline.

The sun is even more severe now. Saibal is sweating profusely. On the left, the dam can be seen at a distance, a little high up. The saffron-painted T.B. Hospital can be seen standing adjacent to it—that is his usual route.

One portion of the bridge is very soft and mushy. Perhaps this is evidence of the heavy shower in the morning. The mat-like cover on the bridge is still wet. Saibal cannot maintain his balance by placing his foot there. He is saved as his right leg gets trapped in a small hole. There is a small hole of the size of his heel. The front part of his foot gets twisted. He cannot muster the strength to walk on.

Saibal transfers most of the weight of his body onto his left leg and starts walking cautiously, taking each step with a lot of care. He crosses one medium-sized hole without much trouble and then another. He can see Banamali road. Just a few steps to climb; a few steps more.

Perhaps Saibal loses his concentration for a few seconds. He has moved his eyes away from the bridge. The bridge cracks, making a horrible sound, due to the weight of the whole body on one leg. Saibal's right leg goes through the cracked portion and sinks upto his thigh.

The bridge swing dangerously. Saibal holds on to a bamboo with his left hand. The left leg has been twisted till the knee. Gradually Saibal pulls himself up, shifting his weight on his hand. Meanwhile, the swinging of the bridge hasn't stopped.

The palm of his left hand is bleeding. There is a burning sensation in his right leg upto the knee. Perhaps the skin has peeled off. The hip joint has also received a nasty blow.

Saibal places his feet on the ground and stands there for a while.

After quite some time, a smile appears on his lips. Turning back, he looks at the bamboo bridge once. Then he starts walking towards his office, holding his head high.

Translated by Mohua Chakraborty

About the Authors

Shyamalendu Chakravorty was born in 1937 in Meymansing in pre-partition India, and moved to Silchar, Assam just before the Independence of India. He served as a teacher of English in a higher secondary school and has been writing short stories for the last five decades. He edited a Bengali little magazine for more than 25 years. His stories have been published in different little magazines and have been incorporated in a few anthologies.

Badarujjaman Choudhury was born in Karimganj, Assam in 1946 and was a school teacher by profession. His short stories have been published in different magazines and have been included in many anthologies. *Lakh Takar Manush,* his short story collection was published in 2003. He has received several literary awards and honours for his works.

Mithilesh Bhattacharjee was born in 1946 in Silchar, Assam. He has been engaged in creative writing for thirty years. Several of his short stories have been published in different little magazines from the North-East and West Bengal, and a few have been included in anthologies. *Kakshapath,* his only short story collection, was published in 2003.

Ranabir Purkayastha was born in Silchar, Assam in 1949. He worked with a nationalised bank till his superannuation. He has been writing fiction in Bengali for the last five decades. His stories have been published in different literary magazines and newspapers and some of them have been anthologised. *Boka Kashiramer Katha*, his only short story collection, was published in 2001.

Arijit Choudhury was born in 1950 in Karimganj, Assam. After a stint as a journalist in the newspaper *Jugashakti,* he joined Assam State Government service. His first story was published in a school magazine in 1962 when he was in class eight. From that time several of his stories have been published on a regular basis in different little magazines and included in collections within and outside the North-East. One of the stories from the collection *Poo Gosh* was included in the PG syllabus of the Department of Bengali, Calcutta University.

Kajal Demta was born in Cachar district of Assam in 1951. She teaches in a school. Apart from being a creative writer and the editor of a magazine, she is a social activist. Several of her short stories have been published in different little magazines and newspapers, and a few of them have been included in different anthologies.

Swapna Bhattacharjee was born in 1952 in Silchar and works in a nationalised bank. She has done her Ph.D. on the poetry of Jibanananda Das and received recognition from Bangladesh as the first woman researcher on the famed poet. She contributes short stories to the literary magazines of the North-East and West Bengal. A few of her stories have been selected in different anthologies. *Notebook*, her short story collection, was published in 2007.

Shekhar Das was born in 1952. A school teacher by profession, he began his literary career in 1973. His short stories were published in different literary magazines and included in various anthologies. A few of his short stories have been translated into different Indian languages and English. His first short story collection *Koshagar* was published in 2000, followed by two novels, *Mohana* (2000) and *Bindu Bindu Jal* (2001).

Amalendu Bhattacharya was born in 1954 in Karimganj, Assam. He teaches Bengali at a college in Silchar. His Ph.D. dissertation was on the folk literature of Cachar district. He has presented papers in national and international seminars and has extensively published research articles in reputed journals. Till date he has edited (individually and jointly) 14 books of literature.

Moloy Kanti Dey was born in Karimganj, Assam in 1954. He serves in a nationalised bank and has been writing short stories for the last three decades. Several of his stories have been published in little magazines and newspapers and have found place in different anthologies. A film has been made on his short story *Asraf Alir Swadesh,* and a play was staged based on the same story.

Bijoya Deb was born in 1959 in Cachar, Assam. She teaches Bengali in a higher secondary school at Silchar. She is a prolific writer whose work is regularly published in the literary magazines of Barak Valley and the North-East. Several of her short stories have been included in different anthologies. She has two short story collections, *Nilanjana* (2003) and *Bhedrekha* (2005), and one novel *Srotaswini* (2008) to her credit.

Debabrata Chowdhury was born in Silchar in 1960. He serves in the Tea Employees' Provident Fund Association at Silchar. Several of his short stories have been published in different little magazines and have been incorporated in different anthologies. He has written quite a few plays and has also made films based on his own stories.

Saumitra Baishya was born in Silchar, Assam in 1962. His short stories have been published in the little magazines of the North-East and West Bengal. He has also contributed articles on different contemporary issues in newspapers and magazines.

Jhumur Pandey was born in Hailakandi in 1962. A prolific writer, her short stories have been published regularly in the little magazines of Assam and West Bengal. Her publications include three short story collections, *Geram Thaner Manush O Dulia* (1997), *Swapna Gandhar Khonje* (1999), and *Sukh Gacher Galpo* (2005); a collection of poems *Kichu Balar Chilo* (2005); and a novel *Alaxenderpurer Kathakatha* (2007).

Amitabha Dev Choudhury was born in Silchar in 1962. An MA in English from Jadavpur University, Kolkata, he teaches English at a higher secondary school at Silchar. He has published two novels—*Uponyaser Khonje* (2003) and *Udas Mahal Shunya Gali* (2007); one poetry collection—*Amitabha Dev Choudhuryr Kabita* (2006); and a book for primary level students—*Ha Re Re Re Re Re Re* (2008). His short stories and poems have been published in different little magazines and major mainstream literary periodicals. He has participated in a national level poetry festival organised by the Sahitya Akademi in Hyderabad in the year 2007 and also in the International Bengali Poetry Festival in Kolkata the same year.

Subrata Kumar Roy was born in 1966 in Karimganj, Assam. He serves as an officer in the State Bank of India. His short stories have been published in different little magazines and anthologies. *Mouno Jogajog, Sandhirag* and *Arshi Nagarer Rupkatha* are his three published works of fiction.

About the Translators

Ashok Kumar Nandy was born in Assam in 1959. He teaches English at a college at Lanka, Assam and writes poetry both in Bengali and Assamese. He is actively engaged in the translation of Bengali and Assamese writings into English.

Susmita Chakraborty was born in Silchar, Assam in 1977. She teaches English at an undergraduate college and is pursuing research on selected fictional writings of Jhumpa Lahiri.

Jaydeep Chakrabarty was born in Digboi, Assam in 1978. He teaches English at Assam University, Silchar.

Rumi Rani Laskar was born in 1983 in Silchar. She is an MA in English and teaches at an undergraduate College at Silchar. Her M.Phil. research work was on the plays of Vijay Tendulkar.

Devashree Bhattacharjee teaches English at an undergraduate college. She has done research on three selected diaspora writers of Indian origin.

Biswajit Sheel was born in Mizoram in 1960. He is a documentary film-maker, radio-TV programme producer and a journalist. He has written a few plays for the stage, radio and TV and has written some short stories. His major documentaries include those on

'Rabindranath Tagore and Northeast', 'Ratan Thiyam', 'H. Kanhaialal' and 'Pramathesh Barua'.

Udayshankar Chakraborty was born in 1977 in Cachar district in Assam. He teaches English at an undergraduate college and is working on the poetry of Jayanta Mahapatra for his Ph.D. thesis.

Subha Prasad Nandi Majumdar was born in Shillong in 1962. He taught mathematics in a college at Silchar before joining the University of Burdwan, West Bengal in an administrative post. He is a well-known singer, a regular radio and TV artist and is a cultural activist of Indian People's Theatre Association. Some of his translations of Bengali short stories and poems into English have appeared in Sahitya Akademi's prestigious journal, *Indian Literature.* His translations of Samaresh Bose's stories for the young adult have been published in 2009 by Ponytale Books of Delhi under the title, *Murder Mystery in the Rajdhani Express and Other Stories.*

Mohua Chakraborty was born in 1978. An MA in English, she has done her M.Phil. research work on the issues involved in the translation of Mahasweta Devi's selected short stories.